HOLMES ON THE RANGE

HOLMES
on the
Range

STEVE HOCKENSMITH

Fic
Hockensm

ST. MARTIN'S MINOTAUR

NEW YORK

www.minotaurbooks.com

Library of Congress Cataloging-in-Publication Data

Hockensmith, Steve.
    Holmes on the range / Steve Hockensmih.—1st ed.
      p.   cm.
    ISBN 0-312-34780-4
    EAN 978-0-312-34780-2
    1. Cowboys—Fiction.   2. Brothers—Fiction.   3. Ranch life—Fiction.
    4. Doyle, Arthur Conan, Sir, 1859–1930—Appreciation—Fiction.
    5. Montana—Fiction. I. Title.

PS3608.O29H65 2006
813'.6—dc22

                                                                                            2005050406

First Edition: February 2006

10 9 8 7 6 5 4 3 2 1

FOR MAR, OF COURSE

HOLMES ON THE RANGE

PRELUDE

Or, The Calm Between the Storms

There are two things you can't escape out here in the West: dust and death. They sort of swirl together in the wind, and a fellow never knows when a fresh gust is going to blow one or the other right in his face. So while I'm yet a young man, I've already laid eyes on every manner of demise you could put a name to. I've seen folks drowned, shot, stabbed, starved, frozen, poisoned, hung, crushed, gored by steers, dragged by horses, bitten by snakes, and carried off by an assortment of illnesses with which I could fill the rest of this book and another besides.

So it's quite a compliment I bestow when I say that the remains we came across the day after the big storm were the most frightful I'd ever seen. Not only had a few hundred cows gone for a waltz over the body, prairie wolves had snacked on whatever hadn't stuck to the hooves. The remaining dribs and drabs of gristle were mixed in with the mud like strips of undercooked beef in a bowl of Texas chili.

"I'll get to gatherin' up the bits," my brother said as he swung down off his saddle. "You head back and grab us a couple shovels."

Usually when Old Red gets bossy with me—which is only about a hundred times a day—I repay his piss with vinegar. But my brother got no sass from me now, as fetching tools sounded a hell of a lot more appetizing than separating innards from earth.

It was a morning as lovely as a Montana spring can produce, so cool and calm and sunny-bright you'd hardly think the blue sky above was the same one that had roiled with black clouds and lightning just hours before. I enjoyed a leisurely ride to headquarters and back, making the most of a rare moment of solitude in the sunshine. Old Red and I had been working the Bar VR ranch nearly two months now, and this was my first opportunity to be alone that didn't involve an outhouse and the attendant odors thereof. True, a man I knew had just died in as messy a manner as one can imagine, but you can't fault me for appreciating a beautiful day while I could. I'd get my fill of ugliness soon enough.

I found Old Red knee-deep in ugly when I returned. Whereas before the "body" had been little more than a colorful circle in the mud, my brother was now shaping the raggedy chunks of flesh and bone into the approximate shape of a man.

"He ain't Humpty Dumpty," I said, tossing a shovel at Old Red's boots. "You can't put him back together again."

My brother made no move to pick up the shovel. Instead, he wiped his hands on his Levi's, pulled off his Stetson, and ran his fingers through his close-cropped, cherry-red hair. He usually wears upon his face an expression of vaguely irritated disappointment, as if he can't stop stewing on what *he* would've done with those six days God took to make a botch of the world. But he didn't look vexed or even disgusted now. He merely looked puzzled.

"It ain't *him* I'm tryin' to piece together," he said, rubbing the back of his head like it was a magic lamp and he was Aladdin trying to coax out the genie.

"What's that supposed to mean?" I asked as I unhorsed myself.

2

"I'm tryin' to put together how he got like this."

"Well, I reckon some *cows* might've had somethin' to do with it," I said, quickly plunging my shovel into the soppy muck. If I had to bury a body that looked like an explosion in a butcher's shop, I wanted to get it over with fast. "That's the only way I can figure it . . . unless you spotted some *elephants* out this way yesterday."

One day maybe I'll get a laugh out of my elder brother. This was not that day.

"I'm just wonderin' if those cows had 'em some help," he said.

I froze mid-dig. Without quite knowing it, I'd been waiting for this moment for months. It was like waking up at the sound of a train whistle—and remembering you'd fallen asleep on the tracks.

"Damn it, Brother," I said. "You're a cowboy, not a detective."

Old Red didn't answer with words. He just turned and showed me that little wisp of a grin he slips under his mustache when he thinks he's being clever.

Oh? his smile said. *A feller can't be both?*

One

THE BEGINNING

Or, My Brother "Deduces" His True Calling

ou can follow a trail without even knowing you're on it. You start out just ambling, maybe get to thinking you're lost—but you're headed somewhere all the same. You just don't know it till you get there.

That's how it was with me and Old Red. We'd got ourselves pointed at that flapjack-flat body a full year earlier, in the spring of 1892. All it took to get us moving toward it was a magazine story.

We were working a cattle drive at the time, and one night by the campfire one of the other drovers pulled out a detective yarn called "The Red-Headed League." It was meant as a jape, as my brother and I form a sort of "red-headed league" ourselves. We've got hair red enough to light a fire, and though our tombstones will read "Otto Amlingmeyer" and "Gustav Amlingmeyer," up and down the cow trails we're known as Big Red and Old Red. (I was branded Big Red for the obvious reason—size-wise I'm just a shade smaller than your average house—while Gustav won his handle more for attitude than decrepitude, having as he does a crotchety side more befitting a man of seventy-two than twenty-seven.)

Old Red not being on speaking terms with the alphabet, it was up to me to read "The Red-Headed League" out loud. And I enjoyed doing so, for I found it to be a dandy little tale. But my brother took it to be a lot more than that. To him it was a new gospel.

Some folks get religion. Gustav got Sherlock Holmes.

As you most likely know, this Holmes fellow's an English detective who's world famous for his great "deductions." Only we'd never heard of him, being out here in Montana where we'll probably only find out about the Second Coming by telegraph a week after it happens.

In "The Red-Headed League," Holmes busts up a gang of desperadoes just about single-handed. But it wasn't the *what* of the story that got under my brother's skin so much as the *how*. Holmes had him this way of digging out facts just by noticing what most people ignore. He could tell where you were born by shaking your hand and what you had for breakfast by how you combed your hair.

"He didn't catch them bank-robbin' snakes with some trick he learned at a university," Old Red said to me. "He caught 'em cuz he knows how to *look* at things—look and really see 'em."

I guess that would appeal to a fellow like my brother, who had his one year of schooling so long ago it's a wonder he can remember one plus one equals two. He asked me to read that story to him over and over in the months that followed, and not once did I refuse, for reading's a skill I wouldn't even have were it not for him. (When I was a child, Gustav and my other brothers and sisters worked extra hours at their chores so at least one of us—me—could get some decent booklearning. I was supposed to hoist the family up into the merchant class, only smallpox and floodwater swept most of us up to heaven before I could do much in the way of hoisting myself.)

The more Old Red heard "The Red-Headed League," the more he got the idea that he had the makings of a fine detective. As I'm his younger brother, you might think I'd be inclined to poke a pin into such puffed-up notions. But I'd always figured Gustav was meant for more than roping steers. While he's every bit as undereducated as your average puncher, he's by no stretch underthoughtful. He's prone to long stretches of cogitation and contemplation on matters he barely even knows the words to put a name to, and I've often thought if he'd been born the son of a senator instead of the son of a sodbuster, he would've become a philosopher or a railroad tycoon instead of a dollar-a-day cowhand.

So I tolerated Old Red's fixation on detecting, even if I couldn't see any practical use for it. As it turned out, there was something else I couldn't see: how much trouble it could get us into.

Not that we were in great shape when that trouble began. The bank in which we'd been saving our trail money had gone belly-up, and we'd drifted to Miles City with nothing left of our nest egg but a few dollars in our pockets and fond memories in our hearts. It was February, so the spring roundups—and the jobs that come with them—were months off. If we were going to get through the winter without selling our saddles and eating our boots, we needed a miracle and we needed one quick.

Now, waiting for a miracle can be a disheartening business. I purchased what solace I could with the two bits Old Red gave me to parcel out each day in the town's saloons. My brother tagged along, though not out of desire for drink or companionship. He wanted to make sure I didn't start a tab anywhere. And he had another reason, too: He was practicing his Holmesifying.

While I shared watery beer and dirty jokes with whatever partners I could rustle up, Old Red sat quietly, casting a cold eye on anyone who came through the door. He was testing himself, trying to make Holmes-style deductions—I wasn't allowed to call them "guesses"—based on a person's appearance. He wasn't bad at it either, though I wouldn't let him forget the time he told me a fellow was a bounty hunter with a wooden leg. Turned out he was a blacksmith who'd dropped an anvil on his foot.

Old Red did most of his Sherlocking in a dingy little hangout called the Hornet's Nest, which caters to drovers whose luck has taken a turn for the unfortunate. Naturally, that's where we were the day *our* luck went from bad to worse. It was well before noon, and I was still nursing my first beer of the day when Gustav sent an elbow into my ribs and whispered, "Take a look at these fellers."

I glanced up and saw two big men moving toward the bar. They had no need to shove—they were rough-looking hard cases indeed, and the crowd before them simply parted like the sea before Moses. When they reached the bar, they barked out for whiskey.

"Those two move with confidence," Old Red said, talking low. "And I'd say they've earned it somehow, cuz they're puttin' a real scare on the boys. They ain't got fancy enough artillery to be gunmen, though. And just look at the wear on those clothes. They're punchers—but not just any punchers. Men in command. A ranch foreman and his straw boss, I'd say."

I shrugged. "Could be."

"No 'could be' about it." My brother lifted a finger just high enough to point out the larger of the two men, a black-bearded, meat-heavy gent even taller than me. "I'd bet our last buck that's Uly McPherson."

I knew of the man. He was the foreman of a nearby ranch: the Bar VR. He had himself quite a reputation—not that I'd heard much specific. I'd simply noticed that anytime his name came up, folks were too busy looking over their shoulders and wetting their drawers to keep talking.

"That'd explain why the boys ain't crowdin' him," I said. "Once he's gone, we'll ask the fellers if you deducted right."

The two men picked up their whiskeys and washed their tonsils. Then the bigger one slapped a coin on the bar, and they started to mosey out. But when they reached the doorway, they didn't push through. Instead, they turned to face the room.

"Listen up," the big one said, not shouting, but with a strong, clear voice that grabbed your ears hard even without a whopping lungful of air behind it. "I'm lookin' to hire hands to work the Bar VR at five dollars a week."

Old Red had been right: It was Uly McPherson.

He looked more like a small-time nester than the top screw of a big ranch. His battered Stetson had lost so much of its shape it drooped over his head like a saddle, and his clothes were held together with the sloppy patchwork you see on bachelor farmers. His large, round face obviously hadn't felt the touch of a razor in months.

I pegged the fellow with him as his brother, Ambrose. He looked to be a tad older than me, which would put him just north of twenty. Folks around town called him Spider, though I didn't know why. With his puffed-out chest and dark, unblinking eyes, he reminded me more of a rooster. His lean face was smooth-shaven, but otherwise he was as shabby as his brother.

They looked like men who didn't give a shit what other men thought of them, and I felt pity for any drover dumb enough to sign on with their godforsaken outfit.

"I need waddies who can ride, rope, stretch wire, grease a windmill, and take orders without backtalk," McPherson said. "If you think that's you, line up."

There was a long, quiet moment while everyone mulled that over. Then a gangly fellow called Tall John Harrington pushed off from his perch and moved to the middle of the room. After that, more men found the courage—or desperation—to do likewise. I turned to Gustav, about to thank God we hadn't sunk so low, only to discover that we *had*.

Old Red was standing up.

"No," I said.

"Yes," he said.

And that was the end of the debate. Gustav wasn't just my elder brother—he was the only family I had left. I'd been stuck to his bootheel for four years, and while he'd walked us into a few tight spots, he'd always walked us out again.

So I got to my feet, and the two of us joined the cowboys trying to form a line. A few were dizzy with drink despite the early hour, making it bumpy work, but we finally got ourselves into a ragged, slouchy row.

We were a scruffy-looking bunch, but you could form a fine outfit if you put us to the test and chose carefully. Some ranches have tryouts that last days, with dozens of drovers busting broncs and throwing calves until all the spots in the bunkhouse are filled. I figured that's what McPherson had in mind. He'd ask a few questions, see if he recognized any names, then take us to a corral to make out whose riding was as good as his talk.

McPherson sized us up, then walked over to the man at the far-right end of the line. *Here we go,* I thought, as the fellow he was moving toward was Jim Weller, a Negro puncher with a reputation as a top-drawer hand.

McPherson stepped right past him.

"One," he said, pointing at the man to Weller's left. He moved to the next man. "Two."

From there he went to three and four and so on in the order you might guess. Gustav was five. I was six. Tall John Harrington was seven—and the last one picked.

"Alright, boys," McPherson said. "You're hired."

Two

OLD RED'S RAVE-UP

Or, My Brother Discovers a Cure for Lockjaw

McPherson told us when to show up at the ranch and the trails to take to get there, and then off he and his brother went, leaving behind a shocked silence that hung so heavy on the room it could've smothered a cat.

This was simply not the way a big outfit picked hands. And why hire up now, with snow still on the ground and the spring roundups weeks off? It just didn't figure.

The cowboy to Tall John's left broke the quiet by swiping his hat off his head and throwing it at the floor. "God damn! I'm eight out of seven! Am I the unluckiest son of a bitch ever or am I not?"

Most of the boys busted out with guffaws, but Jim Weller didn't even unpack a smile.

"If anyone's had the silver linin' swiped off his cloud, that'd be me," he said.

No one had a reply to that, for though the Negro drover was well thought of by those willing to think, not everyone falls into that category—as McPherson seemed to prove. Conversation that separated the open-minded from the muleheaded was best avoided lest you were fishing for a fight.

It was Old Red, of all people, who put some cheer back in the room. Most days he takes to fun like a duck to fire, or you might say like oil to water. But this day was different.

"Here's a silver linin' for you, Jim," he said, and he pulled out a ten-dollar note and handed it to me. "You know what to do with this, Brother."

I stared at him as if he'd just pulled the king of Siam from his pocket.

"You sure?"

"I'm sure."

I let out a whoop and called for the bartender to pour a beer down every throat in sight. Old Red and I were mighty popular while that ten dollars lasted. Once it ran out, other fellows took to buying rounds, either to toast their good luck or drown their bad.

Somewhere in there a twister hit town, or at least it hit me, for when I awoke the next morning our little hotel room was spinning like a top. Yet when Gustav pulled the sheets off me and barked, "Let's go," I managed to roll my aching carcass out of bed, haul it downstairs, and drag it atop a horse—but just barely.

"It ain't fair," I groaned as we rode out of town. "You throw down the last of our money on liquor, and *I'm* the one with the hangover."

"I appreciate your sacrifice, Brother," Old Red said, showing me that little smirk of his. "I knew I could count on you to get a rave-up goin', and you did."

Having a brain pickled in nickel beer, I had to ponder on that a moment before I caught its meaning. Despite the alcohol haze that clouded the previous day, I had dim recollections of my moody, mopey brother laughing it up with the boys in the Hornet's Nest, swapping stories and jokes . . . and gossip about the Bar VR.

"You wanted everybody drunk," I said. "You wanted everybody *talkin'*."

Gustav let his smug smile grow a little larger. He'd used me as his liquored-up Judas goat, and it rubbed on me like sandpaper—though I had to admit I'd had plenty of fun.

"So?" I growled. "That firewater smoke anything out?"

Old Red nodded at the open range ahead and kicked his horse up to a canter. I knew what that meant: *Not in town*. I got my mount moving, too, every jouncing jostle shooting a jolt of pain through me. While I waited for Gustav to slow his horse and open his mouth, I got my mind off my suffering—and my irritation with my brother—by chewing over what I already knew of the Bar VR.

Like a lot spreads, it was owned by Englishmen, lords and earls and such in this case. That's why it even had a name that acted uppity: the Cantlemere Ranche. As is the custom, the outfit was more commonly known by its brand, that being a stubby line over the letters *VR*.

A few years back, the Bar VR wasn't much different from any other big ranch. The winter of '86–'87 changed that. The Big Die-up it's called, for that was the winter more than a million cows froze solid on the plains. At the time, I was trying to keep our family afloat by clerking in a Kansas granary—a job that let me ride out the blizzards as cozy as kittens in a sweater. Old Red was earning money, too, though he didn't have it so soft: He was fighting frostbite in a Panhandle ranch shack. The snow got so high he saw dead steers in treetops when it melted, and the smell of rotting cow flesh hung on the prairie for a year.

Most of the so-called cattle barons sold out after that. The VR's owners stuck firm, though they did make one big change. A new general manager showed up, handed the foreman his walking papers, and brought in his own man—Uly McPherson.

Now, up to here the VR's story was common knowledge. But once McPherson got mixed up in it, details were a lot harder to come by. Apparently McPherson didn't like any flannelmouthing about himself or his outfit, a point he'd made on more than one occasion by decorating the floor with a fellow's teeth. Which is why Old Red had sprung for the rave-up. Fear can freeze men's tongues, but liquor's a surefire way to thaw them out.

"The locals knew of McPherson even before he hired on with the VR," my brother said when we were out on the plains with only prairie dogs around to eavesdrop. "He was a nester with a little spread just south of the ranch. Had him a reputation as a brand artist. The VR's first general manager even accused him of cuttin' wire and helpin' himself to cattle. Then a new manager came over from England—Perkins is his name—and he went and *hired* the son of a bitch."

"Invites the fox into the henhouse."

"Yessir."

"Peculiar."

"It gets more so. When Perkins took over, the VR had thirty thousand head spread over half a million acres. That's enough to keep thirty men busy. But from the provisions they buy in town, the best guess is they've got no more than ten men out there. No one can say for sure, for they run off every visitor they get—even hungry fellers ridin' the grub line in the dead of winter."

"Unneighborly."

"Mighty. The only VR man people see in town other than the McPhersons is the cook. The Swede they call him, for reasons even you could deduce."

"He's from France?"

Gustav ignored my little funny.

"Apparently, he speaks English about as good as a fish can whistle. So folks don't get much gossip out of him. But it ain't always what a feller says that tells you something. One of the boys from the Hornet's Nest saw the Swede go into Langer's Sundries yesterday and pick up the makings of a banquet—canned oysters, a keg of cod, currant jelly, hams. Then McPherson struts in . . . and tells him don't forget the smoked salmon! And in his hands he's got two bottles of thirty-dollar Scotch he just bought at the Gaieties."

I puzzled on this a moment, then gave it a shrug. "I don't see the mystery. McPherson's havin' the Swede lay out an extrafine table the first day we're there so none of us are turned back to town by lousy chow."

Old Red looked at me like you'd look at a man whose britches fell down as he strolled into church. "Brother," he said, "if our first meal at the VR is oysters and Scotch, you can call me Old Shit-for-Brains from now on."

We rode on in silence for a stretch after that. I was thinking I had half a mind to wheel my mount around and head back to Miles, as the VR didn't exactly have a welcoming glow about it.

But I'd been following Gustav's lead so long I didn't even know if I had my own lead to follow. Whatever path in life I'd been on had been washed away the night the Cottonwood River jumped its banks and swept away the family farm—and the rest of our family with it. Who could say where life would've swept *me* if Gustav hadn't offered me an anchor?

Of course, for an anchor my brother sure drifted around a lot. But I'd done fine enough drifting with him. I'd just decided to keep at it—for now—when Old Red spoke up and shook my newfound resolve.

"Don't see the mystery!" he snapped out of the blue. "Feh!"

My doubts came stampeding back, the herd even bigger than before.

I'd assumed we were headed out to the VR on a job. But in my brother's mind, I feared, we were headed out there on a *case*.

Three

THE CASTLE

Or, We See a Cabin Fit for a King

The McPhersons were to meet us that afternoon where the eastern trail crosses the Powder River. When we arrived, the rest of the new hires from the Hornet's Nest were already there: Tall John, lean and long; runty, ruddy Pinky Harris; stooped, cross-eyed Swivel-Eye Smyth; Crazymouth Nick Dury, cocky and full of nonsense; and glowering, quick-tempered Anytime McCoy, the biggest asshole west of the Mississippi . . . or east of it, for that matter.

The boys were keeping themselves warm through the vigorous working of jawbones and playing cards, and I jumped right in. But Old Red just hunkered down next to the fire, lit his pipe, and stared into the flames, content with the company of his own thoughts.

Spider showed up before too long. Riding with him was the strangest-looking puncher I'd ever come across. Everything about the man was yellow-white, even his kinky hair and dead eyes. He looked like he'd been dipped in egg and rolled in flour. When he and Spider got up close, I realized he was an albino Negro.

"We're all gonna ride in together, and I don't want any strays," Spider said without so much as "Hello" as a warm-up. "Around here, you only go where you're told, when you're told. Wander off to pick daisies and you'll regret it."

From the way he glared at us, I couldn't tell whether he meant we'd be fired or fired *on*. His clothes were faded and worn, but his Peacemaker was polished to a shine.

"Before we go, Boudreaux here's gonna collect your artillery," he went on, nodding at the albino. "Six-shooters, hideout guns, rifles—whatever you got."

Boudreaux dismounted and took a couple gunnysacks out of his saddlebag. He shook one out with a quick snap of the wrist.

"In the bag," he said, his voice a lifeless mumble, as if he was speaking to us from beneath six feet of earth.

Tall John unholstered his gun, emptied out the cartridges, and dropped the whole caboodle in Boudreaux's sack.

No one else moved.

"VR hands don't go about heeled. That's the rule," Spider growled. "You don't like it, you can haul your sorry asses back to Miles and starve."

I shot a look at Old Red that said, *I vote we give starving a try*. But my brother was already pulling out his .45. One by one, the rest of the boys did the same—though Anytime McCoy grumbled about handing his hogleg over to a "damned whitewashed nigger."

The albino didn't bat an eye. He just moved from man to man filling his sacks with iron and lead.

My Colt was the last bit of hardware to go in.

Giving up my gun made me feel more like a prisoner than an employee—and that impression stirred in me even more once we got riding. Spider led the way, with us Hornet's Nest boys bunched up behind him and his man Boudreaux riding drag. It struck me as just the way two lawmen might line up a string of rustlers they were taking to the hoosegow . . . or the hangman.

We followed a trail south for more than an hour before we spotted anything other than rolling hills and snow-dusted brush. It started as a speck on the horizon, then grew into what looked like a castle out of a history book, complete with turrets and spires and other fancy doohickeys. As we got closer, I could see that it was built from ponderosa and cottonwood, not stone. It was half-palace, half-cabin.

And totally dilapidated. The paint was peeling, the glass in the windows was sooty and smudged, and someone's boot had put a hole in the steps to the porch. There were a couple of bunkhouses and a barn not far off, and they looked even worse. Whatever the McPhersons had been up to out here, it sure as hell wasn't housekeeping.

"That's your place there," Spider said, naturally pointing to the most beat-up building in sight. "Get yourselves situated . . . and don't go wanderin' off."

Then he did exactly what he'd told us *not* to do. Boudreaux stuck around, watching as we stowed our riding gear, his eyes so cold and hard they could have been yellow marbles.

"I've seen plenty of spooks in my time, but damned if you ain't the *spookiest*," Anytime snarled at him.

The albino didn't take the bait. He just sat atop his horse as motionless as a man sculpted out of chalk.

He didn't follow us into our bunkhouse. If he had, he would've gotten an earful from *all* of us. The dust was thick enough to make a fine mattress, while the wood was so rotted out Swivel-Eye went straight through to the floor when he tried to take a seat on his bunk.

"Home sweet home," he sighed as he hauled himself up.

"God damn," Anytime spat. "They may as well have us bunkin' in a hole in the ground."

"Ain't been nothin' but snakes in here in years," Pinky added.

"Maybe that's a good thing," I replied, hefting my war bags onto a more sturdy-looking bunk. "I bet it's been empty so long even the lice have died."

"That other bunkhouse looked a little bigger," my brother said, heaping his things on the bunk below mine. "I reckon that's where—"

Before Old Red could finish reckoning, someone hollered outside.

"You new boys get out here!"

It was Uly. With him was Spider and another fellow we'd never laid eyes on. Plainly, he wasn't a cowboy, what with his clean white shirt and black frock coat and pale face. In fact, he had every appearance of being a gentleman, which made him seem out of place betwixt the raggedy-assed McPhersons. He was like a cut of choice sirloin sandwiched by two wormy pieces of moldy bread.

"This here's Mr. Perkins, the general manager," Uly said. "Listen up to what he has to say."

We all had permission to stare at the gent now, so I made the most of it. He was a lean fellow, with piercing blue eyes and wavy golden hair that had turned to silver here and there. The gray in his locks notwithstanding, he was no Methuselah, being no older than thirty-five. I'd learned to judge handsome from my sister Greta, who was never shy about expressing her opinion on such things. Her heart would have skipped a beat at the sight of Perkins, as he had the unblemished skin, jutted-out jaw, and general lack of disfigurements she declared essential to a man's good looks.

"Welcome to the Cantlemere Ranche," he said, his cold tone conveying little in the way of genuine welcome. His English accent was still strong after his years in the West, and as he continued the long fingers of his left hand began fiddling nervously with a gold chain that looped down from his vest pockets.

"You are now employees of the Sussex Land and Cattle Company. As such, you will be expected to obey all rules at all times. This means you will not drink, you will not fight, you will not steal. Visitors are not tolerated, nor are unapproved absences. To harbor one or engage in the other is to invite the severest consequence. We do not ask for or reward personal initiative. Quiet obedience is all we want. Mr. McPherson will tell you what to do and what not to do. There is no reason whatsoever for you to speak to me. Am I understood?"

We all mumbled yessirs, and that was enough for Perkins. Without another word, he walked off toward the castle.

"What Mr. Perkins said don't need explainin'," Uly said. "Only I'm goin' to tell you one thing again, cuz I want you to remember it. You go where I say the work is, and that's it. Anyplace else may as well have barbed wire around it. I'd like a 'Yes, boss' on that."

We gave him what he wanted, and he smiled.

"Well, we just might get along then. Now—you see that barn there?"

We did indeed, and an uninspiring sight it was. McPherson must have agreed, for our first job as VR hands was pulling out rotted wood, patching up holes, and slapping on a fresh coat of paint. We were at it until the sun went down and then some after, with no one telling us to stop until a croaky voice called out, "Alright, boyce! You drope dose pentbrooshes end you coom here geeting soom veetles!"

We turned to see a gray-whiskered old coot standing near our bunkhouse. We just blinked at him for a few seconds, none of us knowing what the hell he was yelling about. Old Red broke the code first.

"You say you got vittles?"

"Ya!" the old-timer shouted back. "Veetles!"

That cleared things up—it was the Swede, the cook my brother had heard talk on back in Miles. Fortunately, his cooking was more to be admired than his talking. He'd filled his cookshack with a fine welcome for us—biscuits and beans and sonofabitch stew. But there was nary an oyster nor a drop of Scotch, of course.

Once we had ourselves stuffed, the Swede wished us a good night—or, to be more exact, a "goot neat"—and we ambled on over to our bunkhouse. While the rest of the boys digested over dominoes, Old Red drifted to the front of the shack and leaned in the doorway sucking on his pipe. I got up and joined him.

"What're you stewin' on?"

Gustav answered with a shrug.

Across the way, a light burned in the castle. It put a glow in a couple of the widows, giving them the look of fiery eyes staring at us from a huge, dark face.

"What do you make of him?" I asked, nodding at the big house. "Perkins."

"You know what the man said," Old Red replied, his voice low. " 'It is a capital mistake to theorize before you have all the evidence. It biases the judgment.' "

"The man," of course, was Sherlock Holmes, and the quote was from "A Study in Scarlet," one of the Holmes tales Old Red had found after hearing "The Red-Headed League." Accounts of Holmes's exploits were like strays roaming the prairie, and my brother had rounded up a small herd. They were stuffed in his war bag, the yellow magazine paper worn so thin by my reading and rereading that the words had little more than a sense of duty to hold them together anymore.

"I don't need more evidence," I said. "He's a boiled-shirt son of a bitch."

"Well . . . I suppose *that's* a safe deduction," Gustav conceded.

Jangling footsteps reached out of the darkness to grab our ears, and we turned to see a couple of seedy-looking drovers walking from the corral to the VR's other bunkhouse. They stared back at us, their sneers plain enough even in the dull glow of moonlight.

"You see what I see?"

"I see," Old Red said.

Of course he did. No cowboy would've missed it.

The noise those fellows made as they walked didn't just come from their spurs. There was the squeak of leather and the slap of heavy iron on thigh.

They were wearing holsters—and those holsters weren't packing fresh-picked daisies.

"So that rule about guns—" I began.

"—only applies to us," Old Red finished.

The men we'd been watching disappeared into their bunkhouse just as the light in the castle went out.

Four

A VISITOR

Or, The Law Comes A-Calling and Is Welcomed with Folded Arms

Cowboys," of course, are fellows who work with cows. Along the same track, "housemaids" are gals who work in houses. It follows then that for our first three weeks at the Bar VR, Old Red and I were "houseboys."

McPherson had us new hands shining up the castle, painting, roofing, and even dusting, sweeping, and cleaning windows. We washed linens, we scrubbed floors—and we fought the urge to nip samples from the castle's curiously well-stocked pantry. Pinky Harris was particularly enticed by the impressive store of alcohol, and every few hours one of us Hornet's Nesters had to stop him from sneaking off with a bottle.

Pinky didn't thank us, of course—though he should have. There was little chance a hand could get away with shenanigans in the big house, as Perkins was ever drifting about the place like a ghost. He seemed to be a lonely sort, and he moped around with the doleful air of a man pining for something long lost. One day I accidentally discovered just what that "something" was: a some*one*. I came around a corner upstairs and nearly flattened Perkins, who was gazing down at a small object he held cupped in his open palms. It was a locket attached to the gold chain that ever dangled from the pockets of his vest. He snapped the locket shut and snapped at me to get back to work, but not before I got a look at what he'd been mooning over—a photograph of a slender, dark-haired woman. I saw her upside down and in black and white for all of a second, but that's all I needed to know she had a beauty well worth pining for.

Though I caught Perkins by surprise that time, usually it was him who startled us. His bedroom and office were both on the first floor, and every so often he'd burst from one or the other calling for a McPherson. And there was generally one nearby, for either Uly or Spider was usually on hand to help us with the cleaning. Uly's "help" took the form of comments like "Pardon me, ladies, but you left a smudge on that window." Spider did his part by killing flies—by snatching them out of the air and eating them.

When we'd finished sprucing up the castle, Uly put us to more patch-up work, this time on the bunkhouses and corrals. These new chores were draftier business—though the winter snows had melted to mud, the morning air could still frost a man's whiskers icicle-stiff. We wouldn't have minded if we'd been in our saddles doing as punchers ought, but the cow work was reserved for the VR's old hands.

Aside from Uly and Spider, five other men called the McPhersons' bunkhouse home. Boudreaux was the only one whose name we knew. The others made the albino seem chatty by comparison. They rode off in the morning, rode back in the evening, and wasted no time in between on palaver with us. So we had to come up with our own handles for them—a showy dresser we called the Peacock, a bald fellow was Curly, and so on.

Altogether, seven workingmen didn't seem like nearly enough for a spread the size of the VR, and we wondered how they'd got by before us

Hornet's Nesters came along. Old Red suspected they had help. We caught sight of Boudreaux rattling off to the south in a wagon one day, and my brother was of the opinion that he was driving supplies out to what we cowboys call a line camp—an outpost for hands looking after herds in distant pastures.

If the McPhersons did have line-camp hands, I knew one thing about them: They wouldn't be worth squat. Only once did we see Uly's boys do a lick of labor, and a sorry piece of work it was. The HQ outhouse was as drafty as a pair of flap-assed underdrawers, so Boudreaux and the Peacock built a new one between their bunkhouse and the castle. It kept the wind off you a little better than the old privy, but you were twice as likely to come away with splinters in your unmentionables. On top of that, the door latch was loose, and it would fall into place and lock if anybody let the door slam. The first time that happened, we were making like bears in the bushes the whole day before Old Red figured out the new outhouse was empty.

So to boil it down, working under the McPhersons was equal parts humiliation and misery. But being a cowboy, I'd long ago resigned myself to both, and the mind-numbing routine of ranch life started to wear away the concerns I'd had about the VR. There came a day, however, when that routine was shattered, and the pieces never did fit together again.

It was getting on toward evening, and McPherson's men had already returned for the night. The Hornet's Nest boys were still working, of course, trying to get the smithy shop looking like something other than a tramp's lean-to. Old Red was slapping a coat of whitewash over rotted-out wood, and he stopped midbrush and looked over his shoulder.

"Well, well," he said. "What's *he* doin' here?"

We all turned and saw a fellow on horseback headed toward us— Jack Martin, deputy U.S. marshal out of Miles City.

We gave him a big huzzah. Not that we liked him so much. He had a reputation for puffing himself up around cowboys and wilting himself down around cattlemen. But it didn't matter just then. We were damned pleased to see a halfway friendly face after a month at the VR.

Our salute drew Boudreaux and the rest of the old hands from their bunkhouse, and Perkins, Spider, and Uly came out of the castle looking none too tickled to have unexpected company.

"That is surely the most duded-up ranch house I ever did see," Martin said, nodding at the castle. He turned a bucktoothed smile on us Hornet's Nesters. "So—how're they treatin' you out here?"

"How does the Northern Pacific treat Chinks?" Anytime said.

Perkins jumped in before anyone else could get to bitching.

"What brings you to the Cantlemere?" he said. To us he'd been little more than a shadow in the castle's windows for weeks. If he ever stepped outside, we didn't see it, and his skin had seen such little sun he'd grown as pale as Boudreaux.

"Official business," Martin answered, so full of self-importance it practically dribbled out his ears.

The lawman paused to look around the crowd, obviously savoring the opportunity to keep us hanging in suspense. The sight of Boudreaux's ghostly white hide put a flicker in Martin's grin, but he didn't let it linger. He had big news, and he wasn't going to let some distraction—no matter how freakish—muffle its thunder.

"Bob Tracy slipped out of the Colorado state nuthouse three weeks back."

Nearly every hand murmured the same two words: "Hungry Bob?"

Martin nodded. "The same."

The murmuring got louder, only now the question mark was gone and it was just "Hungry Bob!"

Out West, you'll find more folks who know of Hungry Bob Tracy than can name the president of the United States. Bob was a trapper, a guide, and, most notably, a bona fide cannibal. By his own account, he'd eaten five men when his party got snowed in during the winter of

'77. My mother used to tell me Hungry Bob would get me if I didn't keep up with my studies. I stopped believing her eventually, yet old Bob haunted my dreams for years after.

"He's been spotted twice—once around Fort Collins and again on the Little Bighorn near Lodge Grass."

"Headed for Canada," Gustav announced as if he were the one delivering the news.

"Could be," Martin said. "Or he might be holed up in the hills south of here. If he does push north, that would take him straight through our country here. So we're askin' folks to keep their eyes open."

"That won't be a problem. You know how we feel about folks wanderin' onto the VR," Uly said. "In fact, you're lucky *you* were able to ride in without gettin' . . . stopped."

"We'll be doubly careful from here on," Spider threw in. "In fact, if anybody gets it in their head to track Hungry Bob thisaway, you warn 'em to steer clear. With Bob prowlin' about, we'll be pretty quick on the trigger. Who's to say who might end up with a bullet in 'em?"

Martin frowned and leaned back in his saddle.

"We know you have important work to do. We won't keep you from it," Perkins said, turning and heading toward the castle before he was even done talking. "Good day."

Martin's frown turned into an outright scowl. Dusk wasn't far off, and he'd probably been hoping for a hot meal and a bed for the night.

"It's gonna take you at least four hours to make the next ranch," Uly said. "You best set out *now*." He pointed at the trail Martin had rode in on. "That way."

The lawman stared hard at McPherson a moment. Then he wheeled his horse and galloped off, taking with him any chance that we'd hear more news of the outside world that day.

"Alright, no more gawkin'!" Uly barked. "Back to work!"

Us Hornet's Nesters turned away slowly, unable to tear our eyes from Martin as he rode off. The only exception was Old Red. He was staring in the opposite direction—toward the hills to the south.

I knew exactly what he was thinking. It was the same thought that would weigh heavy on me during the long nights ahead.

Somewhere out there was a monster straight out of my childhood nightmares. It was real. It was loose.

And it was probably hungry.

Five

THE STAMPEDE

Or, A Storm Blows In, and a Life Snuffs Out

For the next few weeks, every owl hooting and bunk board creaking was Hungry Bob on the hunt for a juicy cut of man steak. Tall John almost got himself shot on three different occasions creeping out to drown spiders in the middle of the night. We went to bed jumpy and woke up exhausted, and none of us had much energy for chores.

But then Uly gave us something new to think about—the very orders we'd been hoping for. We were to start breaking horses for the roundup.

We spent the next week getting thrown ass-over-hat busting broncs—and loving every minute of it. At night we dropped into our bunks scraped and sore, and the snores of soundly sleeping men once again rattled the walls.

When we finally rode out looking for cattle, we saw that McPherson's men had been up to something useful after all. They'd stocked a feeding camp with hay and cottonseed and moved a thousand head in from the furthest pastures. We weren't to see those far grasslands ourselves—Uly ordered us to stay within five miles of the castle. Just in case we might drift over the limit, either Spider or Boudreaux was on our heels at all times.

But Old Red managed to unstick our escorts one day. Uly needed a windmill water pump fixed, and my brother stepped up to say he and I knew windmills like the back of our hands—which would have been true had our hands been something we saw only on occasion, and then from a distance.

We wrestled with that wooden monstrosity for hours, slicking ourselves black with grease in the process. Fortunately, there was no audience on hand but thirsty cows, as Spider and the albino were off keeping watch on the other Hornet's Nesters. Somehow we got that windmill pumping water, and after washing ourselves off and taking a ·good, long drink, we let the cows have a taste.

I was feeling pretty pleased with our ingenuity as we headed back to HQ, but Old Red seemed absolutely downcast. He rode slow, leaning out away from his saddle, his head hanging low.

"You feelin' faint?"

"No, I ain't feelin' faint," Gustav growled. "I'm lookin' for somethin'."

"What kinda somethin'?"

My brother stopped his horse and slid from the saddle.

"That kind," he said, pointing at nothing in particular, far as I could see. He went down on his knees and started crawling through the grass.

"Third time in as many days," he muttered.

"Third time in as many days *what?*"

He shot me an annoyed glance. "Third time in as many days I've had to figure I'm the only man here with eyes in his head."

My brother's always had a talent for tracking, but that doesn't mean I'll let him get uppity about it.

"Alright, Chief Eagle Eye," I said. "Just tell this deaf, dumb, blind white man what it is you think you see."

Old Red pointed again. "You're blind alright if you can't tell me what that is there."

Grass was all I saw. I had a feeling that wasn't the answer Gustav was looking for.

"Well, now that you point it out, it's plain as day," I bluffed.

"That it is. Same as this." He pointed at a muddy patch nearby.

"Why, sure. I can't believe I didn't see it right off."

Old Red nodded. "And I *know* you can tell me what this is." He nudged a moist cow patty with his boot.

"Well, of course."

"Yeah?"

"It's . . . well . . ."

"It's bullshit, brother—like half of what comes outta your mouth. Now just grab the reins of my pony and follow behind. I want to see where this trail goes."

I cussed, but did as I was told. For years I'd been letting my brother say things to me no other man could—probably because he was the only other Amlingmeyer left to say *anything*.

He moved off through the grass slowly, stooped over like a chicken hunting for something to peck. I ambled after him with the horses. After we'd poked along like that maybe five minutes, it became clear where we were headed. There was a rocky, shrub-covered bluff half a mile to the east. Whatever my brother was following, that's where it had gone.

We never made it there ourselves. Gustav straightened up and turned to the northwest, and there was Spider bearing down on us hard. It looked like he planned to send his horse right up my brother's chest and down the other side, but Old Red just stood there and watched him come. When Spider finally reined up, his horse was practically stepping on Gustav's toes, yet he didn't get a flinch out of my brother. Me, I jumped enough for the both of us.

"What the hell are you doin'?" Somehow Spider knew to yell this at Old Red. I was just my brother's movable hitching post. "You're supposed to be workin' on a windmill. We've told you dumb bastards not to—"

"I'm trackin' a man," Gustav said calmly.

"*What?*"

"You asked what I'm doin'. I'm tellin' you."

Spider pushed the brim of his sweat-soaked Boss of the Plains up high on his head.

"Say again?"

Old Red pointed at the spot where he'd hopped off his horse a few minutes before. "Someone's been messin' with grouse nests back there. Huntin' for eggs or a nice, tender prairie chicken, I reckon. Funny thing, though—whoever it is, he don't seem to have a mount."

"He's on foot?"

"That's right."

"Hey," I said, putting my two bits in for the first time, "you think maybe—?"

Spider threw those bits right back in my face. "Keep your trap shut." He turned toward Gustav again. "This trail you're on—any idea where it leads?"

Old Red shrugged, which was probably a lie in itself. "Have to keep followin' it to know that."

"Alright." Spider took a good look around—and it wasn't to admire a pretty sunset. He was marking the spot. "Get back to your bunkhouse and don't breathe a word of this to *anybody*. You do, I'll pluck out your eyes and eat 'em like a couple of boiled eggs. You understand me?"

My brother scratched at his ear in a casual, absentminded way, like he was trying to remember where he'd left his pipe.

"You're understood," he said.

Spider stayed close behind as we rode toward HQ. It gave me a creepy feeling, him having such a clear view of our backs. But we made it to the corral without any slugs in our spines. Spider didn't turn his horse out for the night, as we did. He went looking for his brother and Boudreaux, and when he found them they tore out toward the range together.

"You think that's Hungry Bob out there?" I said as they kicked up dust.

Old Red didn't answer.

"There's gotta be a bounty on his head. A big one. Five hundred dollars . . . maybe a thousand."

That didn't get a response, either.

"I reckon that's what the McPhersons are up to," I went on. "They're lookin' to snatch that reward right outta our hands, when it was us who—"

"*Us?*" my brother finally said.

"Alright, *you*. But the point is—"

"There ain't no point. Not when we don't got *facts*. Now hush. I'm thinkin'."

I hushed—and Gustav did the same. The only sound he made the rest of the night was when he struck a lucifer to light his pipe. Of course, silence came easy to him. For me, it was torture. A dozen times I almost blabbed to the boys about what we'd found. But I was anxious to keep my eyeballs from between Spider's teeth, and I managed to limit my conversation to cards and cattle.

The next day Uly gave me something else to talk about. We had new orders. Old Red and I wouldn't be fixing any more windmills. We'd be branding calves with the other Hornet's Nesters.

"Guess they don't want you out where you might see another trail," I said as the two of us stoked up a fire for the irons.

"Or they don't want me to notice there ain't no more trails to see," Gustav said.

"What? You think they caught somebody out there?"

My brother just shrugged.

"Well, if they did, it sure as hell wasn't Hungry Bob," I said.

Old Red looked up from the fire just long enough to cock an eyebrow at me.

"If the McPhersons bagged Bob, they'd have run him straight in to Miles City," I explained. "In fact, they'd be there still, blowin' the reward on wine, women, and song—or whiskey, whores, and more whiskey, more like."

Gustav frowned, making the sort of face a man puts on when he takes a bite of overbaked vinegar pie—a face that says, *I ain't so sure I can swallow that.*

"Could be," he said, and that was all I could get out of him on the subject for quite a spell.

Over the next week, we did so much branding that the whole world began to look like a cow's backside. When we finally got a break from the irons, though, I wasn't happy about it. It started late in the afternoon with a wall of black cloud that blocked up the sun like brick. The sound of distant thunder came with it, and the hair on the back of my neck stood up—and that isn't just an expression. The lightning strikes were still a ways off, but the electricity was already thick in the air around us. A shimmer of green fire danced on every edge, and pony ears and bull horns lit up bright as lanterns.

It was shaping up to be a nasty one indeed, and all the hands—even Uly, Spider, Boudreaux, and the rest of their bunch—headed out to get the cattle to high ground. When the rain came it was going to come hard, with gully washers that flashed up fast. What looked like a dried-out creekbed one minute could be a roaring river the next, and cow, horse, or man caught in the wrong place when the downpour started could easily end up drowned.

And that's not the only way to get yourself killed in a storm. Sometimes that green spark starts jumping from cow to cow, and fear jumps with it. Before long your mount's getting spooky, too, and one good crack of thunder could set everything with four legs to running. If you found yourself unhorsed in the midst of that, there wouldn't be enough of you left to say a prayer over.

These encouraging thoughts had a half-hitch on my brain as me and the boys pushed about three hundred cows up out of a flat. The air was so charged by then I could feel an electric prickle on my eyelashes, and my tongue tasted like a mouthful of pennies. All at once such a wind whipped up I had to dig my boots into my stirrups to keep from taking off like a kite. The rain started soon after that, coming down hard enough to wash the tan off a man's skin.

Through the sheets of rain, an apparition appeared before me—a vision so unexpected I had to wipe away the water blowing into my eyes and stare a moment before I could accept it as something other than a trick of shadow and light. It was a man on horseback wearing not a wide-brimmed Stetson but a derby, and not a yellow slicker but a black frock coat.

"Keep the cattle moving!" he was yelling.

I recognized the voice before I saw the face, and my shock doubled. It was Perkins.

I'd rarely laid eyes on the VR's manager out of doors, and never on horseback. Yet there he was atop Puddin'-Foot, the tamest pony on the ranch. Puddin'-Foot was slow, but he was smart: Leave him blindfolded in any corner of the spread and you'd still find him at headquarters at the end of the day begging for sugar. He was the perfect mount for anyone without much horse sense—and Perkins certainly wasn't displaying sense of any kind by venturing out of the castle on such a night.

"Get them to high ground! *High ground!*"

"Yessir!" I called back. "High ground!"

Perkins nodded, gave me a sort of "Go about your business" salute, and rode off.

That the man had risked life and limb to tell me to do exactly what I was already doing might have struck me as thickheaded indeed—if I'd had time to ponder it. But I was occupied with more pressing business. The ground was turning to thick black muck, and the pinto beneath me almost went down more than once as we struggled through it. Riding in a storm was a fine way to break a horse's leg or a man's back, and I was mighty curious to see which was going to happen first.

After what could have been hours or days far as I knew, another lone rider appeared. It was Spider this time, and though what usually poured from his mouth was pure bile, this time it was sweetest honey.

"Head in! We've done what we can! Go!"

He got no arguments. Us Hornet's Nesters dragged ourselves back to the bunkhouse and fell asleep still slimy as catfish. The next morning we stumbled outside into a world of sunshine and mud. Look up and everything was clear blue, look down and everything was nasty brown. The Swede whipped us up biscuits and ham, and we got to swapping tales of the storm we'd been too tired to tell the night before. I was waiting for the right moment to mention my encounter with our manager when Uly appeared and sped things up.

"Any of you seen Perkins?" McPherson asked.

"Not this mornin'," I said, and the other boys shrugged and shook their heads.

"What do you mean, 'Not this mornin''?"

"I ran across him yesterday in the storm."

"You *what*?"

"I saw him, too," Tall John threw in.

"And me," said Pinky Harris.

"We was about four miles southwest of here workin' cattle up out of the flats," I explained.

"What the hell was Perkins doin' there?"

I shrugged. "I guess he was tryin' to help."

Uly gave me a long squint that let all of us know exactly what he was going to say next.

"Well, I never saw him. And he ain't in the house now."

We put down our plates and got our saddles without a word. We all knew what had to be done. Tall John, Pinky, and I led the rest of the boys out to the spot where we'd seen Perkins, then we fanned out.

It didn't take long. Someone squeezed off a shot, we all circled in on the sound, and there stood Tall John next to a streak of black, red, white, and yellow in the mud. The black was a frock coat.

The rest of it—well, you already know about that.

Just a few hours before, it had been a man.

Six

THE BURIAL

Or, We Finish One Grave, Then Get Started on Our Own

Anytime McCoy summed up what was left to see with his usual eloquence and sensitivity.

"No need for a coffin," he said. "We could bury that in a bucket."

But there was no call for either coffin or bucket, for Uly announced that Perkins would be plowed under on the spot. I was feeling sorry for whoever got fingered for this gruesome chore when Gustav piped up to volunteer *us*. Uly nodded, hollered at the other hands to get to work, then galloped off. Boudreaux lingered by the body while the rest of the boys rode away with McPherson. The albino was either making sure no one powwowed behind the boss's back or fishing for a chance to pocket Perkins's locket and gold chain and whatever other valuables he could pluck from the muck.

"Say, Boudreaux," Gustav said. "How long you been at the VR?"

Boudreaux affixed his piss-yellow eyes on my brother, and I figured that stare was the only answer he was going to give. The albino wasn't just tight-lipped with us. He had little to say to the McPhersons, giving them "Yes, boss" or "No, boss" as required but offering nothing else our ears ever caught. He sort of floated quietly above things, as if speaking might drag him down into the dirt with the rest of us. To men like Anytime, that made him an "uppity nigger freak." But I think my brother almost considered him some kind of kindred spirit.

"You don't exactly seem broken up about Perkins here," Old Red said after a moment of silence limped by.

"Why should I be broken up?"

The low rumble of the albino's voice caught me off guard, like thunder on a sunny day.

"You knew the man," Gustav replied.

Boudreaux shrugged. "Not really."

"Well, still—it's a shame, ain't it? Whether you were friendly with the man or not?"

Boudreaux swept his gaze over the cornucopia of gore spilled out around us. "Yeah, it's a shame alright," he said, his voice as flat as the body. "A goddamn waste." He looked off to the north, making sure all the Hornet's Nesters had cleared out. Then he cleared out, too.

"I wonder what Mr. Holmes would make of him," my brother said as Boudreaux rode off. "That feller . . . he thinks his own thoughts." Then Old Red clapped his hands on the horn of his saddle and un-horsed himself. "Well, you heard the man. I'll get to gatherin' up the bits. You head back and grab us a couple shovels."

And that circles us around to the spot where you, dear reader, came in. I took my time collecting the shovels, found Gustav treating the body like a jigsaw puzzle, and felt obliged to throw out a much-needed reminder.

"Damn it, Brother. You're a cowboy, not a detective."

Old Red was up to his ankles in entrails at the time, yet he curled the corners of his mouth into one of his little smiles.

"That's the real reason we're out here, ain't it?" I went on. "So you can play Sherlock Holmes?"

"I wanted a gander at the body before it got planted," Old Red said.

"I ain't talkin' about *out here* out here! I'm talkin' about out here at the VR, workin' for the McPhersons. Them fellers are snakes, and you just *had* to find out what kind—so you went and threw us into the damn snake pit."

By the time I was done talking, Gustav's grin had wilted down into a frown.

"Where would you rather be right now, Otto?" my brother snapped. "Beggin' for pennies back in Miles? Or out here with a full belly?"

The words *full belly* gave my stomach the flip-flops—probably because Gustav was poking around in another fellow's giblets when they left his lips. I turned away and occupied myself with digging.

"What the hell are you lookin' for over there, anyway?"

"Wounds," Old Red said.

I wasn't in a laughing mood, but I had to pop off a snort at that.

"Sweet Jesus, Gustav—that body ain't nothin' *but* wound."

"I mean somethin' a cow or coyote couldn't do."

"Like what? A knife in his back? A rope around his neck?"

"*No.* I'm lookin' for clues, damn it. Like this here."

I glanced back to see Old Red waving a hand at me—and I don't mean one of his own.

"You notice anything peculiar about this?" he asked, holding the hand up by one rosy-red finger.

"I sure as hell do." I turned my attention back to shoveling sludge. "I see a feller shakin' hands with a *hand,* and that's more than peculiar—it's disgustin'."

My brother heaved a sigh. "If you'd bother to *look* at it, you'd see that Perkins was slippin' out of the castle without us knowin' it."

"How you figure that?"

"The skin on this hand's tanned," Old Red said. "And another thing, there used to be a ring on this finger here."

"I never noticed any ring."

"*You* wouldn't. Your eyes are about as sharp as an egg."

I ignored the dig but stopped digging. My brother was no detective, true enough, but he had eyes in his head and he could use them better than most men. If he said Perkins wore a ring, then Perkins wore a ring.

"Maybe it came off when all them cows used him as a staircase," I said. "If you haven't noticed, he's missin' a few other things, too. Such as, oh . . . most everything from the chest up."

"Hooves can flatten a man. But tuggin' off a gold band?" Gustav laid the hand back in place. "That's work for fingers."

"Just what're you sayin'?"

Gustav shrugged and finally picked up his shovel. "Ain't sayin' nothin'. Just thinkin'."

Then my brother really *wasn't* saying anything. He was digging, the faraway look in his eyes telling me the conversation was over. When Old Red gets lost in thought, Lewis and Clark couldn't find him again.

Before long we had the body—as much of it as we could find, anyway—under a hard-packed layer of earth. Once we were done, Gustav put down his shovel and started spiraling out in wider and wider circles, staring at the ground. My brother's a top-rail reader of trail sign, but I wasn't sure what he could hope to find, as the ground thereabouts had been churned to butter.

Whatever he was in search of, he didn't get to look for it long. The pounding of hooves rose up over a nearby ridge, and Spider appeared, charging at us at full gallop. He hadn't been around when the body was found, but somehow I didn't get the impression he was hurrying out to pay his last respects. He had his horse bearing down on Old Red just as he'd done a few days before. And again my brother didn't flinch. This time he got splattered with mud for his nerve, Spider's horse skidding to a stop practically chest to chest with him.

"Where's Perkins?" Spider spat.

Old Red pointed at the spot where we'd bedded the man down.

"Then why are you out here lollygaggin'?"

"Just makin' sure we didn't miss anything," I said.

"Anything you missed'll be buried in a coyote turd soon enough," Spider snapped back. "Now get goin'."

The way Spider watched as we horsed ourselves made me think it wasn't lollygagging he was worried about—it was snooping. Uly hadn't caught on yet to my brother's nosy nature, but Spider surely had. He rode behind us all the way in to HQ, and once again I felt an uncomfortable itch between my shoulders, like there was a bullet behind me just waiting to dig its way in.

The rest of the day passed as normal as could be, aside from all the gossip. Every other word the Hornet's Nesters spoke was *Perkins*. Yet anytime the McPhersons got close, the boys just took to whistling or talking about the weather. Whatever notions Old Red had—on Perkins, the weather, whistling, or anything else—he kept to himself.

That evening after supper, Spider and Uly dropped in for a visit. They always took their meals separate from us, with their own little circle, and it was rare for us to see them after sundown. As one might expect from such men, they didn't pretend this was some overdue social call.

"Things ain't gonna change around here," Uly said, getting right down to business. "Perkins was nothin' but a glorified clerk. I've been runnin' this outfit, and until the owners see fit to send a new manager, I'll keep right on runnin' it."

Uly moved his gaze around the room, giving each man a chance to take issue with what he'd said. He seemed to give Gustav a few more seconds than the rest. When my turn came, I just stared back as friendly as the face in the mirror. Uly saved the Swede for last.

"I'm sendin' Spider into town tomorrow," he said to the old cook. "You may as well go along and pick up whatever you need."

"Yessir, Misteer Ooly, I do that," the Swede said, sounding none too enthused about a daylong wagon ride with the likes of Spider.

Uly gave him a curt nod, then moved that hard-eyed stare of his around the room again. "Don't keep yourselves up all night with useless gab. You're gonna get called out early for work tomorrow, just like any other day. You understand me?"

The yes-sirs he got were pretty halfhearted, but Uly was satisfied enough to move on. Once he and Spider had left, of course, the Hornet's Nesters threw themselves right into the gab he'd warned against. The main topic of debate was whether things would be better or worse now that Perkins was gone. If put to a vote, worse would've won in a landslide.

"There won't be no rein on the McPhersons now," said Swivel-Eye Smyth. He was the eldest of us—being thirty, he was considered an old man. He was usually one of the last fellows to get downhearted or riled up about our hardships, but now his cross-eyed gaze had lost its usual look of wry tolerance. One eye stared this way, one eye stared the other, and clearly, neither of them saw anything to be cheerful about.

"Too right," said Crazymouth Nick Dury. "Things'll go arse-about-face with those nutters up our Khyber Passes. I've 'alf a mind to scarper—and I would if I 'ad the goolies."

In Crazymouth's hometown—London, England—this might've passed for keen insight or high wit or *something*. But in Montana it meant about as much as a cricket's fart, and Anytime McCoy jumped in as if the Englishman hadn't spoken at all.

"Yeah, those bastards'll ride us harder than ever now." Anytime's perpetually angry eyes smoldered at the thought of insults that hadn't even been hurled yet. "Well, they best not dig their spurs into *me*—them or their pet nigger. They do, and they'll regret it."

"If we're lucky, Uly and his boys'll be too drunk to bother with us for weeks," Pinky Harris said. "Y'all saw how much liquor Perkins had over in the big house. I bet the McPhersons are raisin' a toast to Perkins's memory at this very moment."

"Christ! What is this—a bunkhouse or a sewing circle?" Tall John cried out, a jeering grin cutting across his jut-jawed, crescent-moon face. "Just listen to you gossipy old hens! Why should it make one bit of difference whether Perkins is alive or not? He was always holed up in the castle anyway. The McPhersons'll treat us the same as always—and I don't think that's been half-bad."

"Nope—it's been *all* bad," I said, unable to resist such an opening. "I'm inclined to agree with the rest of the fellers. With Perkins gone, the VR practically belongs to the McPhersons. The owners are halfway around the world. Who's gonna tell Uly what he can or can't do?"

"Well, I agree with Tall John about one thing," Old Red cut in. "Y'all talk too much." And with that he stood, walked to his bunk, and started stripping down for bed.

The rest of us did the same before long. Though we had plenty to think on, that didn't stave off sleep for anybody, for soon enough the boys were singing a chorus of snores. I joined the choir, dreaming of the very things us punchers see so little of when awake—women, good food, women, good liquor, women, and women. I was just about to plant a kiss on one of those lovely ladies from the land of Nod when something clamped down on my lips in the real world. A dark shape leaned in close and whispered in my ear.

"Grab your boots and meet me outside—and do it *quiet*."

Then the hand was gone, and I heard footsteps moving toward the door. I eased myself down silent as I could, snatched up my boots, and did my best to slip out of the bunkhouse without walking into a wall.

When I caught up with Gustav, he was set for my questions—I could see by the dim light of the moon that he had a finger up to his lips to shush me. He began pulling on his boots, so I did likewise, as it was clear we weren't outside just to enjoy the fresh night air. And *cold* air it was, I assure you, for I had nothing covering my goose-pimpled hide but the flannel of my long johns.

Once we were shod, Old Red set off toward the castle. I watched him go, weighing the opportunity to get shot against a good night's sleep wrapped in warm blankets. In such moments of indecision, a memory comes to me that always tips the scales.

The night the Cottonwood River got too big for its banks and swallowed up my family, my sister Greta and I found ourselves perched in the highest branches of an oak tree. We were there for hours, clinging to each other for dear life as the swirling waters swept debris and the dead past our dangling feet. Somewhere in the dark of night she and I both fell asleep, and I awoke in the morning to find Greta gone. I'd been so exhausted I'd let my sister go, and even the splashes of her drowning hadn't been enough to wake me. I never found a body to bury.

Only one Amlingmeyer was left to keep hold of now—and I aimed to keep my grip on him tight.

I sighed and started after my brother.

Seven

BOTTLES

Or, Old Red Finds That Ink and Alcohol Don't Mix

I figured we were a safe distance from the bunkhouses when we reached the back of the castle, so I gave voice to the question that was foremost in my mind.

"What the hell are you up to?"

My brother shushed me again, then turned and set to work on the back door with a short length of wire he'd pulled from his pocket.

Normally Gustav doesn't have any use for American magazine detectives—"all muscle, no method," he calls them. But this lockpicking trick came straight from the pages of a Nick Carter dime novel. That Nick's ever busting into dark mansions or escaping from steel vaults filling with water just by whipping out a toothpick and giving it a twiddle. Frankly, I never believed any of it—and apparently Old Red had doubts himself.

"I'll be damned," he said when the lock clicked, the knob turned, and the door went swinging open.

It was pitch-black inside the house, but that didn't slow my brother. He knew exactly where he was going, and I followed behind more by sound than sight. Before long he struck a lucifer and touched it to a lamp, and when the room lit up around us, I saw we were in Perkins's office.

"Get those curtains, quick," Gustav said, turning the flame down as low as it would go.

"Sure, sure—just jerk me around like a pack mule," I grumbled as I pulled the curtains closed. When I turned around, I found my brother opening the top drawer to Perkins's desk. "You wanna tell me what the hell you're lookin' for?"

"Can't say cuz I don't know," Old Red replied, shuffling through paper clips, pens, and spare bottles of ink.

"What?"

Gustav moved on to the next drawer. "Perkins was holed up in this office for weeks *before* the spring roundups. Far as we know, there weren't any new head counts to record. No sales, neither. So what was he workin' on so hard?"

"How do you know he was workin'? He could've been in here cuttin' pictures of corsets and bloomers out of the Monkey-Ward catalog."

Old Red looked up just long enough to shoot me a frown. "Back when we were sprucin' up the castle, we caught sight of the man every now and again, remember? You mean to say you never noticed he had ink on his fingers?"

"Oh. I guess I *would* have to say that."

My brother shook his head, then disappeared under the desk. When he popped up again, he was holding a metal wastebasket. He peered into it, smiled, and tilted the top so I could look in, too.

Piled up inside were at least twenty empty ink bottles.

"You spent some time hunched over a desk," Old Red said. "What do you make of this?"

Being one of the few boys around Peabody, Kansas, with both a head for books and enough schooling to do anything with it, I'd worked two years as an assistant granary clerk before being dragged back to the farm seven days a week by family misfortune—in this case, my uncle Franz's growing belief that he was Martin Luther and one of our pigs was the pope. That had been years ago, yet I still remembered enough from my clerking days to know Perkins hadn't run through all those bottles without considerable effort.

"With that much ink you could fill up three ledger books and still have enough left over to drown a dog," I said. "But what difference does that make?"

"Could make a lot . . . if Perkins's death wasn't an accident."

"Oh," I groaned. "That again."

"Yes, *that* again," my brother snapped. "Look, we know somethin' strange is goin' on around here. We're put to housework when we arrive, we ain't allowed more than a few miles from HQ, the McPhersons watch us like hawks circlin' a chicken coop, Perkins spends his days scribblin' away at God knows what and then ends up under a stampede. Don't all that make you the least bit curious?"

"Curious, yes. Suicidal, *no*. If Uly and Spider catch us in here—"

"All I wanna do is find whatever Perkins was—"

My brother's eyes suddenly went wide, and I'm sure mine did the same. We'd both heard the back door creak open, and the sound that followed could only be footsteps.

We'd closed the office door behind us, but the faint glow from the lamp might still peek out through the keyhole and give us away. Gustav put out the light, leaving us frozen in a dark as deep as the blind must know.

The hallway from the kitchen splits in two, wrapping itself like arms around the stairway to the second floor. On the north side of the house, the hall passes by a dining room and a parlor on its way to the foyer. Moving around to the south, it takes you by an indoor privy, unused "servants' quarters," Perkins's bedroom, and the ranch office, where we were holed up.

It sounded like whoever was out there was headed straight for us. I suddenly became very aware of the lightness at my hip—where the weight of a Colt would've helped me feel a lot less spooky. Not only were we facing this new danger without benefit of guns, we were facing it without benefit of *pants,* as we were both still in our long johns.

"What're we gonna do?"

"Nothin' . . . yet," Old Red whispered back.

The footsteps slowed, then stopped. We heard a sigh, almost like a ghostly moan.

"Ahhhhhh."

And next, a clink—the sound of glass touching glass. Then "Ahh-hhhh" again.

Much closer now, I heard more footsteps. But this time it was my brother creeping closer to the door. There was a low rattle—Gustav turning the knob—and then a narrow sliver of light appeared. Old Red had opened the door just enough to peek out. I moved up behind him and peered over his head.

Across the foyer, stretched out on an overstuffed divan in the parlor, was the mirror image of Old Red and myself: a fellow in nothing but boots and a union suit. On the floor at his feet were a lit candle and three bottles—one deep amber, one straw yellow, and one bloodred.

Scotch, beer, and wine.

The man had a glass to his lips, and his head was thrown back so as to drain every drop.

"Ahhhhhh," he said.

Then he moved the glass away from his mouth, revealing his face.

He was too small a fellow by far to be Uly or Spider, and his hands didn't have Boudreaux's off-white buttermilk hue. Yet still I'd been so certain he was one of the McPherson men celebrating Perkins's early retirement I almost blurted out in shock when I saw who it really was.

Pinky Harris?

I managed to keep myself stifled long enough for Old Red to close the door.

"Shit," my brother murmured. "I've got serious detectin' to do, and one of the Hornet's Nest boys has to go on a damn bender?"

"I tell you what. I'll step out there and join Pinky in a drink or two. That'll distract him while you finish up your business."

Gustav rejected my noble offer with a snort. "I reckon Pinky's only interested in Perkins's liquor, but we can't take any chances—he might go snoopin' around for tobacco or dirty postcards or who knows what. So we're gonna put everything back just like we found it, then we're goin' out the window."

I heard the sound of a desk drawer sliding shut, and a moment later metal clanked gently against wood as Old Red settled the wastebasket under the desk. In the deep silence of the house, both sounds seemed to echo like thunder. My brother and I stood there a while afterward, motionless, waiting for any sign that Pinky had heard.

"Ahhhhhh," Pinky said.

Clink.

"Alright," Old Red whispered, "get over to the window—and don't trip over anything."

That was easier said than done. We hadn't been in the dark long, but I'd already forgotten every detail of the room around me. Chairs, cabinets, bookshelves—I couldn't remember where they were or even *if* they were. The floor could have been littered with bear traps and roller skates for all I knew. And of course each step got the floorboards creaking like it was a two-thousand-pound elephant bearing down on them instead of a two-hundred-pound man.

Somehow Old Red beat me to the window without making a sound. He pulled the curtains apart slow and easy, then eased the window open. When it was up just high enough, he ducked down and slipped through in one smooth motion.

I followed—though I wasn't so smooth. I had more man to ma-

neuver than my brother, and one of my feet caught on the sill and top-
pled me over. I hit the ground outside with a thud.

Old Red and I stared at each other, two cowboys statue-still in the
moonlight wearing nothing but their Skivvies. A minute passed without
any hint that Pinky or the boys in the bunkhouses had heard us, and we
let ourselves breathe again.

"You go back to your bunk," Old Red said, still keeping his voice
low. "I'll be along in a minute."

"You ain't comin' in now?"

"Somebody catches a peek of one feller tiptoein' in, they figure he
was out waterin' the flowers. Two fellers—that raises questions."

It made sense, so I did as I was told, creeping back into the bunkhouse as silent as I could. My bunk squeaked so fierce as I hefted myself
up into it you would've thought I was stepping on a mouse, but the
sound didn't set a single man off a single snore.

As I stretched out and waited for Gustav, a familiar feeling came
over me. Many's the time my brothers and sisters told me, "Get back to
your books. This here's work for bigguns." They'd be milking a cow or
hitching up a plow, work I eventually learned was every bit as exciting
as watching water evaporate. But as a little nipper it looked like a real
thrill, if only because I wasn't allowed to do it.

Along the same line, I had the suspicion that Gustav had sent me
into the bunkhouse just to get me out of his red hair. That stuck in my
craw, for I was no longer the runt of the litter but was instead a sizable
man with just as much curiosity and pride as the next fellow—unless, I
suppose, the next fellow is Old Red.

I figured it was that pride that drove my brother to act alone. It
must be galling indeed to be both uncommonly intelligent and utterly
unlettered. A fellow might feel he had to *prove* he had a brain, and
mystery-solving would be a pretty showy way to go about it. Not to
mention deadly.

It vexed me to think I'd been dragged into danger by mere vanity.

If Old Red wanted to poke his big nose into other people's affairs, it wouldn't be my fault if that nose got shot off.

On the other hand, I owed my brother everything I had. Hell, he *was* everything I had. He'd been my guardian angel after the last of our family got swept away. Maybe it was my turn to wear the wings.

I'd just about decided to hop from my bunk, search out Old Red, and either force some help on him or kick his scrawny ass, when . . . well, I fell asleep.

When I awoke the next morning, I realized I'd never heard my brother come back in.

Eight

SPIDER'S BITE

Or, A Hornet's Nester Gets Hot Under the Collar

The day started in the usual way—with the Swede banging a pot and shouting, "Eats! Eats! Eats!" at the top of his lungs. That always jerked me from my slumber with a jolt, but this particular morning I had even more reason to wake up jumpy.

The second my eyes popped open, I rolled over and pointed them at the bunk beneath mine. I was half-expecting to see it empty, my brother having been caught by the McPhersons and strung up like a piñata. Yet there was Gustav, sporting that little smirk of his.

I opened my mouth, but Gustav shut it by souring his smile into a scowl that said, *Not now*. I was so glad to see he'd survived his snooping I didn't even get mad. I just holstered my questions and did like the other boys, racing out to get at the Swede's flapjacks before they were all gone. I figured I'd get an explanation sooner or later—even if I had to beat it out of my brother with a stick.

Old Red always let the rest of us stampede ahead come mealtimes, as he's a bony fellow without the appetite necessary to keep fat on a flea.

But this morning he wasn't the only one to linger. The Swede's grub call barely got a stir out of Pinky Harris. When I walked by his bunk, Pinky was buried facedown in his blankets, the only sign that he was alive a low, muffled groaning. Last night it had been "Ahhhhhh" for old Pinky, but now it was all "Ohhhhhh."

"Somethin' wrong?" asked his bunkie, Tall John.

Pinky's only reply was another groan.

By the time Pinky and Old Red moseyed out to the cookshack, the rest of us were halfway through our second helpings. When the boys weren't stuffing their mouths, they were shooting them off at each other. The topic was Perkins again—specifically, what could've possessed him to gallop into a killer storm when none of us had even seen him in a saddle before.

"Here's what I think," I said as Old Red settled down on a stool nearby, and I saw his eyes narrow, flashing me a warning not to let on about his deducifying. "Perkins just went stir-crazy cooped up in the castle all the time."

My brother's gaze returned to his plate, and he set into his food. The Hornet's Nest gang, meanwhile, set into my theory. Swivel-Eye thought I was onto something, as it was his days trapped in a schoolhouse that had sent him running for a horse and the open plains nearly twenty years earlier. Anytime agreed that hunching over a desk all day would surely sap a real man of his senses, but pointed out that Englishmen start out understocked on sanity in the first place. That put a burr under Crazymouth's saddle blanket, as it was meant to, and the English-born cowpoke shot back some of his mixed-up jabber— something like "'E was a right stuck-up Brighton Pier 'e was, without the Niagara the old sod gave a house martin." While the fellows were scratching their heads over that, Pinky put a stop to the fun by finally saying what everyone else had been trying *not* to say.

"Perkins was crazy alright—crazy to trust Uly and Spider," he croaked, his throat no doubt worn raw by all the alcohol that had washed over it the night before. "*That's* what did him in. Those bastards saw a chance to grab the VR out from under, and they took it. Am I right?"

No one said, "Damn straight, Pinky!" No one said anything at all. We all just stared, as silent and wooden-stiff as the stools under our rumps.

Pinky broke the awkward silence with a hoarse, forced laugh. "Awwww, don't listen to me. I'm just . . . well . . ."

"Hungover?" Tall John said.

"You smell like you just climbed out of a bathtub full of beer," Anytime added.

As his handle implies, Pinky was already rosy-skinned, but he turned even redder now.

"Where you got it stashed, Pinky?" Swivel-Eye asked joshingly, obviously trying to keep things from getting too serious again.

"And how come you won't share it?" I threw in.

"You suspicious sons of bitches think I got liquor, you go search my bunk," Pinky teased back. "All you'll find is lice . . . and you can have 'em!"

We all laughed a little too loud, and the conversation quickly turned to horses and cows and other safe subjects. When it came down to it, most of the boys didn't want to know what had happened to Perkins—not if it meant they had to do something about it. They weren't interested in mysteries or adventure. They just wanted their five dollars a week. I can't say I blame them.

We knew what our work was to be that morning, so we got to it. Pretty soon mama cows were lowing loud as Tall John and Anytime threw rope on their babies and brought them to the branding pen. The he-calves we were making into steers through the removal of certain dangling glands, and before long the fire outside the pen was not just heating up branding irons but cooking up a mess of prairie oysters, as well. Gustav and I were working inside the pen, notching ears and slicing off gonads with Swivel-Eye and Crazymouth, while Pinky kept the fire stoked and handed hot irons through the fence boards.

After we'd been at it maybe an hour, the Swede pulled around to the corral in the buckboard he used to tote supplies in from town.

"Hey, Swede! Bring me back some decent tobacco and a pretty gal, would you?" Swivel-Eye shouted at him.

"Bring me two—of each!" I threw in.

Instead of joshing us back, the Swede gave his head a quick shake, and his eyes rolled around to his left. We looked that way and saw Spider and Boudreaux riding toward us.

Spider's lean face was puckered with a little tight-lipped smile, as if he couldn't wait to start laughing at some joke he hadn't yet told. If Boudreaux knew what the joke was, he didn't find it funny—the albino usually looked pretty sour, but just then he seemed practically *curdled*.

"You set, Swede?" Spider asked.

"Yas, Mr. Spiter. I em ready now to be going."

"Fine."

The Swede raised up his reins. But before he could give the leather a snap, Spider turned toward us and called out, "Jeee-zus Key-rist!"

Gustav had just thrown a calf, and I was moving in with an iron so flamed up it could leave a brand on the air itself. And I gave it every chance to do so, for Spider's words froze me in my tracks.

"I was just startin' to think you pukes were real hands after all, and then I see a discouragin' thing like that," Spider said. "Where'd you learn to run a brand, Amlingmeyer?"

I knew Spider didn't want a real answer. But I also knew the smart thing to do was act thick and give him one.

"Well, the first ranch I got on at was the Cross J down in—"

"The Cross J?" Spider waved his hand before his nose as if shooing away a foul odor. "Those Panhandle shitheads couldn't brand their own asses if their hands were hot iron. Let me show you how it's done."

Spider dismounted, and Boudreaux did likewise.

"Gimme that stamp iron there," Spider said to Pinky.

Pinky obliged, pulling an iron from the fire and handing it over just as Boudreaux stepped around and got hold of him from behind.

"Hey! What're you—?" was all Pinky got out before Spider swung that branding iron like a baseball bat. Pinky's chin was the ball, and the way it whipped to the side at the force of the blow I almost feared the jawbone would fly through the skin and arc out of sight like a home-run hit. Pinky grunted and sagged back against Boudreaux.

"Pay attention, boys," Spider said as he brought up the still-glowing iron and pressed it against Pinky's chest. "This is how you lay down a good brand!"

Pinky's shirt began smoldering, and pretty quick we heard the sizzling we knew to be fired metal on flesh. Pinky writhed and screamed in Boudreaux's grip, but after the swat he'd taken he was too weak to escape.

For once, the albino was having a hard time floating above it all. The marble hardness of his pale features finally broke, at last revealing a real feeling—disgust.

Spider was giggling.

The iron in my hand had cooled down some, but it was still hot enough to char a Bar VR across Spider's forehead. I started toward the fence with exactly that in mind, but a hand caught my forearm and pulled me to a stop.

"Wait," Gustav said.

I tore my arm from his grip. "Wait for what? For them to kill him?"

I turned back toward Spider and Boudreaux, but the branding was over, and they let Pinky sink to the ground in a whimpering heap.

"You're fired," Spider said to him. Then he looked up at the rest of us, and his right hand settled a few inches from the grip of his spit-polished six-gun. "We don't need thieves or bigmouth troublemakers around here. Any of you forget that, you'll get the same treatment . . . or worse."

I managed to keep a rein on my anger while Spider and Boudreaux loaded Pinky in the back of the wagon—where they'd already piled his saddle and war bags, we now saw. Once they had him stowed, Spider walked back to the fire, snatched up a smoldering pair of huevos, and popped them in his mouth. He grinned as he chewed, and after he'd swallowed and given his lips a big wet lick, he and Boudreaux horsed themselves. Spider gave us a jaunty wave of his hat as they set off for Miles City.

When they were out of sight, I roared like a grizzly passing a kidney stone.

"God damn! What is wrong with us? Standing by and watching a thing like that!"

The boys just shook their heads or stood there, frozen, their eyes still wide with surprise. Even Anytime was quiet for once, simply turning away and kicking at the dirt.

"We're nothin' but a bunch of cowards!" I hollered.

"Button your lip, Brother," Gustav said.

"Oh, to hell with you! I'm sick and tired of your bull—"

Old Red grabbed a fistful of shirt and jerked me down so our eyes were but inches apart.

"I said *shut up*."

I've felt like taking a poke at Gustav many times over the years, though I'd never been quite mad enough to do it—until that moment. My fist was clenched and ready to shoot up to the side of his skull. But when Old Red spoke again, his words took the fight right out of me.

"Damn it, Brother, don't you see? We gotta watch our step," he whispered. "One of the Hornet's Nest boys is a spy."

Nine

HORSE SENSE

Or, A Clue Gallops Right Under Our Noses

Somehow us Hornet's Nesters managed to brand calves for the next two hours with barely twenty words passing among us. What did get said was on the order of "That one next" or "Hot iron here." I reckon most of the boys were feeling guilty about not helping Pinky. I was trying to figure out who *didn't* feel guilty.

I'd picked up on Old Red's point about a spy right off. Given Pinky's bloodshot eyes and rummy breath, it would've been easy to peg him as the thief who'd helped himself to the castle's liquor the night before. But Spider wouldn't know he was a "bigmouth troublemaker" unless he knew what Pinky had said at breakfast—which meant someone had tattled.

The easiest fellow to point a finger at would be the Swede. He was a VR man before any of us, and he could've gone running to Uly after we'd headed out for work. But given that English for the old cook seemed to be less a second language than a fifth or sixth, I couldn't believe he'd be much good at eavesdropping. With Pinky hardly a sensible candidate and my brother and myself disqualified for equally obvious reasons, that left the other Hornet's Nesters to consider: Tall John, Swivel-Eye, Anytime, and Crazymouth.

Unfortunately, once I'd tallied up all the jaunts to fetch saddles and catch mounts and take pisses and squats, I realized every one of them had been out of my sight that morning at one point or another. In the end, I settled on Anytime as my main suspect for the not exactly airtight reason that he was a nasty son of a bitch.

Despite my irritation with Old Red—it still chafed on me that we hadn't stood up for Pinky—there was nothing I wanted more just then than to pick my brother's prickly brain. I didn't see how I'd get a chance, though, as we were still branding calves with Swivel-Eye and Crazymouth, and neither man was more than a dogie-length away at any given moment. I was trying to figure how to get Gustav alone when my brother let out a mighty *"Damn it all!"*

We'd just mugged a calf, twisting her head and bringing her down on her side—and it looked like we'd brought her down on Old Red's foot, as well. Since punchers find nothing more amusing than humiliation and pain inflicted on another, this gave the boys a good guffaw. As usual, Anytime was the first to get a dig in.

"You're supposed to wait till the skin's leathered up before ya try to wear it!"

"Yeah!" Tall John called out from his spot by the fire, where he'd taken Pinky's place. "That boot's got too much beef in it yet!"

"Haw haw," Gustav yelled back, taking a wobbly step toward the fence. "Help me out here, Brother."

I wrapped an arm around him, and together we hop-walked to the far side of the pen. Old Red sat in the dirt and tugged at his boot.

"Damn, that smarts." Then, in a much softer voice, he added, "Quick—what do you want to know?"

"What?"

Gustav got himself unshod and took to inspecting his toes as if to make sure they were all still there.

"I could tell you were bustin' apart with questions. So I'm givin' you a chance to ask 'em."

"You sayin' you dropped that calf on your foot on purpose?"

"I didn't drop that calf on my foot at all. Now spit it out—I didn't go to all this trouble so we could squat here and play pat-a-cake."

A low growl rumbled in my throat. Even when my brother was doing me a favor, he had to be high-handed about it.

"Alright," I said. "Why'd you take so long gettin' back last night?"

"Didn't you notice somethin' missin' yesterday mornin'? Somethin' we should've found when we were buryin' the body?"

"I don't know. A head? I believe men usually have such things attached to their necks, but Perkins seemed to have misplaced his."

"I'm not talkin' about the body itself." Gustav's voice took on an edge of exasperation. "I'm talkin about—"

"Oh." I nodded, embarrassed that it had taken any prodding to get me pointed in the right direction. "His mount. Puddin' -Foot."

"Thank God. I was beginning to worry about you. Thinkin' of the man's horse don't call for detective know-how—it calls for cowboy know-how."

"Yeah, well, so," I said, eager to move beyond the subject of my mental shortcomings. "If Puddin' -Foot had gone down in the storm, he would've made an even bigger mess than Perkins."

"And if he didn't go down, why, Puddin' -Foot bein' gentle-broke the way he is and smart as a sheepdog, he would've come back to headquarters to get the saddle off his back."

"So you went lookin' for him?"

"And he wasn't anywhere around HQ."

"He could still be south of here somewhere, runnin' free or flat as a frying pan."

"Could be. If so, one of the boys'll run across him sooner or later."

"And if they don't?"

" 'It is a capital mistake to theorize before you have all the evidence. It biases the judgment.' "

"Well, how do you expect to gather *any* evidence with a spy doggin' us?"

Old Red started to pull his boot back on, and he made a big show of grimacing as the leather slid up over his shin.

"I ain't got that figured yet," he whispered. "We gotta be careful, that's for sure. If I'd known Uly had such a sharp eye on us Hornet's Nesters . . ."

Gustav let his words trail off, leaving me to wonder *what* if he'd known. Would he have stayed in his bunk last night? Would he have unhitched himself from his notions about detecting? Would he keep his eyes and ears and *mind* closed, the way the McPhersons wanted?

I didn't think so. Pinky proved otherwise. My brother didn't get in fights often, but he wasn't shy about setting people straight if they couldn't tell right from wrong. There'd been a time when he would have set Spider straight *con mucho gusto*—and *con mucho* knuckles to the nose. Instead, he'd stood by while a man was beaten and branded. And what's more, he'd made *me* stand by.

Thinking of Pinky got me heated up to quite a blaze again, and I was just about to singe Old Red's eyebrows with some hot talk, spy be damned, when Anytime put out a shout that rescued my brother from the barbecue.

"Hey, Big Red—get back to work! Just cuz your brother can't keep his feet out from under don't give *you* an excuse to lollygag!"

"We'll *both* get back to work," Old Red snapped, hauling himself off his duff. "If I sit here much longer, you'll make such a mess of things it'll take the rest of the week just to fix your mistakes."

My brother mock-limped to the center of the corral while the boys fed him more sass about his supposed clumsiness. The only talking he and I did after that was about hot brands and fresh-cut balls—not the sort of thing a spy would feel the need to report back to Uly.

Despite his "sore foot" (which he remembered to fake long after I would've forgotten), Gustav volunteered to tend to the saddle horses at the end of that day and the beginning of the next. Each time, he came back and gave me a quick shake of the head when he was done. I knew what he was looking for, so it wasn't hard to figure what that signal meant.

Puddin' -Foot had not returned.

Ten

NEWS FROM ENGLAND

Or, Old Red Is Reunited with One Partner and Loses Sight of Another

Spider, Boudreaux, and the Swede returned from Miles City the next afternoon. Though Spider and the albino were hardly a welcome sight, we were mighty pleased to see our biscuit rustler. While the Swede was gone, Uly had Tall John doing the cooking, even though the man couldn't so much as pop corn without scorching it black. On top of that, most of us Hornet's Nesters had put in special wink-and-a-handshake orders with the Swede in the hopes of getting around the VR's "company store"—aka Uly, who charged prices for tobacco, rolling paper, chewing wax, and other necessities that would've gotten a cowtown shopkeeper lynched.

Unfortunately, the second I laid eyes on the Swede, I knew the company store wouldn't be losing my business. The old cook had a sheepish look about him, and as soon as he was free of Spider and Boudreaux he began handing out money and apologies.

"I em sewry, boyce. Spiter vas over my shoulder all de time looking."

The only fellow who got a smile instead of a refund was my brother.

"Ahhhh, Old Red! I have what you ask fur, I tink."

The Swede had brought back a pile of newspapers, which we would soon put to use as reading material, kindling, wallpaper, and asswipe. Buried at the bottom of the stack were three magazines, and when the Swede pulled them out I knew exactly how I'd be spending the next few evenings.

They were copies of *Harper's Weekly,* the "Journal of Civilization"—and, much more important as far as my brother was concerned, the journal of Mr. Sherlock Holmes.

The magazine had begun printing accounts of Holmes's cases in January. Prior to that, Gustav had run across but two Holmes tales: "The Red-Headed League" and "A Study in Scarlet." Thanks to *Harper's,* he acquired several more. These weren't tattooed on my eyeballs to the same extent as the first two, for Old Red had stopped pestering me for repeat readings once we were bunked at the VR. I knew his reason, though he never spoke it.

Cowboys can be uncommonly open-minded on many a surprising subject, but there is one upon which their minds snap shut like a steel-jawed bear trap: They hate an "uppity" man. For one of their number to grudgingly admire a gentleman like Sherlock Holmes might be tolerated. To aspire to *become* him would invite scorn of the most venomous variety. So Old Red had kept his detective stories—and his dreams—out of sight.

But I knew the temptation of three new Holmes cases would be too much to resist. And sure enough that night in the bunkhouse Gustav handed me one of his treasures and said, "If you feel up to it, Brother, I'd sure enjoy a little oratory."

Now I'm not one for holding grudges. They usually slip through my fingers within a day or so. I'm especially apt to let them wriggle free if they involve my brother, as I've had years to accustom myself to his cussedness, just as he's had more than enough time to get used to whatever flaws I might allegedly possess.

But I was still stewing on what Spider had done to Pinky—and what we *hadn't* done to stop him. So while I always feel obligated to read when Gustav requests it, that doesn't mean I can't roast him over the fire a bit before I do so.

"Why, sure," I said. "This here *Harper's* has got a story on that World's Columbian Exposition they're plannin' in Chicago. Gonna be like ten state fairs and a hundred carnivals rolled up in one. And you'd never guess how much *concrete* they're shippin' in to build the exhibit halls and such. This article just goes on and on about it. It should only take an hour or so to get through."

Hats, boots, and curses came flying my way, while Old Red suffered in stone-faced silence.

"Well, my goodness! If you fellers don't have strong opinions about literature!" I said. "This next story looks like it's about a stolen racehorse, so I don't suppose you'd want to hear that. Now here's an article about the Idaho Populist Party. How about if I—"

As I expected, there were cries of "Whoa there!" and "Back up!"

There are two things cowboys can talk on all day long: horses and gambling. Combine them into one story—and throw in the appeal of crime to boot—and you'll have any puncher downright hypnotized. So naturally the boys were anxious to hear that racehorse tale . . . which just happened to be "Silver Blaze" by Sherlock Holmes's pal John Watson.

The story had much to grab the ears of my audience. There was that stolen Thoroughbred, a death, a crooked bookmaker, and even Gypsies. Yet while keeping the Hornet's Nesters happily diverted, all this was but trimming as far as my brother was concerned. The meat of the matter was how Holmes found that missing horse. As I read certain passages, I slowed my pace and glanced at Old Red, certain that he'd be doing his best to commit these words to memory:

"The difficulty is to detach the framework of fact—of absolute un-deniable fact—from the embellishments of theorists. . . .

"I follow my own methods and tell as much or as little as I choose. That is the advantage of being unofficial. . . .

"See the value of imagination. . . . We imagined what might have happened, acted upon the supposition, and find ourselves justified."

When I was finished, Gustav stretched out on his bunk looking like a man who's stuffed himself full of duck and pudding on Christmas Day. The rest of the boys seemed pleased enough, though the story lacked the perils and bloodshed they consider essential to truly rousing tale-telling. Still, the next night I was able to talk them into hearing two more Holmes cases: "The Stock-Broker's Clerk" and "The 'Gloria Scott.'"

Though these stories struck me as skimpy on the instructive deduc-tions my brother craved, Old Red had no complaints. In fact, he had little to say on anything at all, acting so distracted in the days that fol-lowed that the other hands began ragging him for his "sleepwalking."

Unlike Gustav, the rest of the Hornet's Nesters were in uncom-monly high spirits just then. We were almost done branding the calves McPherson's men had brought up from the distant pastures that had so far been barred to us, and the boys hoped we'd soon be out on horse-back pushing cattle ourselves.

No sooner was the last calf running back to mama than Uly came to the pen to lay out exactly what our new chores would be. I almost didn't recognize him at first, for he'd finally scraped off his dark thicket of beard and given his face and hands a splash of water. If he ever de-cided to change his raggedy britches and put on a clean shirt, he'd prac-tically look respectable.

But one thing about Uly hadn't changed: He wasn't a man to waste time on niceties.

"McCoy, Dury, Amlingmeyer," he barked, pointing at Anytime,

Crazymouth, and Old Red. "Take the fence wagon south and mend the wire wherever it needs it till you get five miles out. The rest of you I want ridin' bog north along the creek. That gully washer a few days back might've left some new sinkholes. You see any cattle in 'em, you get 'em right out. No dawdlin' now—hop to it."

I was so pleased to be getting out of the corral and horsing myself, the full meaning of Uly's words didn't hit me straight off. I turned to fetch my riding gear and then stopped dead in my tracks, my mouth slowly falling open and just dangling there, slack with surprise.

For the first time since we'd been at the VR, I realized, Old Red and I were being busted apart.

Eleven

THE BOG RIDE

Or, I Encounter Some Very Small Sinkholes and One Whopper of a Shock

As peevish as I'd been feeling toward my brother, I didn't like having him out of my sight for long. He might've steered us into some kind of shitstorm, but that didn't mean I'd ride off and leave him to face it alone. In fact, striking out on my own was an option I rarely even remembered I had. I'd become accustomed to thinking of Gustav and myself as a team, like two old mules ever hitched up together. I might squawk about it from time to time, but in the end whatever Old Red did, I did.

The trail bosses and foremen we'd worked for had always taken the same view. Even at the VR, which was hardly typical in many a matter, we were generally set to the same task.

So Uly's sudden break with tradition had an unsettling odor about it. When I swiveled around to look at Gustav, I saw that he'd caught a whiff of it, too. He cocked an eyebrow at me that said we needed to talk—alone. We got our chance half an hour later.

"Be careful," Gustav said as we heaved a spool of barbed wire up onto the back of the wagon. "We don't know who's to be trusted."

"I'll be alright. I'm headin' out with two fellers. If one of 'em's the spy, well, he won't try anything when he's outnumbered, will he?"

"Brother—we don't know there's only one spy. Could be two. Maybe Uly's decided—"

Crazymouth and Anytime appeared just then with the horses for the wagon, and our conversation came to a quick end. I didn't need to hear any more to know what my brother was driving at, though.

Every day, cowboys are presented with fresh opportunities to get themselves killed. The job Uly had just handed me and Tall John and Swivel-Eye—pulling beeves from sinkholes—is one of the easiest ways to go about it. A steer can stick to swamp like a fly on gluepaper, and by the time you find him he might be half-crazy with fear. Getting him out isn't as simple as throwing on a rope and kicking in spurs. I've seen drovers pull horns, legs, and even heads off the critters they're trying to save. So you've got to get in close and work it scientific—which gives the bull a chance to gut you with his horns, brain you with his hooves, or just crush you under his big, beefy butt.

If someone wanted to help him do it . . . well, it wouldn't be hard. So as I rode north, I kept my eyes open for two things: bog holes and stabs in the back.

Most days I was friendly enough with Tall John and Swivel-Eye— particularly the latter, who hailed from Kansas farming folk like Old Red and myself. Still, either or both could be working for Uly, and I grew so wary of saying the wrong thing to the wrong fellow I ended up saying nothing at all.

"I can't believe it," Tall John said after we'd ridden a couple miles seeing nothing more noteworthy than a few largish puddles. He cupped a hand to his ear. "You hear that?"

"Hear what?" Swivel-Eye asked.

"Nothin'. Absolute silence." Tall John grinned. "I never thought I'd hear *that* when I was within a mile of Big Red Amlingmeyer."

Swivel-Eye chuckled. "What's the story, Big Red? Tall John's right—you're as tight-lipped as your brother today."

"Can't a man just roll up his tongue every now and then and listen to what the songbirds have to say?" I said.

"My goodness," Swivel-Eye replied, shaking his head. "We have a goddamn poet in our midst."

Tall John cocked his head and gave a mock-serious nod. "I think Big Red might be onto somethin'. Just listen." He lifted his cheeks from his saddle and gave the beans he'd had for dinner a chance to speak their piece. "I do believe that was a duck. What do you think he was singin' about, Big Red?"

This busted Swivel-Eye and myself into such hysterics Tall John stuck out his butt and gave us an encore.

Amongst cowboys, this is what passes for wit.

"But in all true seriousness," Tall John said once our laughs wound down into wheezy giggles, "I can understand why a man might think twice about openin' his mouth with . . . you know . . . events of the day bein' as they've been."

Swivel-Eye gave that a neutral "Um-hmm" and pointed a cross-eyed stare in my direction. He might have been hoping I'd join in with some square talk. Or he might have been looking to see if I'd stick my head in the noose. Either way, I didn't give him what he was looking for. I just acted like I was listening to the birds again.

"Alright then," Tall John muttered, disgusted, after the resulting silence had gnawed at us for almost a minute. "I thought maybe with us being away from HQ and all—"

"Shut up," Swivel-Eye said.

Tall John squinted back at him. "What did you say?"

Swivel-Eye shushed him.

And then I heard it—the clatter of wagon wheels and the jangle of hitched horses coming at us from the north.

Headquarters and the VR's wire wagon were to the south.

Without a word, the three of us got our horses to a gallop and headed toward that noise.

Before long we saw what was kicking up the ruckus—a stagecoach, a surrey, and a wagon, all moving along the trail that winds down from the Yellowstone River valley to the castle. As we approached, the stage driver stood and waved his hat.

"Don't shoot, boys!" he called out. "We got women here!"

With that, what had been a mere surprise turned into an absolute miracle. It had been two months since I'd laid eyes on a female who didn't sport hooves, and I'd assumed I'd be waiting several more before I got my next chance. Yet there in the buggy drawing up behind the stage I spied the unmistakable outline of a woman. When we got close enough, I could see she was a real beauty, too. Swivel-Eye, Tall John, and I rode straight toward her, racing for the honor of saying how-do first.

Swivel-Eye won. By the time I trotted up to the buggy, he was already bidding the woman and her companion good afternoon, hat in hand. The woman—and that's what she was, being a number of years past the point at which she could wear the tag *girl*—nodded and favored us with a smile that, while small, lit up the sky brighter than the noonday sun. She might have been too old to be considered a fresh young filly, but she was one hell of a beautiful mare.

The fellow with her, on the other hand, was simply a horse's ass. He looked about the same age as the lady—in his midthirties, I'd guess—though he had the rounded, doughy features of a child and the impatient scowl of a crabby old man. He was kitted out in a tweed suit with matching cap, argyle socks almost up to his knees, and spectacles that perched on his bulbous nose like two birds on a turd. His ways were as uppity as his clothes—when he spoke, his voice was more starchy stiff than his spotless white collar.

"You are employed with the Cantlemere Ranche?" he asked.

He used the pronunciation *raunch* instead of *ranch,* prompting us hands to titter like little girls.

"No, sir," Swivel-Eye said. "We work for the Bar VR."

"It's what you would call a *ranch,*" I explained.

"Never hired on with no *raunch* before," Tall John added. "What sort of work they do there?"

Our giggles straightened up the fellow's spine so fast it's a wonder he didn't bust his suspenders.

"We're here to see Mr. Perkins," he snapped with all the cold fury a rich man can muster when people stop licking his boots.

"Oh," Swivel-Eye said, and our chuckles evaporated. As much as we didn't like this duded-up juniper, it would reflect poorly on us to give disrespect to a dead man's friends or relations—especially a friend or relation as pretty as the lady.

"I'm afraid we have bad news, folks," I said. "You're too late. Mr. Perkins was taken in an accident just a few days ago."

" 'Taken in an accident'?" the woman asked. She didn't speak like Perkins, and certainly not like Crazymouth, but something about her voice told me she was from England. If she was our former manager's sister or fiancée or some such, it had fallen to me to deliver sad tidings indeed.

"Yes, ma'am," I replied. "He was caught out in a storm and . . . he didn't make it back. He's dead."

"Oh my. How unfortunate," the woman said, her poise only the slightest bit ruffled.

Mr. Fancy-Pants didn't shed any tears, either. He seemed not so much distressed by Perkins's death as annoyed that the man should presume to die at such an inopportune time.

"Dead?" he said. "Then who's in charge?"

"That would be Mr. McPherson, the foreman," I said. "He'll be runnin' the place for the rest of the season. The owners are all the way back in England, so it'll be months before we hear who's to take over."

"Hardly," the man sniffed. "*We* are the owners. We have come to see our *ranche*—and apparently we have arrived not a moment too soon."

Twelve

"MR. BALMORAL"

Or, The King and His Court Lay Claim to Their Castle

Before I could figure out the proper response—the best I could manage on the spur of the moment was a pop-eyed stare—an older gentleman climbed out of the stagecoach. He had a number of years (and pounds) on the first fellow, but his haughty manner was just the same.

"What's this about Perkins?" he demanded in a tone that told me *demanding* was something he did a lot. Like the lady, he had an accent I took to be English. And like the man with her, he was dressed up fancy, wearing a cream-colored suit, blinding white puttees, and a high-peaked helmet. He looked like a European explorer gone to fat, as if he'd spent the last few years lost in somebody's kitchen as opposed to the deadly jungles of darkest Africa.

"Well, sir, it's like this," I said, and I told of Perkins's ride the night of the storm and his condition the next morning. As I spun out the story to the blustery old gent and the lady and her snooty companion—not to mention the wagon drivers and shotgun riders, who were plainly enjoying an opportunity to eavesdrop—I noticed that my audience had grown even further. Two more passengers were in the coach the old man had exited: a gangly young fellow and a golden-haired girl, both of them about my own age. They stared out at me with the wide-eyed wonderment of children at their first circus.

The old man seemed considerably less impressed. When I was finished, he gave me no thanks, but simply snapped that I should lead his party to the manor house without delay. Then he heaved himself back up into the stagecoach before I could ask what the hell a "manor house" was. I made my best guess and headed for the castle.

Swivel-Eye, Tall John, and the rest of the caravan followed behind, and before long we were back at HQ. That many harnesses and horses will put up a noise that stretches out quite a ways before them, so Uly had a bit of warning somebody was coming. When we arrived, he was waiting for us in front of the castle looking as slick as I'd ever seen him, in clean clothes and polished boots and a brand-new Stetson.

I didn't pause to wonder why Uly would have such finery just lying about, for my brain was brimming with gleeful anticipation—I couldn't wait to see the conniption that would befall our foreman when he realized the VR was no longer under his thumb.

"What is this?" he called out. "I send you lookin' for sinkholes and you come back with guests?"

"That's right! And wait'll you hear who!" I shouted back.

The little wagon train slowed to a stop before the big house, and that gruff, puffy old geezer stepped out of the coach again.

"Who are you?" he huffed at Uly.

"My name's McPherson. I'm the foreman here," Uly explained, his voice and manner shockingly polite. "And who might you be?"

"This is His Grace, the Duke of Balmoral," snapped the swell in the surrey, apparently offended that there were actually folks in the world who didn't recognize the old man on sight. His beautiful riding companion had the decency to look embarrassed by his presumption.

"Mr. Balmoral?" Uly said, swiping the hat off his head. "The chairman of the Sussex Land and Cattle Company?"

"Mr. Balmoral" nodded brusquely. "I have in my party two other stockholders." His gaze darted to the uppity fellow who'd just introduced him. "There's Mr. Edwards." Then the gawky young man I'd seen in the coach stepped out behind the Duke. He was dressed like a gentleman, though one in need of a better tailor—his overly ample jacket and baggy trousers gave him the look of an understuffed scarecrow. The Duke turned, glaring at him the way you'd look at a bug floating in your beer. "And young Brackwell here. We have come to inspect the Cantlemere."

"Did Mr. Perkins know you were comin'?" Uly asked with such meekness it nearly knocked me from my saddle. I'd been expecting fireworks, but what he was giving off so far wouldn't light a candle.

"That no longer matters," the Duke harrumphed. "Now I need you and your men to get us situated."

Behind him, the situating had already begun. The stage driver had hit soil, and his shotgun rider was easing a trunk down into his hands. They were quickly joined by the final passenger from the coach—the blond girl I'd seen peeking out at me a few minutes before. She was considerably younger and fleshier than the lady in the buggy with Edwards, with less of the china doll about her. But she was pretty in her own sturdy way. As she didn't hesitate to start hefting boxes, it was plain she was a servant.

Edwards and the lady stepped down from the surrey, yet the only help they offered with the unloading came from the gentleman—in the form of reminders not to bust anything. He seemed to be an American, though his words were warped by an accent I couldn't place. The skinny kid, "Young Brackwell," kept his distance from any work, as well. He took to wandering around staring at all there was to see, peering in astonishment at every hitching post and horsefly as if they were carved from purest gold.

Tall John, Swivel-Eye, and myself were quickly drafted into service lugging trunks. The lady took charge of assigning rooms, and it took us a good three-quarters of an hour to get everything stowed where she wanted. She had us deposit the maid's things—little more than a small case and a carpetbag—in a tiny room on the first floor, next to Perkins's old bedroom. Naturally, the biggest, heaviest items all had to go up the stairs to the second floor. If they'd brought a cannon with them, I'm sure the lady would've wanted it on the roof.

Not that she gave us any real cause to grumble. Her commands were firm but never harsh, and she even favored us with the occasional *please* and *thank you*.

It was the servant girl—Emily, the woman called her—who finally told me the lady's name. She'd overheard us cowhands talking about getting "Mr. Balmoral's" gear settled where "that pretty gal" wanted, and she pulled us into one of the bedrooms for a little lesson on how to address our betters—and also to flirt, which she did with an enthusiasm we were keen to match.

"His name's not 'Mr. Balmoral.' Oooooo, he'll bark like an old bulldog if any of you call him that again!" Emily told us, somehow managing to cackle no louder than a whisper. "No, he's Richard Brackenstall de Vere St. Simon. Whew! Turns me blue in the face just saying it. Fortunately, he's just 'His Grace' to the likes of us—'*Your* Grace' if you're speaking to him face-to-face . . . which I don't recommend! Ho! Best to stay out of the big boar's way, if you can."

"You know, I knew a woman named Gracie once," Swivel-Eye said, winking one of his squinty peepers. "Never met a man went by that handle."

"It's 'Your *Grace*,'" the girl corrected, the smile on her face telling us she was in on the joke. "Don't forget or you'll regret it."

"Thank you for the advice, ma'am," I said. "Just so you know, folks around here refer to me as 'Sir Red, the Earl of East Kansas.' Naturally I expect you and your bunch to do likewise."

Emily hiccuped out a "Ho!"

"And everybody knows me as . . . ," Tall John said, upon which he unleashed a mighty thunderclap of flatulence. Being one of the many men who consider the breaking of wind to be the perfect punch line for any joke, Tall John immediately doubled over laughing.

Such buffoonery would have the chippies back in Miles City busting a gut. But I assumed a woman who spent her days in the company of the hoitiest, toitiest folks on earth would surely be scandalized. I assumed wrong.

"Oooooo, you must be a friend of the Duke's then," Emily said. "I heard him mention you by name just this morning! Ho!" And then she blew a raspberry and doubled up laughing herself.

When the snorting and snickering finally faded, I asked the question that had been on my mind for the past hour.

"So what about the lady? Who's she?"

"You may refer to her as Lady Clara," Emily said, sounding awfully prim and proper for a girl who'd been trading fart jokes with cowboys a moment before. "When speaking to her directly, 'My Lady' or 'Miss St. Simon' will do."

" 'Miss St. Simon'? So she's the old man's daughter?"

I tried to keep my voice neutral, but the relieved smile that creased my lips gave me away.

"You were afraid maybe her name was Mrs. Edwards?" Emily said, her stiff airs disappearing with a leer.

I shrugged and blushed. "Well . . . it would be kind of a shame. Not for her to be married, I mean. For her to be married to a feller like *him*."

"Oooooo, it'd be a shame, alright—which isn't to say it won't happen," the maid replied, rolling her eyes. "Not if that Edwards gets his way, nasty bugger."

Tall John leaned in and planted an elbow in my ribs. "So who do you propose the lady *should* marry, Sir Red?" he said. "The Earl of East Kansas, maybe?"

I was getting ribbed—literally—and if I didn't act fast it wouldn't let up for days. I decided the best thing to do was give the conversation my spurs and point it in another direction.

"So how 'bout that beanpole—'Young Brackwell'? What are we supposed to call him? 'Your Royal Highness' or 'Your Majesty'?"

Emily giggled and filled us in. Though his family had titles in spades, Brackwell didn't carry any himself. Nevertheless, as the youngest son of the Earl of Blackwater, he was due the respect afforded a nobleman. He was no older than any of us hands, but we were to address him as "Mr. Brackwell."

I was about to ask what we should call Edwards—simply "Jackass" or "*Mr.* Jackass"—when Lady Clara got to calling for Emily. Our little sewing circle broke up, and Tall John, Swivel-Eye, and I headed downstairs to grab the last of the trunks. In doing so, we found that the stage and wagon crew had finished watering their horses and were getting set to roll out. That was a big disappointment, as we'd been looking forward to hearing news from town.

"You can't even stay for supper?" I asked.

"Wish we could, friend," the fellow riding shotgun on the stage said. "But we gotta get back. The old man wouldn't hire us out for two days—he'd only pay for the one. That cheap son of a bitch might look rich, but he pinches pennies till they bleed."

"But your horses could surely use more of a rest," I pointed out. "And there's no way you'll make it back to Miles before sundown anyway. If you don't have business callin' you back to town, you really oughta stay the night."

It was true enough, and for a second it looked like they were giving it real thought. But then Uly came outside, glared at the drivers, and snarled, "What the hell are *you* still doin' here?" Then he turned to me and Swivel-Eye and Tall John and added, "And you three—get back to work."

That settled that.

"Don't let Hungry Bob get you!" I called as the stage and wagon clattered away from the castle.

The shotgun rider looked back from the stagecoach and waved. "Don't let the McPhersons get *you!*"

I turned to see how Uly would take that crack, but he'd already gone back inside, no doubt to apply more lip varnish to the Duke's seat cushions.

While Lady Clara and Emily had been setting up house, the old man, Edwards, and Young Brackwell had holed up with Uly in Perkins's office. Snoopiness having become a habit by now, I found every excuse I could to tarry at the bottom of the stairs, outside the office door. But all I heard from the other side was the rumble of the Duke's deep voice and the occasional "Yes, sir" or "No, sir" or "I don't know, sir" from Uly.

All this kowtowing apparently had Uly a bit buffaloed, for he'd made a rare mistake when he'd been barking at us a moment before. Unaware that the lady was through using us as her personal pack mules, he'd simply told us to get to work—without telling us what to do. As we saw it, that made us our own bosses for as long as we could make it last.

Tall John volunteered to take care of our horses, something he could do at as leisurely a pace as he pleased with Uly occupied and Spider out on the range somewhere. Swivel-Eye said he was going to help the Swede get supper going, which really meant he was going to hang around the cookshack and see if he couldn't get an early meal. And I chose to go back into the house to check on Lady Clara. After all, there might have been more heavy lifting to do, and it wouldn't be very gentlemanly to leave such work to the women.

Swivel-Eye and Tall John saw right through me, of course, but they didn't give me any guff but a couple of wicked grins.

After the boys left, I lingered outside the office door again. All I heard this time was the opening of drawers, the rustling of papers, and a low murmur of voices that just about lulled me to sleep. After a minute or so, I began making my way to the second floor to avail my-self of the decidedly more stimulating company we'd been blessed with that day.

When I was about halfway up the stairs, I heard a door below me open, followed by the *clop-clop-clop* of someone taking the steps two at a time. I whipped around to see the rail-thin form of Young Brackwell flying at me—and then past me. When he reached the second floor, he hurried to the room Lady Clara had claimed for herself.

"You must come downstairs immediately," I heard him say.

"What is it?"

Brackwell sighed. "They're already going over the ruddy bookkeep-ing and the tedium is simply *killing* me. I made an excuse to slip out and—"

"They weren't supposed to start without me."

"Edwards and old Dickie just couldn't contain themselves. And you know how that horrid Edwards feels about women and—"

Before he could finish, Lady Clara came storming out of the room and swept past me without so much as a glance in my direction. I didn't mind being overlooked just then, for there was enough fire in her eyes to melt a man.

Brackwell followed at a slower pace, dragging his heels like a fellow on his way to the gallows. When he saw I was eyeing him he brightened up, and he actually gave me a nod and a smile as he passed by. Why a high-class aristocrat, even as gawky and poorly tailored a one as this, should favor a low-class hand like myself with such friendliness I didn't know.

Downstairs, the lady went marching into Perkins's office, and I managed to catch only two sharp words before Young Brackwell slouched in after her and closed the door.

"Gentlemen!"

"Clara!"

Slam.

I started down the stairs again to catch what tidbits of conversation I could, but just then the front door flew open and Spider came striding in. He was still in chaps and spurs from saddle work, and clouds of dust gusted off him with each stomping step.

"Amlingmeyer!" he snapped before he'd even seen me, leaving me to wonder how he knew I was in the house.

I didn't have time to wonder long. He caught sight of me on the staircase and waved me outside with an angry jerk of his hand.

"Listen good, you big, dumb son of a bitch," he said once we were out on the porch. "You stay away from them Britishers. Shoot off your mouth around 'em, and I'll shoot off your damn *face*. Understand?"

I restrained myself to a simple nod as opposed to the punch to the gut his words warranted.

"Good. Now get over to the barn and help Tall John with the horses."

I nodded again and got on my way. As I trudged along, taking out my anger on whatever rocks I could get my boot toe under, I saw Swivel-Eye and the Swede coming from the cookshack, their arms piled high with kitchen gear.

"You fellers goin' to a bar-b-q?" I called out.

The Swede answered in his usual gibberish, which Swivel-Eye quickly translated into regular English.

"We're headed to the big house. Spider told the Swede to get set up there for some fancy cookin'."

I stopped dead in my tracks. "Who's gonna cook for us then?"

"Talla Yon!" the Swede said.

Swivel-Eye didn't need to decode that for me. I knew who the Swede was talking about. And I knew what that meant for my stomach: hard times. Putting Tall John in charge of a skillet made about as much sense as putting an Eskimo in charge of a cattle drive.

I found our new pot-rustler in the barn. It looked like Tall John had fared better shirking work than I had, for he'd barely begun putting away the saddles, bridles, harnesses, and whatnot. We got to it together. By the time we'd finished with the horses, Old Red and the rest of the fence crew came rolling in on the wire wagon.

I'm sure my brother was overjoyed to discover that Swivel-Eye and Tall John hadn't sunk me in a bog hole. Yet when he saw me he simply said, "How'd it go?" so casual you might've thought he was making chitchat with a hand coming back from the outhouse.

"You ain't gonna believe it, Gustav!"

"The owners are here!" Tall John cut in.

Being one who's reluctant to give up the stage when there's a tale to be told, I cut right back in, trotting out the detail that was sure to be greeted with even greater amazement.

"And they brought women!"

There was little variation in the responses, most of the boys opting for either "What?" or "Holy shit!" Old Red being Old Red, he stuck with silence.

For once there were fellows fighting to help with the end-of-the-day chores, as the boys didn't want to leave the barn until they'd heard everything. Naturally, I held a few choice details in reserve for some later time when my audience would be reduced to one. Just when that time might come was unclear, as hot gossip is strong glue, and it looked like nothing was going to break apart the Hornet's Nest bunch until these new developments had been totally talked out.

I only got one moment alone with my brother. It was later that night in the bunkhouse, and the boys were deep in debate. Half of them hadn't laid eyes on our guests, yet they'd already broken into two camps: the ones who favored the delicate, raven-haired maturity of Lady Clara and those who found themselves stirred more by the bawdy, blond girlishness of the maid, Emily. Old Red didn't weigh in himself, except to say that pining for either woman made as much sense as trying to can sunshine. Then he got up and drifted to the doorway, puffing on his pipe. After throwing in a few more words on the lady's be-half, I ambled after him.

It was dark by then, and we could see squares of light shining from the big house. One of those squares was the window to Perkins's office.

"Just when we thought things couldn't get more cockeyed around here," I said, "all of a sudden we've got lords and ladies in the castle. I'll bet even your Mr. Holmes wouldn't have seen *that* comin'."

Old Red shook his head. "I ain't so sure about that. Now that the Duke and them others are here, certain things make a lot more sense."

Before my brother could spell out what exactly those "certain things" were, the boys started yelling for me to come back—Swivel-Eye and Tall John were having a tough time describing the women's clothes, and they needed my help. The rest of the night was eaten up by such talk, and the fellows wouldn't let me go to sleep until I'd described those gals' every hair, tooth, and dimple ten times over. When I finally hauled myself up into my bunk, my jaw was throbbing from overwork.

As the other hands settled in for the night, I tried to make use of the quiet and dark that settled over the bunkhouse to focus my thoughts. I meant to puzzle out the meaning behind Old Red's remark, but that *focus* I was aiming for kept straying elsewhere—onto Lady Clara. I'd worked so hard to construct her image for the boys, it was now burned into my brain like a brand. After a while, I stopped fooling myself. The only thinking I was going to do just then was about her. I affixed my mind to the lady's likeness in my last waking moments, hop-ing she would do me the kindness of visiting me in my dreams.

Whether she did or she didn't I don't know, since I can never recall what I've been dreaming if I'm startled awake. And that's exactly what happened the next morning.

Just after dawn, I was jolted from my slumber by the sound of gun-fire.

Thirteen

THE DUDE

Or, The VR Gains a Hand More Fit for Kid Gloves

Tall John's bunk was closest to the door, so he had his head poked outside before the gunshot's echo had even died away.

"Who or what in the hell is that?" he said.

In a flash, five more bodies were pressed up against the doorway. What we saw outside was straight out of Buffalo Bill's Wild West Show.

By the nearest corral was the most prettified cowboy I'd ever laid eyes on. His knee-high boots were sky blue with white stars. Tucked neatly into the boot tops was a pair of fringed buckskin trousers around which was slung at the waist a jet-black two-gun holster. Above that the man wore a buckskin pullover with an eagle done in red and blue beads across the back. Around his neck was a red silk bandanna and on his head a tall-domed ten-gallon hat so pure white it looked like a snowcap atop some distant, rainbow-streaked mountain.

And in his hand was a shiny silver peacemaker, smoke still slithering from the barrel. There seemed to be nothing around for the fellow to be shooting, and after a moment it became clear that's exactly what his target was—nothing. He held up the gun and stared at it, in apparent surprise that such doodads would make loud noises and emit fire and fumes and nuggets of lead.

As the man's profile came into view, Tall John, Swivel-Eye, and myself chuckled in chorus.

"I'll be damned," I said. "That's Young Brackwell."

"He's gussied up more than a twenty-dollar whore," Anytime said.

"What kind of stock you think a hand like that would work?" Tall John asked. "Poodles?"

"I'd like to see his saddle," Swivel-Eye added. "I bet it's purple velvet stuffed with swan feathers."

"Too bloody right," Crazymouth threw in, " 'e's a Christmas caboose served as bangers and mash, and no one what knows 'is bum from his ooh-me-little-thumb is apt to be fooled by it."

A silence followed while we tried to dig the meaning out of this remark. But the man who spoke next didn't offer a translation or yet another funny aimed at Brackwell.

"Strange that Uly and his boys ain't takin' note of this," my brother said. He was looking at the McPhersons' bunkhouse, the doorway of which was surprisingly free of giggling cowboys.

"I don't think they're around," Swivel-Eye said. "I heard 'em up and about extra early. Sounded like the whole gaggle pulled out half an hour ago."

Old Red cocked an eyebrow at me, the meaning of which I didn't grasp until he hopped into his britches, walked out of the bunkhouse, and headed for Brackwell.

When the cat's away . . . , he'd been saying.

I sighed and set off after him, dressing myself on the run. Once it had been Gustav's job to keep me out of trouble. Now it looked like the boot was on the other foot—except it didn't fit me very well. At least this particular morning I'd have help, for every other hand followed along behind me, no doubt anxious to get a closer look at our clown-cowboy.

You don't have to be a Blackfoot scout to hear a herd of half-asleep punchers stumbling up on you, and Brackwell turned toward us when we were still a good many yards away, his slender face going as red as any Blackfoot's at the sight of us.

"Good morning," he said with a sheepish nod.

"Takin' a little target practice, were you?" Old Red asked.

"Well . . . why, yes. Yes, I . . . yes."

"Those are some mighty fine sidearms you got there." Gustav held out his right hand. "May I?"

The gangly young aristocrat's expression changed from embarrassed to wary.

"Of course," he said, slowly handing over the gun he'd been holding.

The Hornet's Nesters stirred with anticipation, no doubt imagining some gratifying humiliation Gustav was about to visit upon this silk-and-satin cowboy. But that just showed how little they'd come to know my brother. Though the trading of petty indignities is a much beloved pastime amongst drovers, he took little pleasure from such sport himself—unless perhaps it was *me* who was getting the ribbing.

Gustav inspected the gun—a gleaming silver-plated Colt .44-40 with a mother-of-pearl grip.

"Very nice."

He popped the cylinder open and inspected the cartridges inside.

"Loaded it with six bullets, did you?" Old Red shook his head. "That takes guts. I never keep more than five in my iron. I'm always worried I'm gonna catch the hammer on somethin' and send a shot flyin' out Lord knows where. So I keep the chamber under the hammer empty. Some other fellers are known to do likewise."

"Some other fellers" would be every man with a lick of gun sense in his head, but Old Red didn't say so. He was taking care to gentle-break our duded-up guest.

He closed the cylinder, spun the Colt around, and handed it back grip first.

"Yes, I can see how that might have its advantages," Brackwell said. "Perhaps I should think about loading my revolvers as you do."

Gustav shrugged. "They're your guns."

Having by now figured out that Gustav meant to help Brackwell save face, not rub his face in the dirt, the other Hornet's Nesters took matters into their own hands. Despite the Englishman's buckskin and beads, he had an air of fragility about him, and rowdy cowboys are drawn to such vulnerability like wolves to a lame cow.

"If you want to play it truly careful," Swivel-Eye said, "maybe you oughta leave out the bullets altogether."

"Or the guns," Tall John added.

"Awwww, don't listen to them," Anytime said. "I think you need even *more* guns. You could probably fit five or six on that belt of yours."

"No, Tall John hit it on the bunk. The guv 'ere don't need any hot-cross at all," Crazymouth said. "That gear of 'is would blind any geezer what tries to shoot 'im."

I could've added some brilliant, biting witticism of my own here, of course, but the Englishman struck me as a decent enough fellow, despite his foolish choices in matters of fashion. On top of that, I didn't want to bring Old Red's wrath down upon me. For whatever reason, my brother was taking the young man under his wing, and he spun on the boys looking as ruffled up as a gamecock in the ring. Before he could speak, however, something behind us caught his eye, and he held his tongue.

We looked over our shoulders to see Edwards marching toward us. He was again attired in tweed, with a cap and brightly shined shoes and a pince-nez flashing sunlight in our eyes. Though well-tailored, the outfit couldn't conceal the thick lumpiness of the man's body. He dressed himself like caviar, but beneath the tweed he was pure potato.

"What's happening here? What was that noise?" he asked, aiming his questions at Brackwell.

The Hornet's Nesters tomfoolery had turned the Englishman kind

89

of wilty, but the closer Edwards got, the more he straightened up. By the time Edwards came to a stop in front of him, Brackwell had added four inches to his height.

"Just a little target practice. These fine lads were sharing their insights on the use of firearms."

"You've no time to be socializing with the help," Edwards replied, sounding like a not-so-loving father talking to a feebleminded stepchild. "Now run along and change out of that ludicrous costume before His Grace and Lady Clara see you." A snort of disgust erupted from his big spud nose. "You know, I never understood why your family would send *you* as their representative—until now. If you've harbored a secret desire to be a 'cow-boy,' you should have said so sooner. I can have McPherson hire you on. You won't earn as much as from your allowance, but hopefully you'll find a way to make yourself useful at last."

Brackwell's face went crimson with barely restrained rage—or shame. Before he could make any reply, Edwards turned and addressed us hands.

"Bring the buggy and two good riding horses around to the house. Emily will bring out our saddles."

He began to walk away, leaving Brackwell glaring after him impotently.

"Hey, Edwards!" Old Red shouted.

The man whipped his stout frame around looking ready to spit. He obviously wasn't used to hearing "the help" hollering at him.

"Are you American or British?" Old Red asked.

Edwards simply glowered for a moment, obviously weighing whether to answer.

"I'm from Boston," he finally said.

"Oh?" Gustav rubbed his chin, his left eyebrow arched up high. "You know, I'm not sure if that really answers my question."

"I expect to see those horses in five minutes," Edwards growled, then he turned and stomped toward the castle.

"Hey, Old Red," Swivel-Eye said. "Why'd you ask him that?"

"With that accent of his I couldn't tell where he was from," my brother replied. "And I figured it was my right to know exactly what kind of asshole I was takin' orders from."

That got the boys laughing, and Brackwell actually joined in. Old Red gave the Englishman a hearty slap on the back, which was like seeing a cat ride a horse—you just wouldn't think it was in its nature.

"Come on, pardner," Gustav said to Brackwell. "Let's pick you out a pony."

And with that they headed for the corral, the two of them looking so chummy they may as well have been walking arm in arm.

The boys were thunderstruck to find this new Old Red in their midst, and when he was out of earshot they asked me what he'd eaten that morning to get himself so spiced up. I just shrugged and said whatever it was, I wished he'd eat it more often.

By the time we pulled the buggy around to the house, my brother was already there with Brackwell. They were throwing what looked like leather mittens on the back of a couple horses. Upon closer inspection, those mittens were revealed to be saddles of the type we punchers call postage stamps.

Whereas a cowboy saddle's got good stiff wood under the leather, the moneyed classes do their riding on little more than a doily. I hoped for Brackwell's sake that our visitors were heading out for a quick pleasure ride—covering real ground with nothing under you but a quarter inch of cushion would kink up your back so bad you'd end up rubbing your nose on your knee. I was about to say as much when Uly came riding in behind us.

"You sure you wouldn't rather take one of our wagons, Mr. Brackwell?" he asked.

"Absolutely. I'm looking forward to trying one of your fine Western horses."

Young Brackwell and Old Red exchanged a look that said they'd just been talking on that very subject. Their ease with each other wasn't lost on Uly.

"Well, I hope you enjoy the ride," he said to Brackwell, sweet as sugar. Then he turned toward Gustav and the rest of us, and the sugar turned to salt. "Finish with them saddles and get to your own. There's cows in the west pasture with screwworms. I want 'em doctored before we're back."

We swallowed our moans and groans, though this assignment was about as stinky as ranch skunkwork could get. Uly obviously wanted us away from the Duke's lot, and it seemed best to accommodate him before he handed us some even nastier chore—like cleaning out the privy with our tongues.

We were still gathering up our riding gear when the parade passed us by. Uly led the way, while Edwards and Brackwell (still in his fancy "cow-boy" duds) rode close behind, bouncing up and down off their little saddles like a couple of Mexican jumping beans. The Duke and Lady Clara clattered after them in the surrey. The old man was again wearing his puttees and pith helmet, and he would've looked like a little boy playing soldier if not for his bushy side-whiskers and two-hundred-plus pounds of girth.

It was a peculiar party indeed, and I couldn't resist throwing a whisper at my brother despite the danger that our spy was nearby.

"Brackwell tell you where they're goin'?"

"Nope," Old Red replied. "He didn't need to."

"What do you mean?"

"Take a gander to the southeast and you'll see."

I did as he said.

In previous days we'd seen huge swirls of dust due south where McPherson's men had been bringing up more cattle. Today there was a new cloud, a distant pillar that streaked the sky brown far to the south-east, deep in the VR territory us Hornet's Nesters were forbidden to enter.

Somewhere out there, something was on the move.

Fourteen

BOUDREAUX

Or, The Albino Shows His True Colors

By noon, we'd rounded up the most pathetic little herd you could ever lay eyes on. More than a hundred cows were milling about in a pen adjoining the main corral, and every one was afester with screwworm maggots.

We drew straws to see who'd stay on horseback and push cows over for their dose of medicine. Anytime and Tall John won, which made them the luckiest sons of bitches in Montana that day. The rest of us would have to do the hands-on nursing. And when you get your hands on screwworms, they get their little teeth in *you*.

Screwworm flies won't make a distinction between dead meat and live as long as they can get at it, and fresh brands and castration wounds are the perfect nursery for their young. A man might look at a brand and get the impression it was laid on with whitewash until he got close enough to see that it was *moving*—the "paint" being hundreds of squirming maggots. The only way to keep the poor cow from going crazy with pain is to smear a handful of axle grease and carbolic acid over the raw flesh. And if you let any of those little screwworm bastards wriggle inside your glove while you're at it, you'll find your hand's become a hatchery.

Even doing the job in teams—with me and Old Red on one cow while Swivel-Eye and Crazymouth doctored another—it was going to take hours to send all those maggots to meet their maker. And though Spider and his boys were up to who-knew-what who-knew-where while Uly was off with the Duke's bunch, we wouldn't have the luxury of lollygagging. Somebody had been left behind to keep a yellow-white eye on us.

Boudreaux was about a hundred feet from the corral, leaning back in a chair propped up outside the McPherson gang's bunkhouse. His legs were splayed out, his hands were folded on his chest, and his battered Stetson had been pushed down over his face. But we knew the albino wasn't out there taking a siesta. We were nursemaiding cows, and he was nursemaiding *us*.

"Boo sure landed himself the cushiest chore to be had today," Swivel-Eye said, using one of the nicer nicknames the Hornet's Nesters had for Boudreaux.

"Lazy, goddamn Spook," Anytime grumbled, using one of the meanest. "If he's gotta spy on us, least he could do is make himself useful while he's at it."

"That's easy for you to say," I threw back, talking over the top of a calf I was slathering with black goo. "You're on horseback. I bet you wouldn't be so anxious to help out if you had to dip your delicate little fingers in this." I held up my muck-covered gloves, and dozens of tiny white squiggles wriggled in the sunlight.

Anytime brought his horse ambling toward me.

"You stickin' up for that bleached-ass nigger?" he said.

"I'm just sayin' you—"

"Anytime, get back to the shoot," Old Red butted in. "You got cattle to mind over there."

Anytime gave us his best glare—which was pretty damn good—then jerked his reins to the left and trotted away.

"Try not to rile him up, would you?" Gustav said.

"He riles himself up. You know how he is about Boo."

My brother nodded. "I know."

Anytime's hatred for Boudreaux was kindled our first day on the VR and had smoldered ever since. The albino's skin might have been fish-belly-white, but all Anytime saw was Nubian black. He didn't miss a chance to call the albino Spook or Ghost or Whitey to his face. Yet he never got any satisfaction for his trouble. Boudreaux had grown even more unreachably distant after Perkins's death and Pinky's branding. Before, he'd floated above us like a cloud. After all that, he was as far away as the moon.

"That," my brother had whispered as Boudreaux drifted silently by one day, "is a man stewin' on somethin'."

If so, it was a slow simmer indeed—or the man was exceptionally good at doing his boiling under the surface. I stole a glance at him now through the fence rails and saw him rise up off his chair. He was too far away to have heard my exchange with Anytime word for word, but it was entirely possible the phrase *bleached-ass nigger* had reached his ears. For a moment, I thought he was coming over to give Anytime the ass-whupping he'd been asking for all these weeks. Instead, he strolled off toward the outhouse.

I turned back to the calf Old Red and I were working on, but before I could lay my glove on her again, my brother was letting her loose.

"This critter's done," he announced to Anytime and Crazymouth. "Hold off on the next one—I gotta drop a pie." I felt his boot toe prod my ankle. "And you do, too," he added under his breath.

Naturally, Anytime got to fussing when the two of us went over the rail and headed for the privy, but he hushed up when he saw that Boudreaux was gone. The Hornet's Nesters had been handed an opportunity to loaf, and within seconds every one of them was rolling a cigarette and hunting for shade. I was more than a little annoyed that I was missing my chance to do the same.

"I know you've got a lot of faith in Mr. Holmes's methods," I said as we hustled away from the corral, "but I don't think you can solve any mysteries by listenin' to Boo cop a squat."

Gustav gave me the sort of look that makes you think something unpleasant's dangling from your nose. Then he pointed ahead of us, and I saw that the albino had breezed right by the outhouse, headed for the back of the castle. We stopped at the jakes and watched him.

"Get inside," Old Red said.

"What?"

"We can't both stand here starin'. You go into the privy. I'll make like I'm waitin'."

"Is that why you brought me along? So I could sit in the shithouse while you spy?"

"*Get inside.*"

"Alright, alright."

I stepped into the outhouse and slammed the door. As was its habit when jostled, the latch fell on its own, locking the door tight.

"Christ, Gustav," I said, pushing my face up against the crescent-shaped ventilation hole. "The smell in here could smother a skunk."

"Light yourself a smoke," my brother suggested.

I pulled out my tobacco and rolling papers, but it was too dark to put them to use. Half my makings would end up in the dirt—or somewhere worse. I sighed and leaned close to the vent hole again.

"What's Boo doin', anyway?"

"He went down into the storm cellar."

"The storm cellar? What would he be doin' down there?"

" 'It is a capital mistake to theorize before you have all the evidence. . . .' "

"Yeah, yeah. It biases the goddamn judgment. Right. So I'm supposed to just stand here till Boo comes out of the cellar?"

"Not necessarily," Gustav said. "You could take yourself a seat."

"Oh. A joke. Pardon me if I don't laugh. If I so much as breathe in here, I'll pass out."

"Don't worry—he won't be long."

"What makes you so sure?"

"There's a spy amongst the Hornet's Nesters, remember? Boudreaux probably knows it—which means he'll try to finish up quick." Old Red glanced over his shoulder. "The boys can't see the cellar doors from the corral, but he can't be sure they'll stay over there long."

"Hold on. Why would *Boo* worry about the spy . . . unless he was puttin' somethin' over on the McPhersons himself?"

"Maybe he is. I don't mean to theorize, but he did wait till Uly and Spider were gone to . . . hold on. He's comin' out. And hel-lo. Would you look at that?"

"Look at *what*? All I can see from in here are flies and a crazy-ass cowboy who thinks he's—"

Before I could finish, Gustav gave the door three quick kicks. "Hurry up in there!" he shouted. "I'm fit to bust!"

It wasn't a very dignified part my brother had dragged me along to play, but I knew when the time had come to play it.

"Go and bust then!" I shouted back loud, for Boo's benefit. "I've got a hell of a lot more bricks to stack in here yet!"

"Hey, Boudreaux!" Old Red called out. "You got a second?"

Soon I heard footsteps getting closer, and I slinked away from the ventilation hole, huffing out a grunt to cover the sound of my movement.

"I swear I'll never . . . touch Tall John's cookin' . . . again," I moaned.

"I told him those beans were trouble, but the boy just don't listen," Old Red said, apparently to Boudreaux.

"What do you want?" the albino rumbled, his low voice as mumbly as ever.

"Oh, I'm just curious about our guests," Gustav replied casually. "Do you know where they set off to this mornin'?"

"I do."

There was no sound for a long moment but tree branches creaking in a gust of wind. Old Red finally broke the silence with a wry chuckle.

"Alright, you don't have to tell me."

"That's right—I don't," Boudreaux said. "If you were meant to know where they were, you'd be there yourself."

"Oh? Then how come *you* ain't there?"

"Things to do here."

"So I saw."

My brother chuckled again. Boudreaux didn't join in, and *I* certainly didn't see what was funny. In fact, I felt about ten seconds from a dead faint. The stench in that little pine box was starting to fog my brain like the fumes from an opium den.

"Look, Boudreaux—I like you," Old Red said, sounding uncommonly chummy. "You ain't dumb. You got your own view on things, I can tell. So why's a feller like you workin' for the McPhersons? You're one of their top hands, so you must've been with 'em a couple years, at least. How could you stick with those bastards so long?"

Rough fabric rustled—the sound of a shrug. "It wasn't so bad."

"Wasn't?" Old Red shot back, pouncing on the word like a bobcat on a hare. "So things have changed? Maybe in ways you don't like?"

"A man looks out for himself. What's 'like' got to do with it?"

For the first time, I heard emotion in the albino's slurred words—irritation, or perhaps fear, or perhaps both.

" 'Like' can mean a lot—to the right kinda feller," Gustav said. "For instance, you didn't seem to *like* it when Spider was puttin' a brand to Pinky Harris."

"A man looks out for himself," Boudreaux repeated.

"So is that what happened to Perkins?" Old Red asked, prodding hard now. "Somebody was just 'lookin' out for himself'?"

They say every man's got his limits—and my brother had just pushed Boo up against his.

"Get back to work!" Boudreaux snapped, his words strong and clear for once.

"But I gotta use the—" Gustav began.

"No, you don't."

Knuckles rapped hard on the outhouse door.

"You, too," Boudreaux said. "Get outta there."

I pushed up the latch, staggered outside, and put my hands on my knees, sucking in deep lungfuls of sweet, fresh air.

"Just . . . let me . . . collect my wits," I gasped.

"That shouldn't take long," Old Red said. "Ain't much to collect."

"Hey—"

"As long as we're waitin', I got one more question—"

"I'd start mindin' my own damn business if I was you," Boudreaux said. "Now get." His voice had returned to its usual husky murmur, but the way his hand wrapped around his .45 spoke a lot louder.

My brother and I scurried toward the corral—where, I could now see, the Hornet's Nesters were lined up watching the show. They were giggling and guffawing, obviously assuming we'd just been chewed out for goldbricking.

"I don't get you," I said to Old Red as we showed Boo our heels. "For days, you've had us tiptoein' around because of some supposed spy. But then you spout off just the kind of talk that got Pinky beat and burned. Don't you think Boo's gonna go straight to the McPhersons once they're back?"

"Nope."

"You got a reason to say that, or is that just your natural sunny optimism speakin'?"

"I got a reason." We were almost to the corral by then, and Gustav had to talk fast. "When Boudreaux came out of the cellar, he had a piece of paper in his hand. I saw him stuff it in his pocket—and he saw me see him. So he knows if he blabs on me to Uly, *I'll* blab on *him* about that paper."

"But that won't help us if you ain't deductin' right," I pointed out. "If that paper don't mean nothin'—if Boo ain't up to somethin' behind Uly's back—we're cooked."

We were climbing the railing now, and Old Red paused with his legs slung over into the corral.

"Huh," he grunted. "I reckon you're right."

Then he dropped down to the ground, picked up his gloves, and got back to work.

Fifteen

THE TABLE

Or, Old Red Sets Out Dishes, and Emily Dishes Out Gossip

Before long, Boudreaux took up his perch out front of the McPhersons' bunkhouse again. He spent the rest of the afternoon there doing an uncanny imitation of a bump on a log. He only unstuck himself from his seat twice: once to head out with us looking for more maggoty cattle, and again to tell us to knock off for the day. Each time he spoke, Anytime gave him a salute—with his middle finger. Beyond following orders, Old Red didn't have any reaction at all, and Boo didn't treat him or me any different from the other boys.

The Duke's expedition returned just as the evening dusk faded into night. Us Hornet's Nesters were eating supper at the time, but we had no choice but to hop up to help—Spider and his men still weren't back from wherever they'd gone that morning, and Boudreaux couldn't very well tend to the buggy and horses alone. For supper we'd been served Tall John's tooth-cracking stab at red-bean pie, so the boys didn't feel too bad about putting down their plates.

Our visitors looked dusty but cheerful as they pulled up in front of the castle. Brackwell greeted us with a wave of his huge and now not-so-white hat, Lady Clara beamed quietly, and even the Duke had a look of prideful satisfaction upon his flabby face. The one exception was Edwards, who was scowling even worse than usual.

It was obvious all that bump-ass riding had jumbled up the Bostonian's bones. Uly and Boo had to help him down from his horse and practically drag him into the house. I watched them go, wondering what McPherson and the albino would get to talking about once they'd deposited Edwards in his room.

"You there!" the Duke barked, and I was shocked to discover that these words were directed at *me*. I snapped to attention like I was wearing blue.

"Yes, sir?"

"Tell the cook we've returned. The party will be changing for dinner, which we will expect within the hour. We had discussed *canards à la Rouennaise* this morning, but I think not now. A roast of our own Cantlemere beef should do nicely. Yes, very nicely indeed! And tell Emily to set out one of the ports. And cigars! This is most definitely a night for port and cigars, eh, Brackwell? Well, now—did you get all that?"

I most certainly did not. I feared to admit my shortcomings as a manservant to the Duke, however, and I was prepared to simply nod and set off to make a mash of the whole thing. But Old Red spoke up before I could do so.

"Don't fret, Your Grace," he said, taking me by the elbow and steering me toward the house. "Whatever he don't remember, I'll remember for him."

We were inside before the old man could raise an eyebrow at my brother's initiative, so I did it for him.

"Are you crazy? Boo's off sayin' who knows what to Uly, and you just go strollin' into the castle like you own the place?"

"I ain't gonna sit on my ass when the time comes to act. While the

Duke and his people are here, we've got us a chance to break this thing."

"The only thing that's gonna get broke around here is our necks," I grumbled. "And what difference does it make whether or not them English folks are here? They hadn't even showed up when Perkins got himself ground into powder."

Old Red shook his head with sad, almost perplexed aggravation, as if he'd just observed me trying to eat soup with the wrong end of the spoon.

"That don't mean it ain't all connected," he said. "Haven't you wondered about the *timing* of—?"

The doors behind us opened, and the Duke and the rest of his bunch stepped into the foyer.

"That must be Emily back in the kitchen," Gustav said, cupping a hand to his ear while herding me down the hallway. "Oh, Emily! Emmm-illly!"

As it turned out, Emily *was* in the kitchen. She was harping away at the Swede, who looked as flummoxed by her chatter as we usually looked by his.

"Sir Red!" the maid said when she turned and saw us come in. She smiled and gave me a little curtsy, and I pulled myself together enough to respond with a deep bow.

"My lady."

She giggled in just the way I wanted.

Making gals laugh has always come easy for me. Maybe it's because I'm not exactly underblessed on good looks. Or maybe it's because I spent so much time around women as a boy. After my father and my brother Conrad died and Gustav hit the trail to make money, it was just me and my mother and my sisters there on the farm for the next couple years—and there wasn't much to laugh about. So I did my best to keep everyone bucked up, and I've kept on clowning ever since.

Old Red, on the other hand, can face down rattlesnakes, rustlers, and rabid bears without so much as batting an eye, but put him face-to-face with a *female* and he'll practically bat himself blind. He's no more unsightly than the average drover, with piercing blue-gray eyes and a high forehead and a nose and ears that manage to be "prominent" without spilling over into "enormous." Yet he's always been so bashful around women he could hardly bring himself to shout "Fire!" if a gal's skirts caught flame.

When I introduced him to Emily, she gave him another jokey curtsey, but the best he could do in reply was swipe off his hat and mumble what sounded like "Peas tomato again tents"—I assume it was "Pleased to make your acquaintance." I stepped in quick before things could get even more awkward.

"Your Grits is back, and he's hungry. You're supposed to set out pork and cigars before you go upstairs." I turned to the Swede. "And you're not to worry about whatever you had planned for supper. Just rustle up some steaks."

"You're to set out *port,* ma'am," Old Red corrected, still mumbling but managing to make himself heard. "And the Duke said he wanted a roast."

"A roast, steaks, what's the difference? The man wants beef." I glanced over Emily at the Swede. "What's the matter? You look like you're about to bust out bawlin'."

"All day I em vit ducks cooking, and this one"—he shook a bony finger at Emily—"she say, 'Not goot! Not goot enough for the Duke!' And now I em to broil a roast?"

"You will if you know what's good for you," Emily replied coolly, all brusque business now. "You don't deny a man like the Duke. He gets what he wants, how he wants it—or you'll pay. So you'd better get to that roast. And lay out oysters, boiled potatoes, custards, and a cherry tart while you're at it."

"God damn it!" the Swede exploded, cutting loose with the clearest English I'd ever heard leave his lips. "I em only two hands having!"

Emily gave him an unsympathetic shrug. "They'd better be enough then, hadn't they? I don't have time to help you. I have to go upstairs and dress my lady for dinner."

She started for the door, but an unexpected obstacle appeared in her path—Old Red.

"Looks to me like you and the Swede have your hands full," he said, his words loud and clear now. "Seein' as we ain't got nothin' to do but head back to the bunkhouse and jawbone with the boys, maybe we could help out."

"You?" Emily replied with a skeptical grimace. But her frown slowly blossomed into a mischievous grin. "Well, why not? That fat bastard dragged us all the way out here without so much as a single valet—what more could he expect? Ho! Do you know how to set a table, then?"

We knew how to set plates on wood, but that wasn't quite what she was asking. Nevertheless, Old Red got to nodding and grinning, and he cocked an eyebrow at me that said I should do the same. So I did, and Emily gave us another "Ho!" She showed us where the china and silver had been laid out and then left us to it—provided we *didn't* wash our hands before we started.

"That gal sure don't like the Duke," Old Red mused as I began puzzling over the bowls, plates, cups, saucers, silver, and crystal.

"Tell me why she should. And while you're at it, why don't you tell me what the hell you're up to?"

"Settin' a table," Gustav said. "Let's do the plates first. Them I understand."

The big plates took all of ten seconds to lay out around the dining room table. There were smaller plates, too, and after some debate we stacked these atop their larger siblings.

"Well, that wasn't so hard to figure out, was it?" Old Red said, looking pleased. "Now what do you think about them bowls? On top of the plates or off to the side?"

"They wear 'em on their heads for all I know. Now would you please tell me what we're doin' here?"

"We are waiting," my brother said, speaking slowly and solemnly, like a preacher reading Scripture from the pulpit, "for opportunity to present itself."

Rather than explain *what* opportunity, Old Red placed a bowl on top of a plate and leaned back, beaming at the porcelain tower he was building.

"Now what about these spoons?" he said. "In the bowls or beside 'em?"

I told him exactly where he could stick those spoons, but of course he didn't follow my recommendation. Instead, he started balancing the spoons on top of the bowls. When he was done with that, he criss-crossed the spoons with forks.

Old Red's table-setting sure as hell didn't look right, but I had to admit this much: It did look *interesting*.

Just as he found a home for the last of the saucers—he'd perched them atop a set of crystal goblets—the door behind me opened and I heard Emily bark out a "Ho!"

"If only old Ousby could see this. He'd drop dead on the spot, he would," the maid said. "It's a good thing the lady wanted to finish dressing herself tonight. . . ."

Emily started around the table, tittering as she undid the work Old Red had put into it. My brother bugged out his eyes at me, and I realized the *opportunity* he'd been awaiting had just presented itself. We were alone with an eager young flirt—and it doesn't take much canoodling to turn flirtation to gossip. And as canoodling with women is more my line than Gustav's, it was up to me to get things rolling.

"So," I said, favoring Emily with a smile, "who's this Ousby feller you speak of?"

"The gruffest old goat in all England, that's who. He's the head butler back at Cantlemere. The real Cantlemere, I mean. The Duke's estate in Sussex."

"How come he ain't out here with the rest of you?"

"Oooooo, he's got the household to run, don't he? And he's hardly got the staff to do it anymore. And anyway, he's too old to be dragging his bones halfway around the world. That's for the likes of poor me."

"You ain't excited to see America?"

"Excited to see the Columbian Exposition maybe. After all, that's the reason we came over, innit? Or so they tell the servants."

Emily flashed me an exaggerated wink that seemed to imply the secrets and lies and inherent sneakiness you always had to expect from your employers.

"But now we've missed the opening. And why?" she went on. "So we can come out to Mandana or Montini or whatever you call it and let the savages have a chance at our scalps! Ho! I'll have you know the Duke actually gave me a *gun* before we left Chicago. A little silver thing hardly bigger than a pocket watch. Everyone got one just like it—Lady Clara, Edwards, Brackwell. Old Dickie made a joke of it. 'In case of Red Indian attack or train robbery,' he said. Oooooo, he thinks he's a regular Oscar Wilde. If only he were. Ho!"

Old Red was getting exactly what he'd wanted—information. There was such a deluge, in fact, I felt myself drowning in it. I grabbed hold of a stray bit of flotsam and tried to ride out the flood.

"If the Duke wanted to inspect the ranch, why didn't you and the lady just stay behind in Chicago for the Exposition?"

"Oooooo, you don't know 'Lord Clara.' Headstrong, that one is. She *insisted* on coming along—to keep the old man from making a cock-up of things, I'd wager. She's got more sense with a pound than all the men in her family combined . . . little good it can do them now. Now look—it's fork fork fork, then knife knife spoon."

Soon she was instructing us on the proper placement of "finger bowls." Old Red gave me a glare that told me to get her back to gossip.

"It's a shame Mr. Perkins ain't here to see all these beautiful eatin' wares laid out like this," I said. "The Duke and the rest of 'em must be mighty downhearted they came all this way to see the man only to find he's dead."

"Oooooo, you wouldn't know it from their moods tonight. I've never seen them more cheery. Except that Edwards. The only time he bothers with a smile is when he can use it on my lady. Everybody knows what he wants—and he just might get it. After all, she can hardly make a match with a nobleman, can she? Someone's already taken a bite of that plum, and the gentry won't touch a commoner's leftovers. Although I can think of one who wouldn't mind a taste. Ho! That puddinghead Brackwell's got as much money as Edwards, but to my lady he's nothing more than a pet. The boy's family would never stand for it, anyway. Even their black sheep's too good for the likes of her. Ooooooo, I'll never understand the high and mighty. If they've got respectability, they want money. If they've got money, they want respectability. And if they've got both, why, then all they want is more of each! Ho!"

We were getting more gossip alright—though not much I could make any sense of. Trying to steer Emily in conversation was akin to riding a buffalo without benefit of a bridle. You were sure to go someplace fast, but you had little choice in where.

Nevertheless, I hoped to get Emily's tongue pointed in the direction of the Duke's daughter again. Lady Clara's social woes would probably be the last thing Old Red wanted to hear about, but I didn't care. I was smitten with the lady, and I couldn't defend her honor if I didn't know what had stained it.

But before I could fire off a question, the door to the parlor opened, and the Duke stepped in looking like he was on his way to an opera house. He was decked out in formal evening clothes, complete with tie and tails, and his fat fingers were wrapped around a smoldering cigar.

Given that he'd just stumbled upon two dirty ranch-hands pawing over his silverware, I expected rage to overtake him, or at least shock. Instead, the old man shocked *me* by hanging a grin betwixt his mutton-chops.

"Well, well," he said. "Just who I've been looking for."

Sixteen

THE PARLOR GAME

Or, Old Red's Brain Is Put Through Its Paces—and Comes Up Lame

he Duke told the three of us to follow him into the parlor. We found Edwards there awaiting us, slicked up like the old man in a high-collared white shirt and black suit, his thick lips making a pink *O* around the butt of a cigar. He was leaning back stiffly upon the very divan Pinky Harris had made himself so comfortable on the night my brother and I sneaked into the castle. Like Pinky, Edwards was putting a glass of hooch to good use, though he was limiting himself to just one, ruby-red liquid.

The Duke had a glass of his own waiting for him, and he picked it up and took a slurp as he settled into an armchair so large and ornate it could've been a throne. Sitting there together, he and Edwards almost looked like portraits of the same man—one as he came into the full bloom of maturity, the other as he faded into decay.

Neither one invited us to have a seat.

"You can't use both," the Duke said to Edwards. "Pick one."

By *both,* the Duke evidently meant Old Red and myself. Edwards got to inspecting us like he was judging cows at a county fair. His eyes narrowed to dark slits behind his spectacles as he looked at my brother, reminding me of the lip Gustav had given him that morning.

"That one," he said, stabbing his cigar at Old Red. Even as small a movement as that seemed to pain him—a grimace twisted the lumpy loaf of sourdough he used for a face. Evidently his back was still buckled up from the pounding it had taken on horseback that day.

"I'll go first," the Duke announced, sounding like a man who *always* goes first. He pointed his jowls at my brother. "What's your name?"

"Gustav Amlingmeyer."

"That question doesn't count," Edwards said, managing to smile as if this were a very clever remark indeed.

The Duke grunted out a gruff chuckle. "Tell me, Amlingmeyer," he said, "where is the seat of the British Empire?"

"The seat, sir?"

"The center. The capital."

"You mean to say you don't know?" Old Red said, deadpan.

"I want *you* to tell *me*," the Duke growled.

"Alright . . . I suppose it must be London."

The old man leaned back in his plush chair, jutting out his equally plush belly.

"Very good," he said.

"Emily," Edwards said, "what is the capital city of the United States?"

The servant girl blushed and brought her fingers up to stifle a giggle. "Ooooo, I'm not much for geography, Mr. Edwards. Is it New York, then?"

The Duke wheezed out a mirthless grunt that was apparently a laugh. "That's fifty dollars for me!"

"I'm sure Emily's American counterpart will even the score quickly enough," Edwards replied, throwing a sneer my brother's way.

Emily kept up her tittering, blissfully unaware that she was a pawn in some cruel game. But Gustav's face was beginning to burn as red as his mustache.

"Amlingmeyer," the Duke said, lifting his glass for another slurp. "Can you tell me who rules the British Empire?"

"You folks've got yourselves a queen."

"Yes, but what's her name?" Edwards asked.

Gustav's face went another shade darker, almost appearing purple by this point.

"Do the letters *VR* mean nothing to you?" the Duke prodded, incredulous. "Victoria Regina?"

"Now, Your Grace—no hints, if you please," Edwards chided gently. "Answer the man, Amlingmeyer."

Of course, *I* knew the answer. Anyone who'd ever read a newspaper would, what with the woman running half the world and all. But to Old Red, a newspaper was just something you used to swat a fly or light a fire. I had to hope his deducing would see him through, as the Duke had waved the answer right under his nose.

"Well . . . I suppose this Mrs. Regina must be the queen," Old Red said, making exactly the deduction I'd hoped he *wouldn't* make.

The Duke and Edwards nearly burst their starched collars they got to cackling so, and Emily added her own shriek of a laugh to their howls.

"Behold—the common American!" Edwards hooted. "That's fifty for *me!*"

I just barely kept myself from stomping across the room and herding Edwards's teeth from his face with my fist. Not only did he have some sort of bet going as to my brother's ignorance, he was kissing up to the old Englishman by cutting down Americans. One might expect a highborn European so-and-so like the Duke to feel more pride in his class than his countrymen, but for Edwards to do the same struck me as akin to treason.

For his part, Old Red seemed less enraged than shamed. He'd always been sensitive about his lack of learning. I figured that had something to do with his desire to detect and deduct—a lot of folks assume "uneducated" and "stupid" are one and the same, and he aimed to prove them wrong. He just stared down at his boots now, looking like he was counting off the seconds till the laughter would stop.

"Now, Emily," Edwards said after one last giggling snort. "Who is the president of the United States?"

"Oooooo, I know that one," the maid said proudly. "It's Mr. Lincoln, innit?"

Her answer didn't set Edwards and the old man off into hysterics as had Gustav's, but it did give them another chuckle.

Emily blinked at her employers, an unsure smile dimpling her round cheeks. "Is that not right, then?"

The men didn't bother explaining their amusement.

"Nervous, my boy?" the Duke said to Edwards. "You're falling behind again."

"Falling behind? Whatever are you two up to?"

We all turned toward the doorway, finding there a vision of loveliness so breathtaking it could've stepped straight from the canvas of some master painter. It was Lady Clara, of course, entering the parlor in a white evening gown so dazzling yet demure a rough-tongued son of a farmer like myself couldn't describe it without despoiling it.

And it wasn't just her beauty or the elegance of her attire that made her the very picture of feminine perfection. A shallow man might point to the faint lines around her mouth or the slight shadows beneath her eyes or the stray strand of gray in her ample dark hair and say that time had tarnished the lady's charms. Yet with age had come a poise that runs deeper than mere looks, and she carried herself with a combination of delicacy and strength, grace and steel, that elevates a woman from pretty or even beautiful to *ideal*.

The two gentlemen sat up straight in their seats, Edwards paying for it with another jolt of pain that curled his face into a wince. The Duke suddenly became curious about his cigar, inspecting it with the same air of innocence adopted by little boys trying to hide mischief from the schoolmarm.

"We've just been settling a debate," His Grace said.

Lady Clara arched an elegant eyebrow. "And a wager, as well, I expect."

"Nothing wrong with making things a little more sporting."

"That depends on *how* sporting," the lady replied coolly.

"Just a trifle. Five dollars a point—eh, Edwards?"

Edwards backed up the old man's lie with a quick nod and a feeble smile.

"Surely you can't begrudge me that," the Duke went on. "Not after seeing . . ."

He suddenly remembered us peons, and he washed away whatever he was about to say with a gulp from his glass.

". . . what we saw today," he finished after giving his lips a wet smack.

Lady Clara didn't speak or move or even change the expression on her face, yet a chill descended upon her so icy cold I could feel my toes go frostbit. Edwards, on the other hand, was sweating worse than a preacher in a whorehouse, his gaze darting back and forth from the lady to her father. He obviously wished to please each, but smooching two sets of backsides can be a tough feat indeed if the people they're attached to are going toe-to-toe.

My brother, meanwhile, was watching all this like it was a night at the theater, his red-faced humiliation replaced by open fascination. If he could've pulled up a chair and opened a bag of peanuts, he would've.

"So, what is this debate of yours?" Lady Clara asked.

The Duke squirmed his fleshy behind around in his chair, leaving it to Edwards to explain.

"His Grace and I had been comparing the relative merits of hired help in Europe and America—or their relative *de*merits, to be more precise."

The smirk Edwards unfurled at his own play on words went limp quick—Lady Clara was not amused. As Edwards forged on, he finally had the decency to look embarrassed.

"I felt that American workers lack the requisite mental . . . well . . ." He shot a glare at Gustav and myself, apparently unhappy with us for placing him in this awkward situation. "That one can't find common Americans with . . . ummm . . . that English servants would be superior in certain—"

Oh, just spit it out, you stuck-up son of a bitch, I wanted to say. You think we're dumb, but the old man thinks Emily's dumber.

"Yes, yes, she understands," the Duke interrupted, to Edwards's very apparent relief. "I think we've settled the matter—wouldn't you say, Edwards?"

It was easy for the old man to call an end to the game—he was fifty bucks ahead. But Edwards didn't argue. He just nodded and said, "Oh, yes. Most definitively."

"You may go," the Duke said, and from his sharp tone it was clear who he was speaking to, though he didn't trouble himself to look at us as he said it.

Emily curtsied and scurried toward the dining room, while Old Red headed for the door to the foyer. I followed him, pleased that we'd be passing close to Lady Clara on our way out.

Perhaps it was for her benefit that I paused in the doorway. Perhaps it was for my brother—or Amlingmeyer family honor. Whatever the reason, it was a whim that hit me so fast I was acting on it before I could stop myself.

"In case you're still wonderin'," I said as I swiveled around to face Edwards and the Duke, "the queen of England is just plain *Victoria*. Her kin are the Hanovers, not the 'Reginas.' There ain't no king. The lady's husband—Albert was his name—he died years ago. Most likely their son Edward'll take over the family business when his mama passes on. And if there's anything else you need to know, why, just come out to the bunkhouse and ask me. I'll set you straight."

I topped it all off with a wink.

The men stared at me, slack-jawed, and I turned to go before they could get those jaws working. On my way out, I gave the lady a nod and a polite "Good evenin', ma'am."

Old Red was waiting for me in the foyer.

"Jee-zus Christ," he snapped. "Must you be so goddamn—"

Whether I'd been goddamn *stupid* or goddamn *reckless* or goddamn *foolish* I didn't discover, for the next words stuck in my brother's throat as he caught sight of something behind me.

"I sincerely beg your pardon, Miss St. Simon," he said, blushing.

Lady Clara had followed me. She acknowledged Gustav's words with a slight bow of her head.

"I believe I owe an apology to *you*. My father can be . . ."

As she searched for the proper word, a look came over her face that suggested the phrase *a big, fat asshole* might actually escape her lips. But good manners prevailed, of course.

". . . ungracious," she said.

Old Red gave her a shy little shrug.

"Don't trouble yourself over it, ma'am," he managed to mumble.

Unlike my brother, I'll seize any opportunity to bandy words with a comely woman, and I couldn't resist now.

"But your concern is most deeply appreciated, my lady," I threw in, placing both hands over my heart. It made me feel like a character out of *Ivanhoe*. If I could've gotten away with it, I would've planted a kiss on the back of her dainty hand.

Lady Clara graced me with a smile that instantly became the highlight of my life up to that point.

"You certainly took the gentlemen by surprise," she said. "Are all 'cow-boys' so well versed in England's affairs of state?"

I let loose with a not particularly modest chuckle. "Oh, hardly. I'm a special case. My mother pushed a book in my hands every chance she got. And before takin' up with cattle, I clerked in a granary for a spell, which gives a feller plenty of free time for newspapers and magazines and other edifications." I shot what I thought was a sly glance at my brother. "But even the drovers without as much learnin' as myself can surprise you. They might look like a drawer of dull blades, but there's usually a sharp one mixed in there somewhere."

"I'll remember that," the lady said, looking both amused and remarkably sincere, as if I'd offered advice she actually planned to follow.

Footsteps echoed down from above, and we turned to see Brackwell descending the staircase, done up in dark tails and tie like Edwards and the Duke. Though his clothes probably cost as much as I've earned my entire life, it still draped over the young man's lanky form like a sheet thrown over the back of a chair. Oddly enough, the only outfit I'd seen the kid wear that truly fit were his crazy circus cowboy duds.

"Well," Lady Clara said to us, "good night, gentlemen."

Gustav and I offered goodnights in return, and the lady moved off to the foot of the stairs to meet Brackwell. We threw a couple of hello/good-bye nods up at him ourselves, then we left.

"Did you hear that?" I said as we headed toward the bunkhouse. "'Gentlemen' she called us."

Old Red rolled his eyes. "We walk out of there with a regular banquet to chew on, and you pick out that measly little crumb?"

"Oh, no—it ain't no crumb. Anything from the lady's lips is sweetest sugar to me."

"While most of what comes from yours is steamin' horseshit."

"Awww, you're just jealous cuz she obviously fancies me over you."

Gustav went from eyeball rolling to head shaking. "Better get it through your head, Brother—people like that don't 'fancy' people like us."

"Oh, I don't know. Emily said somethin' about the lady bein' 'a commoner's leftovers.' What do you think that means?"

"You really want to know what I think?"

"Yes, I really want to know."

"Alright. I think"—Gustav took in a deep breath and let it out slowly—"it is a capital mistake to theorize before you—"

"Oh, shut up."

We were almost to the bunkhouse by now. Tall John and Swivel-Eye stood in the doorway gabbing over cigarettes, so I had to keep my next words low.

"And you say *I'm* full of horseshit."

Once we got inside, I quickly fell into conversation with the boys about the day's happenings, giving them a heavily expurgated account of our adventures in the castle. Predictably, they were most interested in the food and the women. Gustav retired to his bunk, lying there stiff as a board, his hands folded over his stomach. This was the position he sometimes assumed when he had vigorous cogitating to do, and I was happy to leave him to it. I didn't bother with a "Good night" when I climbed into my own bunk an hour later.

Sleep didn't come quickly. I kept thinking about that "banquet" of facts Old Red had spoken of. What we'd heard in the castle didn't seem like any banquet to me—it was more like the stale bread and scraps of gristle dive saloons lay out for their "free lunch."

So the Duke couldn't resist a good wager—or a bad one. So the lady had some kind of scandal behind her and felt a bit frosty toward her father. So Edwards was a social climber and Brackwell was the "black sheep" from a noble flock. It was good enough gossip, I suppose, but how any of it tied in with Perkins's death was beyond me.

Thinking of Perkins reminded me of my brother's little chat with Boudreaux earlier in the day—and the possibility that Boo had already repeated every word of it to Uly. That line of thought didn't exactly put me in a relaxed, restful state of mind, so I herded my brain along to a far greener pasture.

I finally drifted off to sleep thinking of Lady Clara, of course, dreaming myself into the center of a whole new scandal for her. But somewhere in the night, my mind took a less pleasant turn, and my dreams were spiced with the sound of gunfire.

The noise of it rang so loud and so real it popped my eyes open. I stirred, awakened just enough to be aware of dim light and snoring men.

Soon enough I settled into slumber again, certain it had been nothing more than a nightmare.

Seventeen

THE PRIVY

Or, Something About the Outhouse Doesn't Quite Smell Right

As the boys began rolling from their bunks the next morning, Tall John announced that Buffalo Bill had returned. Young Brackwell was out near the corral, once again duded up like a cross between a Texas cowboy and a Denver pimp. He was attempting to master the use of a throwing rope by hurling one hungry loop after another at a fence post.

If that post had been a bull, the critter would've had little to worry about. Brackwell's throws were eating dust six feet away at their closest, coming down so limp and lifeless the man may as well have been tossing dead snakes instead of good hemp.

The boys drifted to the doorway to take a look—and one of them kept right on going out to the corral.

This was, of course, my brother.

As tempted as they might have been to guy poor Brackwell again, the rest of the Hornet's Nest bunch chose not to follow. Spider was back, him and his gang having returned to headquarters just as we'd been turning in the night before. But Old Red was tossing caution to the wind, and after a few antsy moments I decided I should be out there caution-tossing with him.

"What are you doin' now?" I asked when I'd caught up to him. "If the wrong person sees us—"

"I'm just goin' to have an innocent little chat with Mr. Brackwell," Old Red replied, his pace slacking off not one whit. "It's plain to see the kid's taken an interest in droverin'. I'm sure he'd appreciate a few pointers that don't come from a dime novel."

"Well, *I'd* appreciate it if you'd stop tryin' to get us killed."

"I'm not tryin' to get us killed. I'm tryin' to unmask a murderer."

" 'Unmask a murderer'? Christ, Gustav—do you hear yourself? You're the one livin' in a dime novel."

That finally jerked my brother to a stop.

"I know this ain't no dime novel. It's real—and a real man is dead. And the only way we're gonna find out *why* is if we get closer to them folks in the castle."

"What the hell do they have to do with it?"

My brother squinted at me as if trying to figure out why such a featherlight thing as my head doesn't go drifting off my shoulders with the slightest breeze.

"Has Mr. Holmes taught you nothin'? It's plain enough if you apply a second's thought to it."

Old Red gave me a few seconds to apply that thought, but I still didn't have any idea what he was jabbering about.

"When the Duke showed up, he and McPherson made out like this was a surprise inspection," he finally said. "But Perkins knew it was comin'—knew it for months. Why do you think we put so much time into fixin' up HQ? Why do you think we got hired at all? It's a show for the stockholders. And Uly must've known about it, too. Didn't you notice how he got himself washed and shaved and done up in new duds *before* the Duke arrived? And once you get to chewin' on all that, don't it strike you as a powerful coincidence that Perkins died when he did—just days before the Duke and them others got here?"

Old Red's explanation made sense—and left me more confused than ever. Tucked away inside his answer were at least a dozen more questions begging to be asked. But before I could unpack even one, my brother was moving again.

"You're never gonna catch him like that!" he called out to Brackwell. "Them fence posts can be mighty wily. You'd be better off just shootin' the son of a gun."

Brackwell turned and gave my brother a bashful grin. The young Englishman had picked up a touch of color in his travels in the West, but he didn't show it now. He was as pale white as the fine linen the folks in the castle slept on. Under his eyes were bags so large you could pour oats in them and strap them to a horse's muzzle.

"Perhaps you're right," he said, his words dribbling out slow and unsteady. "I'm certainly not having any luck with this lariat."

"Well, maybe my brother and I can change your luck. If you're interested, we could learn you how to make that rope dance."

Brackwell gave a nod that instantly turned into a grimace, and I knew then what was ailing him. He was suffering from a condition the German farmers back in Kansas call a katzenjammer. To you and me, that's a hangover.

"Alright then," Old Red said, holding out his hand. Brackwell handed him the rope. "First thing you gotta do when you're building a loop is shake out the noose like so."

The next five minutes were taken up with nothing but rope talk, all of it kept to a low volume so as not to box poor Brackwell's tender ears. Gustav did most of the speaking, having me whir and dab with the rope so he could stand back and point out what I was doing right and (by his account) wrong. Brackwell turned out to be a fine pupil, for when he got a chance to throw again he looked pretty good—even if his aim was still off by at least three feet.

"Not bad. Now that you know the ropes, as they say, all you need is practice," Old Red said. "Of course, it's a whole other kettle to rope a steer from a horse at full gallop. And the kidney beans you and Edwards seat yourselves upon wouldn't do at all. There ain't no *hold* to them puny things. I'm surprised you can even stand up straight after ridin' through all the rough country we got south of here."

"Oh, the ground we covered wasn't so horribly bad. It was grassland mostly—nothing more rugged than a few hills." Brackwell's thin, pale lips curled into a wobbly grin. "I'd wager I was more comfortable on my saddle than old Dickie and poor Clara in that rickety carriage."

"I don't know if Mr. Edwards would agree with you on that," Gustav said, chuckling. "Looked to me like he won't be in a saddle for quite a spell. I hope you ain't plannin' on another outin' today."

"Oh, no. We saw what we n—" Brackwell's grin went stiff. "Today we shall be otherwise engaged."

"Well, I'm sure Mr. Edwards will be pleased to hear it," Gustav joshed, putting on like he didn't notice the change in Brackwell's tone. "Now, why don't you have a go at that post again. Only this time, I want you to try somethin' different. You ain't gonna toss rope like a cowboy unless you can move like one. Loosen up! Let your shoulders droop a bit. Put a little bend in your knees. And don't jerk the rope out there. It ain't a harpoon. It's rope, good and limber, like you oughta be. Sling it out there nice and smooth."

Brackwell tried to do as Old Red instructed, loosening and drooping and bending until he'd assumed the doubled-up hunch of a ninety-year-old squaw.

"Tougher than it sounds, ain't it?" I said.

Brackwell nodded. "It goes against everything I've been taught."

"You been taught to walk around stiff as a damn totem pole?" my brother asked.

"Oh, absolutely. Even when . . . one doesn't feel one's best. Where I come from, that's called good breeding."

Gustav made a face like a child with a mouthful of week-old but-termilk. "Breedin's for cattle. A man picks his own path."

Brackwell gaped at my brother, obviously not expecting philoso-phizing from a simple drover. "I see your point," he said.

"I know you do." Old Red clapped his hands under Brackwell's arms and pulled the young man up straighter. "I said I wanted you loose, not limp as a rag doll. You're tryin' too hard. Relax. Let it come natural."

Brackwell cocked an eyebrow at my brother. It was plain that "re-laxed" and "natural" were *not* conditions he'd ever been encouraged to strive for. But strive for them he did, and before long his throws were even better. Though he still wouldn't have stretched out a steer, he fi-nally got his loop on that fence post.

Old Red was congratulating his student with a clap on the back when a heart-stopping shriek pierced the morning air. It wasn't a scream of pain or terror. It was more a kind of wild, yipping yowl. An-other screech rang out, then another, and by the time their echoes died away it was clear where they were coming from—the outhouse. Gustav and I raced for the privy, the gentleman as close on our heels as he could manage with that katzenjammer weighing him down.

When we got to the jakes, we found Anytime peeking through the ventilation hole in the door while Swivel-Eye staggered around behind him, doubled up laughing.

"Me see you, white man!" Anytime yelled. "Me break down door and scalp you good!"

Swivel-Eye's laughter choked to a stop as we approached, and Any-time turned and saw us coming.

"Oh," Anytime said. "Good mornin', Your Highness."

Before Brackwell could respond, a new voice boomed out behind us. "What the hell is goin' on?"

It was Uly. He threw Brackwell a nod as he approached but quickly shifted his glare back to Anytime and Swivel-Eye.

"Well? Speak up."

"Just a little fun, boss," Swivel-Eye said.

"What kind of 'fun'?"

"I came by to use the shithouse, but somebody was in there already," Swivel-Eye explained with a nervous grin that was as helter-skelter as his eyes. "Anytime was passin' by and . . . well, we thought it might be one of them swells from the big house. So we thought we'd have us a little fun. No harm intended."

Uly shook his head and growled, "Get to work," sparing us the ear-blistering bluster he might have employed had Brackwell not been present. No doubt thankful that he'd been spared a tongue-lashing—for now—Swivel-Eye hurried away from the privy, offering more muttered apologies as he went. Anytime went with him, too stiff-necked and surly to beg forgiveness, but avoiding Uly's gaze all the same.

"That goes for you, too," Uly said, turning toward me and Old Red. "Make yourselves useful."

I wasn't aiming to buck the man. I had yet to get any breakfast down my gullet, so I was looking forward to a trip to the cookshack—even if it was still under Tall John's tyranny. But something about the way my brother stayed so absolutely still put roots down through *my* boot soles, as well.

"What the hell are you waitin' for?" Uly asked, his voice running up higher with each word, like a finger dragging up the keys of a church organ.

"I'm worried about whoever's in there," Gustav said. "We still haven't heard a peep from him."

"Oh, bullshit," Uly spat, starting to lose control of his temper, Brackwell or no. "You know that door's got a cranky latch. There's probably not even anybody in there."

"There is," said Anytime, who was still close enough to overhear. "Enough light gets through the peephole to show him sittin' there."

"There you go," Old Red said to Uly. "I tell you, I'm concerned. Anytime's war dance probably scared the poor man shitless."

"Ain't no better place for it," Anytime said.

"Shut up," Uly snapped without taking his eyes off my brother.

Gustav didn't seem to notice. He walked over to the privy and went up on his toes to peek through the crescent vent hole in the door.

"Yeah, I can see somebody . . . barely," he said. "That you, Mr. Edwards? There ain't no Indians around—just some damn fool cowboys. Why don't you come out of there?"

We waited for a response, but the only thing to be heard was a steady buzzing coming from the other side of the door.

"Lot of flies in there," Gustav said. He took a big sniff. "Quite an odor, too."

"What do you expect?" Uly cried, throwing up his hands. "It's an outhouse, for chrissakes!"

Uly usually wasn't a man to give in to exasperation when cold condescension would suffice, and his bluster now struck me as forced—almost desperate. That thought must've struck my brother just as hard, for instead of letting McPherson's huffing and puffing blow him away, he bent down and scooped up a handful of dirt and gravel. He sorted through it until he found a small stone, then he stood, brought his hand up quick as a flash, and threw that rock through the crescent moon. It must've found its target, for we didn't hear it clatter against wood.

Old Red got up on his toes again and took another look.

"That feller in there ain't *scared*, is he, Gustav?" I said, already feeling my stomach hitch itself into a queasy knot before my brother even answered.

"He ain't scared in the slightest," Old Red replied. "He's dead."

Eighteen

THE TURNING POINT

Or, The West Loses a Drover and Gains a Detective

When my brother stepped away from the ventilation hole, Brackwell and I took turns peeping through it. All I saw was a dark, shadowy shape slumped away from the single shaft of light that penetrated the cramped (and powerfully odiferous) privy.

"Could be a body," Uly said after he finally stomped over to take a look himself. "Could be a sack of taters."

"In the outhouse?" my brother said. "With the door locked?"

"Maybe it needed some privacy," I suggested. "Right, Uly?"

McPherson turned on me with a look that could curdle milk, but before he could repay me for my sass, Brackwell cleared his throat with a dainty cough.

"McPherson . . . I think it might be best to get a good look at . . . whatever's in there," the young gentleman said, sounding a tad nervous about handing out orders to the likes of Uly. "Just so we can be certain nothing's amiss, you understand."

For a moment, it looked like the only thing Uly *understood* was that

Brackwell, Old Red, and I were each in need of a swift kick in the ass. But instead of getting busy with his boot, he rolled his eyes and barked out a bitter laugh.

"I guess it's a good thing there's no *work* to be done this mornin' so we can just while away the hours chewin' the fat around the outhouse," he said. He turned on Swivel-Eye and Anytime and set them to running: Swivel-Eye was sent to fetch tools to get the privy door open, while Anytime was dispatched to the castle to see who might be missing.

"Damned waste of time," Uly said, shaking his head as the two Hornet's Nesters scurried off. "If I might say so, *sir*."

Brackwell fidgeted with his holster for a moment, picking at the leather near his six-guns, then turned away and occupied himself with another look inside the privy. When his back was turned, Uly shifted his gaze to my brother—and that gaze went frigid cold. It might have just been a foreman giving the evil eye to an uppity hand, but I wasn't so sure. There was an unsettling odor about this business and it seemed to me Uly'd been waving his hat awfully hard to dispel the stink of it.

While Old Red and Uly stared each other down like a couple of tomcats waiting to see who was going to swing his claws first, I was left to wonder about that shape inside the outhouse. If that was a body in there—and I sure as hell didn't think it was a sack of taters—then whose body was it?

Swivel-Eye and Anytime came back fast, and neither one came alone. Swivel-Eye had obviously been unable to keep such news as this bottled for even the minute it took to grab a couple hammers, for Crazymouth and Tall John were on his heels. The three of them kicked up such a commotion they drew Spider and a few of the other McPherson men from their lair. A moment later, Anytime came rushing back with the Duke and a limping Edwards not far behind. Everyone from the Duke's party had been accounted for, Anytime said, and the Swede was scrubbing pots in the kitchen.

If the mystery was to be solved, that door would have to come off.

Even before Uly or the Duke could order it done, Gustav snatched one of the hammers from Swivel-Eye and shoved the claw in just below where the latch held firm on the inside. Swivel-Eye slipped in next to him, working the other hammer in a foot higher. After a minute of sweating and growling, they finally got the wood to splinter, and the door clattered open.

The morning sun streamed in, revealing what would have been a truly nauseating sight if Perkins's pancake cadaver a few days before hadn't steeled me to less messy displays of human gore.

Propped up over the poophole was the albino, Boudreaux. He had a bit of extra color about him now: a dark circle in the center of his forehead. His yellow eyes were rolled up high in their sockets.

Anytime was the first fellow to state the obvious.

"Well, I'll be damned," he said, not sounding particularly shocked . . . or saddened. "Somebody went and shot Spook."

Most of the other boys had the same reaction—which is to say not much of a reaction at all. Boudreaux was a Negro, and not a well-liked one at that. Nobody fell to his knees weeping bitter tears.

The only fellow who seemed to take Boo's death personal was Old Red. His eyes blazed with the fire of indignation, and he moved his hot stare from man to man, as if trying to burn a confession out of one of them right then and there.

"I think I heard it," Brackwell whispered hoarsely, looking twice as nauseous as when we'd first seen him that morning. "The shot, I mean."

"I heard it, too," Swivel-Eye added. "Not too long ago neither—a couple hours, maybe."

Brackwell turned toward the cowhand as if he were about to say something, but the Duke broke in first with an impatient growl.

"This is unacceptable! Intolerable! Men gunning each other down on *my* ranch? I won't stand for it!"

Beside him, Edwards looked every bit as perturbed as the Duke—

though maybe that was because the old man seemed to forget in the heat of the moment that the VR didn't belong to him and him alone.

"Well, sir, I don't think you'll have to worry about any more fellers 'gunnin' each other down,'" Uly said, stepping up to Boo's body. "The only killer we've got around here is already dead." He scooped something up off the ground near the albino's feet.

It was a hideout gun—a derringer. One that had seen better days, too, by the looks of it. It was an ancient single-shot Colt .41, mottled and gray with grime.

"Looks like he did himself in," Uly said, holding up the little gun for all to see before slipping it casually into his coat pocket. "He always was moody. Ain't that right boys? I guess he decided this was the end of the trail."

Uly sure was cooking up an explanation in a hurry. All of a sudden he seemed as keen on deducifying as my brother. I shot a glance at Gustav to get a bead on his reaction to this turn of events, expecting perhaps a frown or a cocked eyebrow. But what I saw I wasn't expecting—or happy about—in the slightest.

They say action speaks louder than words, and ninety-nine times out of a hundred they're right. On this occasion, however, I witnessed the one-hundredth time out of a hundred, for my brother managed to upend our world without lifting a finger. All it took was one word— two innocent little letters that, when combined, changed absolutely everything.

"*Ha,*" Old Red said.

Awwwww, hell, I thought.

"Ha?" Uly asked, too surprised to be angry at first.

"Ha," my brother confirmed, nodding.

Uly's expression shifted from puzzled to pissed. "*Ha?*" he asked again, cawing the sound out like some huge crow.

"You heard me," Old Red said. "Ha!"

Every man there who had to sweat for his bread knew exactly what this exchange meant. To put it delicately, my brother had formally challenged his foreman's veracity.

To put it with less delicacy, Old Red had just told Uly he was full of shit.

Though Edwards, Brackwell, and the Duke were not themselves workingmen, they could surely piece together that some kind of face-off was at hand. The old man dealt with the situation in his usual fashion—by opening up his big mouth and shouting.

"What's the meaning of this? You there! Do you have some other explanation for this man's death?"

"You there" was Old Red.

"An explanation? No, sir," my brother said. "But I do have some questions that bear askin'."

"Such as?" the Duke prompted with his typical impatience.

"Well, for one thing, why's he wearin' his spurs?"

We all turned to gape at Boudreaux's boots. Attached at the heels were work spurs, the rusty, star-shaped rowels digging into the dirt of the outhouse floor.

"Why would a feller on the verge of shootin' himself take the trouble to strap on his spurs before sneakin' out to do the deed?" Old Red asked.

"Well, obviously when a man ups and kills himself, he ain't thinkin' straight," Uly replied. He'd wiped the scowl from his face, affixing in its place an expression of tolerant bemusement similar to the one my dear old *Mutter* used to wear when Uncle Franz would get to telling us ducks can talk, pigs can hear your thoughts, and God had just dropped by to talk politics. "There's no use lookin' for any *why* to what he might do."

"But it ain't just the spurs," Old Red said. "Look at Boudreaux's holster. He's got a perfectly fine Peacemaker tucked away there. He could've placed that up against his ear and done the job with more certainty than he'd have with that little stingy gun. If he was downhearted enough to kill himself, I don't think he'd be too concerned about makin' a mess of the privy. So why not use the .45? And that brings us along to somethin' else."

Uly was rolling his eyes now, trying to get his boys to lay in with catcalls. But they were as wrapped up in Gustav's chatter as us Hornet's Nesters. Even Spider was hanging on every word, though he looked ready to hang Old Red from the nearest branch.

As for the gentlemen, no two were reacting the same way. The look of put-upon amusement on Edwards's face suggested he was inclined toward the view Uly was pushing—namely, that my brother was crazy. Brackwell, on the other hand, was gazing upon Old Red as if he were a conquering hero, not a raving lunatic. And the more my brother worked his mouth, the more the Duke puckered his own into a prodigious frown.

"There ain't a lick of powder scorch on the man," Gustav went on. "Blastin' yourself in the skull ain't sharpshootin'. You'd have to get your hand right up against your noggin. And if you did that, not only would you end up wearin' your brains for a glove, you'd give yourself a heck of a powder burn. But his hands and forehead are as white as ever, aside from that bullet hole. So to my eyes, it's clear. Boudreaux didn't shoot himself. Somebody did the shootin' for him."

"Ha!" Uly spat out.

Gustav folded his arms across his chest and gave McPherson the sort of coldly appraising, vaguely disappointed look he usually reserves for me.

"And what is there to 'Ha' about?"

"You, that's what," Uly replied with cold scorn of his own. "You got a reputation for bein' an odd bird, Amlingmeyer, and now I see why. I've heard cow farts that made more sense. What exactly are you hintin' at, anyway? Someone got in there with Boudreaux, shot him in the head, dropped down into the shit pit, then dug his way out? That's the only way it could happen, cuz in case you forgot that door was locked from the inside."

Old Red blew out a breath and shook his head. The outhouse door was still open wide, and he surprised us all by walking around to hide behind it.

"Otto," he said, "give this door a knock."

I'd been keeping quiet and trying to look small—neither of which comes naturally to me. But there was no way around it now. My brother wasn't just asking me to play along with his Sherlockery again. He was asking me to do it right there in front of everybody. If I was going to tell him to shut his trap and forget this detecting nonsense—and maybe keep us in the frying pan as opposed to the fire—now was my last chance to do it.

So I had a choice to make, and it was splitting my brain like an ax through a watermelon. All Gustav wanted me to do was knock on a door, but it felt like I'd been told to march through one—knowing there was a cliff on the other side. I had to face up to a none-too-flattering truth about myself just then: I've always had opinions on things, yet choices I've left to others.

Well, I thought, *maybe it's time to change that.*

I walked up and gave the wood a rap.

Old Red's eyes appeared in the ventilation hole.

"Who's there?" he said.

I'm not always lightning-quick about catching on to my brother's ideas, but this one I got hold of straight off. I stuck out my index finger and pointed it at my brother's forehead.

"Bang," I said, snapping my thumb down like the hammer of a pistol dropping on a round.

Gustav's eyes went into a crinkle, and I knew he was favoring me with a small but approving smile.

When he stepped back around the door, of course, all trace of that smile was gone.

"I say again—this man did not shoot himself."

I thought that was a pretty neat display of deducting, but Uly was having none of it. He'd been working hard to save face in front of his employers—or maybe save his neck from a noose—and he wasn't about to give up now.

"Fiddle-faddle!" he declared. "If someone shot Boo like you say, why on God's green earth would they leave the gun in the outhouse?"

"That I don't know," Old Red admitted, meeting McPherson's contemptuous glare with a steely stare. "I'd surely love to ask the man who did it."

Uly curled up his lip, but before he could get out another word, he was interrupted by the sound of applause.

"Oh, bravo, *bra-vo,*" Edwards said, clapping his fleshy, soft-palmed hands. "That was quite a performance. Will you next offer definitive proof that the sky is blue?" He faced the Duke. "I don't see how the death of some Negro laborer can have any bearing on us, no matter what the circumstance. I suggest we send word to the proper authorities and get back to our business."

I gaped at the man, utterly boggled by the bluntness with which he revealed the hardness of both his heart and his head.

If I'd been looking to the Duke to balance Edwards's jackass callousness with a little simple human decency—and I wasn't—I would've been sorely disappointed.

"Quite right, quite right," the old man said, giving Edwards a nod so firm it set his chins to quivering. "This is obviously no concern of ours. McPherson—see to it."

"Yes, sir," Uly said, triumph gleaming in his eyes.

The Duke and Edwards turned toward the castle, no doubt keen to move on to matters more important than mere murder—namely, the ones that might make them *money.*

"Wait!" Old Red called out.

The Duke spun around looking like a boar who's had his tail yanked.

"Please," Gustav added quickly. "Your Grace. Sir. You'll have to pardon my sayin' so, but I don't think you should be so quick to assume this has nothin' to do with you."

"What do you mean?" the old man snapped.

"Well," Old Red said, and though the pause that followed was mere seconds in length, I aged a good ten years as they dragged themselves out. It was hardly the time to throw down our cards about Perkins.

As it turned out, my brother had an entirely different card up his sleeve.

"I'm wonderin', sir," he said. "Has anyone warned you that we may have a madman loose in these parts?"

"A madman?" Edwards scoffed. "What in heaven's name are you talking about?"

"Why surely even all the way back in Boston you've heard of Hungry Bob Tracy," Old Red replied. "The Colorado Cannibal? The Mountain Maneater? He was spotted not too far from here. This body don't look like Bob's work, bein' uncooked and free of salt and pepper, but who knows? Maybe that's just cuz ol' Bob couldn't get at it. Like I said there's good reason to think Boudreaux didn't kill himself. And if there's even the smallest chance Hungry Bob did him in, it ain't just a county matter. You tell the sheriff you got a death you can't account for, he's gonna have to tell the federal marshal in Miles City. And then you're gonna have deputies out here turnin' over every blessed rock on the spread."

The more Gustav flapped his gums, the more the Duke got to looking like he'd swallowed a frog. He clenched his jaw hard, as if trying to keep his breakfast from hopping up his throat and out through his mouth. Edwards looked equally queasy—you could almost see his waistcoat bulging and rippling with all the flip-flops his stomach was doing.

Setting eyes on a dead man hadn't so much as ruffled a one of their feathers. But the prospect of a posse on the VR had them practically plucked clean?

"That would be . . . an unwelcome disruption," Edwards said.

Old Red nodded sympathetically. "No doubt. Course, it don't have to roll out like that. You send one of the boys off after the law, they're not gonna be back for at least a full day. All we'd have to do is use that time wisely."

"By determining the manner of this man's death before the authorities arrive," said Brackwell, who now looked decidedly less green around the gills than Edwards or the Duke.

"That's the only way we're gonna avoid that there 'disruption' Mr. Edwards spoke of," Gustav said. "Put our finger on what happened or have lawmen swarmin' around here like so many honeybees."

"And who exactly would conduct this investigation?" Brackwell asked, though he seemed to have guessed the answer already.

"Why, I would," Old Red said.

"*You?*" Edwards looked my brother up and down as if laying eyes on him for the first time. "I'd like to know what inspires such confidence in a . . ."

All indications pointed to words along the lines of "ignorant ranch hand" being the next to exit Edwards's mouth. As he was *surrounded* by ignorant ranch hands, Edwards reconsidered, ending his sentence instead with the words "man such as yourself."

"I've made a study of the science of observation and deduction," Old Red answered. He didn't acknowledge the snickers this drew from the McPhersons and some of the other men—including, I was disappointed to observe, the boys from our own bunkhouse. But he did raise his voice a touch louder to add, "And I'll point out that you wouldn't even be askin' that question if I hadn't kept everyone from jumpin' to conclusions."

"He's right enough about that," Brackwell said. "I say we give him a chance."

"Don't be ridiculous," Edwards sneered.

"What's ridiculous about it? I don't see what we have to lose."

"I don't see what we have to *gain*." Edwards gave Brackwell's colorful costumery a look of open disdain. "This man's no more a detective than you are a cow-boy."

Brackwell's cheeks flushed so pink you'd think he'd just been slapped.

"If you fellers feel so strongly opposed on this, maybe you oughta settle it like gentlemen," Old Red said. His gaze drifted over to the Duke. "You know—make things a little more sportin'."

"A wager?" the old man mused. His gray, watery eyes suddenly lit up bright, taking on the same sheen they'd had the night before when he'd tried to square Old Red and Emily off in a battle of half-wits. "Yes! If you have faith in this man, Brackwell, you should back it up!"

"Well, I . . . I will then," Brackwell replied, trying to sound defiant despite a nervous quiver in his voice. "Two hundred pounds says he can provide a satisfactory explanation for what's happened before the authorities arrive."

"Done!" the Duke crowed, and Brackwell's face went from livid red to ghostly pale in a heartbeat. I tried to imagine what shade Lady Clara's face would turn when she heard of the bet, as the previous evening she hadn't seemed happy about a wager of five dollars, let alone one of two hundred pounds—however much *that* was.

Edwards managed to toss in his own "Yes, done!" before the old man turned to Uly and began barking out instructions.

"Send word to whatever authorities you must—they should come as quickly as possible. In the meantime, you are to excuse this man from his regular duties so that he may"—the Duke pointed a smirk at Gustav—"pursue his investigation."

"One more thing, Your Grace," Old Red said. "I'll need my brother's help if I'm to have a fair shot at this."

"Your brother?"

I stepped forward—this time with no hesitation. "That's me, sir."

The Duke glowered at me. "Why do you need *him*?"

"Well, someone's gotta take down notes and such," Gustav replied. "And I can't do nothin' with a pencil beyond scratch my nose."

"You can't write?" the Duke asked.

"Nor read, sir. No."

Brackwell gave my brother a pained look that said, *What have I done?*

"Fine. The brother, too, McPherson," the Duke said, his smirk returning.

For a fellow who'd been so unnerved by the thought of lawmen on his land a minute before, he looked awfully chipper now. Uly'd wanted Boo's death swept under the rug, but the old man seemed perfectly happy to snatch that rug up and toss it out the window—provided he might win a bet in the process.

Perhaps Uly was just more cautious. Perhaps the Duke was blinded by his contempt for a mere workingman like my brother.

Or perhaps Uly and the Duke simply had different things to hide.

The Duke and Edwards turned and headed back to the house, the old man moving with a new spring in his stride while the younger man struggled to keep up, his back stiff and his legs like rubber. Brackwell watched them glumly, no doubt thinking of all the hastily wagered cash that would soon be walking off with them.

Uly and Spider weren't wasting their stares on Edwards and the Duke, however. They were focusing all their attention on my brother and myself. And unfriendly attention it was, too—glares of the sort that would turn any normal fellow's blood to ice.

"Alright then," Old Red said, slapping his hands together and rubbing them with cheerful excitement. "Let's get to it."

Nineteen

CLUES

Or, Someone Sticks His Nose Where It Doesn't Belong

After the Duke left, Uly scattered the Hornet's Nesters with a few bellowed commands. But he and Spider lingered behind with their men, no doubt waiting to see what Brackwell would do. Should he return to the castle, our newly sanctioned investigation would most likely come to a quick end—along with our lives.

Old Red set to work as if his audience wasn't there, walking up to the outhouse door and practically putting splinters in his eyeballs he got to looking at it so close.

"Would you mind steppin' over here, Mr. Brackwell?" he said. "I'd like to hear your thoughts on these scratches by the door handle. They look pretty fresh, wouldn't you say?"

Brackwell seemed confused by this request, having little knowledge, I would guess, of pinewood and carpentry. But he complied. As he stooped in to take a look, Old Red straightened and turned his gaze on Uly.

"You know, boss—seein' you there reminds me. With Hungry Bob or some other mad-dog killer runnin' around, you oughta let me and my brother strap our irons on. You wouldn't want us caught short, would you?"

"I'll think on that," Uly said, his tone suggesting he was just as likely to consider setting himself on fire.

"You do that," Gustav said. "And as long as y'all are just standin' there, you may as well answer a few questions for me. Did any of you happen to notice when Boudreaux—?"

"No time to lip-flap," Uly broke in. "We've got *real* work do to."

He turned and barked at his boys. His orders were of the usual sort, with a solitary exception: One of his men, the little strutting runt we called the Peacock, was to take word of Boudreaux's death to Sheriff Staples in Miles City.

McPherson's men hurried about their business, and Uly and Spider went with them, obviously anxious to avoid any other awkwardness Old Red might send their way while he had Brackwell on hand.

Our young dude, meanwhile, had finished his inspection of the door and stepped away with a shrug.

"Yes, I see the scratches. You and that other fellow had to do quite a bit of work to get the door open. I don't see why that should be significant."

"Well, the thing is, *we* didn't put all those gouges there—I think someone else had a go at this door," Gustav said. "Now could you two do me a favor and paste yourselves down for a spell? There's already been enough boots layin' tracks around here."

Old Red hunched over, screwed his gaze to the ground, and got to walking in a ring around us. His circle gradually grew wider, taking him farther and farther from the privy. When he was about fifteen feet out, he spoke the same words Mr. Holmes uses when encountering a fresh clue: "Hel-lo! What's this?" Then he threw himself on the ground and started shuffling around on his hands and knees.

"Mr. Brackwell, is two hundred pounds a lot of money?" I asked while my brother crawled around like a kid playing horsey.

Brackwell nodded sadly. "It is. To be honest, I was hoping it would be so much that even a man of the Duke's tendencies couldn't accept the wager. Obviously, I was wrong."

"You'll have to pardon my askin', but . . . well . . . are you good for it?"

Brackwell would have been within his rights to take offense, but he just offered me a rueful smile.

"*I'm* not 'good for it'—not at the moment, anyway. But my family is."

"Oh," I said. "I understand."

I finally had Brackwell pegged. He was what we Westerners call a remittance man—a fellow who's packed off to the frontier by wealthy relations who wish to be rid of him. The average remittance man lives off an allowance from back home, squandering the majority of it on hard drinking, reckless wagers, and crackpot fixations. Given what I'd seen of Brackwell, I had to conclude he was prone to all three.

"Tell me," he said. "This 'study of deduction' your brother mentioned to the Duke—what form did it take?"

I tried to think of an answer that wouldn't sound ridiculous. I gave up pretty fast.

"It took the form of him sittin' on his ass while I read out detective stories. But I assure you—he's serious about the art of deducifyin'."

Gustav was now on his belly, wriggling along the ground back toward the outhouse.

"I don't doubt it," Brackwell said.

Upon reaching the door, Old Red hopped up and ran his fingers over the ventilation hole. He pushed his nose in, gave the door a sniff, then let out a low, frustrated growl.

"Damn. That's what I get for theorizin'."

"What is it?" Brackwell asked.

Old Red rapped on the door. "There ain't no scorch marks."

"So?" I said.

"*So*, if Boudreaux was shot through the vent hole, there'd be some burn on the wood. You know derringers—a man can't hit a barn at ten paces with one of them little things. They're for killin' up close."

Brackwell sighed. "So you were wrong about how the man died."

"Only the details," Gustav said, shooing away the gentleman's concerns with a wave of his hand. "He didn't shoot himself, I'm still sure of that. The rest of it . . . well, it's a puzzler alright. A regular three-piper."

Those last words—a twist on one of Mr. Holmes's little sayings—seemed to simultaneously amuse and alarm Young Brackwell.

"These stories you've been reading," he said. "Surely some of them detail the adventures of my countryman Sherlock Holmes?"

"The best of 'em do," Old Red replied, looking deeply gratified to encounter someone who knew of his hero. "His is the only method worth mindin' when there's detectin' to be done."

"That might be," Brackwell said. "All the same, I wouldn't repeat such praise in the Duke's presence."

Gustav cocked an eyebrow. "Don't care for Mr. Holmes, do he?"

"That would be putting it mildly. And he has good reason. You haven't read 'The Noble Bachelor' then?"

Old Red and I exchanged a puzzled glance.

"No, sir," my brother said. "I could see that my Holmesing a while back was puttin' a twig up his snoot. But I figured that was just his way anytime a man don't play the hand he's dealt at birth."

Brackwell looked confused for a moment, then nodded slowly. "Yes . . . I see what you mean. But there's more to it than that. About four years ago, one of the Duke's sons, Robert St. Simon, came very close to marrying into an American fortune. It would have been . . . a useful alliance for the St. Simons. Unfortunately, your Sherlock Holmes uncovered a most embarrassing fact about the bride-to-be: She was already married. Of course, the scandal tainted the entire family. And just as the whispers were beginning to fade, Holmes's biographer, Dr. Watson, had the bad taste to publish an account of the affair."

" 'The Noble Bachelor,' " Gustav said.

"Precisely."

"That's one we ain't run across yet," I said. "Looking for Holmes tales out here's like pannin' for gold in a trickle of piss."

Brackwell may have been done up in cowboy duds, but such language was still a tad overly earthy for him. "Yes, well," he said with an uncomfortable cough, "it's plain to see you've found enough to acquaint yourselves with his theories and habits. So much so that old Dickie was probably reminded of a man he blames for a blemish on his family's honor."

"Though I reckon he's done his part to blemish things up, what with all his bad bets. Is that why his family's strapped for cash?"

Brackwell gaped at my brother. "You astonish me. Yes, actually all the male St. Simons are prone to an excessive love of gaming. And it has affected their fortunes over the years. How could you know that?"

Old Red shrugged casually, the very picture of false modesty. "Simple observation and deduction. Child's play for Mr. Holmes, I imagine."

"Possibly. I never met the man, but I understand he was—"

"Mr. Brackwell!' "

We turned toward the castle to see Emily heading in our direction. Instinctively, the three of us moved between her and the outhouse, attempting to shield a delicate female from the gruesome sight within. But Emily didn't want any shielding, and she went up on her tiptoes and swiveled her neck like a snake to get a peek at the body.

"Breakfast is being served," she said.

"Thank you, Emily. I'm not hungry," Brackwell replied.

Emily kept coming closer. "Lady Clara would like to speak to you," she said, dropping her voice down a notch. "At your earliest convenience, sir."

"Very well," Brackwell said with a sigh. "I'm in the soup now," he added to us under his breath. "I'm not supposed to encourage the Duke's bad habits. Well, gentlemen . . . good hunting."

He took one last look at Boo, shook his head, and started off for the house with Emily—who turned for another peek herself as they walked away.

That left Old Red and me alone at last. But as much as I wanted to put our privacy to use by unloading a wagonful of questions and complaints, I knew there was more important business to attend to first.

"Uly and Spider'll be back any second now," I said.

"Most likely. So we'd best move quick."

Gustav stepped into the outhouse and began fussing with Boudreaux's body. When he came out a moment later, he was carrying the man's gunbelt. He slipped out the .45, checked the cylinder, and gave the barrel a sniff.

"Been used?" I asked.

Old Red shook his head. Then he jammed the iron back in its leather and handed the whole caboodle to me.

"Strap that on."

As I pulled the holster around my waist and cinched it loose, the way I like it, my brother moved back to Boo, grabbing him by the boots and dragging him out into the light.

"That ain't a very respectful way to treat a feller's remains," I pointed out.

"You wanna sing a hymn, you go right ahead. I got work to do."

Gustav commenced that work by lifting Boudreaux's pale paws and giving them a quick going over.

"No scorch, no scratches, no busted knuckles," he mumbled. "He didn't put up a fight."

"Hungry Bob or whoever must've got the jump on him."

"Just make that 'whoever,'" Old Red said, dropping Boo's hands.

"You don't really think Hungry Bob's tied up in this?"

"If I were a bettin' man like 'His Grace,' I'd wager ol' Bob is two hundred miles north of here roastin' himself a nice, juicy Mountie at this very moment."

"So you were just guyin' the Duke about Bob payin' us a call?"

"Got a good jump out of him, too. Only it wasn't Hungry Bob that had him sweatin'. It was the posse that . . . *hel-lo!*" Gustav pushed his face in so close to Boo's he could've smelled the man's breath had he any left in him. "I sure wish I had one of them 'magnifying glasses' Doc Watson writes of."

"What is it?"

"I don't know."

My brother reached his hand out slowly and plucked something small and dark from the crusty wound in Boudreaux's forehead. He squinted at the little ditty for a minute, holding it pinched betwixt his forefinger and thumb, then motioned me over for a look.

It was a feather—a fluffy bit of down blackened by gunpowder and blood.

"Well, that wraps up the mystery," I said. "Boo got himself gunned down by a *goose*."

Gustav sighed. "Brother, I'll never know how you got hold of the crazy notion that you're funny."

"Oh, a feller just knows."

Old Red stuffed the feather into one of his pockets, then started searching those belonging to Boudreaux.

The first items he pulled out were the inevitable rolling papers and pouch of tobacco—the man had been a puncher, after all, and not finding makings on his person would be akin to discovering a porcupine free of quills. Gustav put it all back where he'd found it and moved on.

Now many qualities can be credited to my brother, and chief

among them is a powerful fortitude: He's got enough backbone for three men and a mule. This has served him well over the years, for farmboy and cowboy alike can ill afford to go weak-kneed in the face of the unsavory.

So a display of squeamishness from Old Red is something I would expect about as much as a display of courage from a turnip. Yet when he pulled something pink and rubbery from one of Boudreaux's pockets, his fingers went fluttery and he dropped it, hissing out a shocked "Sweet Jesus!" I peered over his shoulder and blurted out a blasphemy of my own.

The albino apparently had mighty unwholesome tastes when it came to mementos and good-luck charms.

Tucked in his Levi's had been a man's nose.

Twenty

THE TRAIL

Or, We Follow in the Footsteps of a Dead Man

It took my brother but an instant to regain his usual air of unflappable calm. I, on the other hand, remained *flapped* for a good many moments.

"Goddamn what the hell holy shit," I panted. "Is that what I think it is?"

"That depends," Old Red said. "What do you think it is?"

I pointed at the nose, which had dropped onto Boudreaux's shirt, coming to a stop sitting upright like a pair of extra nostrils growing out of the albino's chest. It made a considerable mound resting there, being neither a noble "Roman" nose nor a cute "button" nose but rather a huge, hairy, hooked honker adorned with a mole the size, shape, and color of a pinto bean. The flesh had been dusted liberally with coarse salt, no doubt to keep the gruesome keepsake from smelling (so to speak).

"Well, I know that's a nose. I'm just surprised Boo would be carryin' around a spare," I snapped. "Now don't give me any crap about 'theorizin'.' What's goin' on?"

Gustav shrugged. "I couldn't theorize if I wanted to," he said, pulling out a bandanna. He draped it over the nose and scooped it up, bundling it like our *Mutter* used to wrap biscuits and ham for my lunch at school. "I have no earthly idea what this means."

Old Red stuffed the nose in his vest and got back to exploring Boudreaux's pockets. I took a step back, fearing he might turn up ears, fingers, or eyeballs next. But all he found was an ordinary pocketknife.

Gustav flipped out the blade. It was covered with a dark, flaky film.

"Dried blood?" I asked, peeking over my brother's shoulder.

"Yup. Looks like Boudreaux didn't just find that nose on a Christmas tree. He barked it himself." Old Red folded up the pocketknife and put it back where he'd found it. "Help me get him back in his coffin."

It was a bit of a struggle, but after a minute or so we had the man propped up in the privy again.

"Now what?" I asked.

"Well, you'll remember in 'Silver Blaze' one of them police inspectors talks about 'the scene of the crime.' I reckon that's what we got to find."

" 'The scene of the crime'? You mean this ain't it?"

Gustav sighed, looking like a schoolmaster about to explain for the fiftieth time why things fall down instead of up.

"Just try walkin' through it as Mr. Holmes would," he said. "Boudreaux didn't shoot himself, he wasn't shot through the vent hole in the privy door, and he sure as hell wasn't shot by somebody there in the jakes with him—that little thing can barely hold one man, let alone two. Now that only leaves one other way to go, don't it?"

"Boo . . . was . . . shot someplace else?" I ventured. "And . . . the killer . . . stowed the body in the privy?"

Old Red nodded. "There you go, Brother," he said, looking almost pleased for once. "We just might make a detective out of you yet."

I grinned, feeling pretty proud of myself—until I realized there was one more step to take if I was to walk through the mystery Holmes-style.

"Hold on, Gustav," I said, my grin suddenly gone. "Why in God's name would anybody try to hide a freshly murdered man in an out-house?"

"Damned if I know," Old Red replied, completely unfazed that we'd deducted ourselves smack-dab into a brick wall. "It ain't just a three-pipe problem—it's more like a thirty-piper."

He turned and wandered away, his eyes on the ground again. This time he headed for the creek that winds behind the castle and the privy, and before long he went down on his knee and spread his fingers in the grass. Though I couldn't see anything but dirt and scrub, I knew my brother was reading the sod like I read a book. He'd been in the drover-ing business nearly ten years, and in that time he'd learned to recognize every hoofprint, hair, toenail, tooth, scuff mark, piss puddle, and shit pile on the plains.

"I thought so," he said. "Boudreaux brought a horse along here last night. That's why he had on his spurs. He aimed to . . . hel-lo!" He crawled around a bit, stopping over a hoofprint so bold and deep even I could see it. "*Another* horse. Someone else rode up this way." He stood and stared back along the creekbed. "Followed the creek in from the south. Well . . . that's a wrinkle."

Old Red spun on his heel, moving quickly back toward the privy, his eyes down. He went past the outhouse, not stopping until he was under a green ash tree near the castle. The ground around the tree was pocked with horse turds. After a moment, Gustav moved on, finding more of the same behind a stand of buffalo-berry bushes not thirty feet away.

"Looks like Boudreaux and that other feller didn't picket their horses together," I said.

Old Red nodded. "Good, Otto, good—you're using your eyes now."

"That means they probably weren't travelin' together," I went on, feeling encouraged to follow up my observation with a touch of deduction. "I bet somebody was trailin' Boo . . . probably the man who shot him! He came right up behind him here and—"

"Whoa there! Slow down! We're supposed to *walk* through the clues, not go ridin' roughshod over 'em," my brother chided.

Before he could remind me that my guesswork constituted theorizing—and get a boot up his butt for doing so—the back door of the house opened and someone leaned out to shoot us a "Pssssst." We turned to find Emily's pleasingly rounded form in the doorway. She motioned us closer. From behind her in the house I could hear the murmur of conversation and the clinking of silver on china. The recent unpleasantness apparently hadn't diminished our employers' appetites.

"So who snuffed it then?" the maid asked.

"Excuse me?" I said.

"Who *died?*" Emily explained, rolling her big, blue eyes. "Who's the stiff?"

"Oh. It's one of the hands. A feller named Boudreaux. You've probably seen him around—the albino Negro."

"Oooooo, it was that one, was it? You know, I used to think all coloreds looked alike until I laid eyes on *him*. Not much 'colored' about him, I'd say. Ho!"

Neither Old Red nor myself gave her a *Ho!* back.

"Well, go on then," Emily prodded. "Tell us what you know."

I looked at Old Red, and he gave me a nod, so I spun out the morning's events, skipping over our more gruesome discoveries. To judge by the look on Emily's face, I needn't have worried about protecting her ladylike sensibilities—she didn't have any. In fact, she seemed positively exhilarated by the few bloody details I did dole out.

"The Duke and Lady Clara and the rest of 'em must be in quite a lather, havin' a dead man on their doorstep and all," Gustav said when I was done, his voice cool and steady despite the nerves that usually jangled him up around women.

"Oooooo, so you might expect," Emily replied. "But the way the Duke and that icicle Edwards are talking, you'd think that Negro back there was no more than a dead cat. 'Probably some meaningless quarrel amongst the strongbacks,' says the Duke. 'Yes,' says his lapdog. 'These Westerners are little better than the filthy aboriginals they drove out.' And then it's on to breakfast and business talk! Well, my lady gave them a right scolding for their lack of feeling. And then when she heard about the gentlemen's wager—oooooo! She dressed them down all over again, even her pet Brackwell. She's a true lady, despite what some say. But when she gets on her high horse, why, she could ride down 'Mrs. Regina' herself! Ho!"

I worked up a "Ho!" of my own to keep things friendly, and my brother even coughed up a good-sport chuckle himself.

"Speakin' of Brackwell, what's the story with him, anyway?" Gustav said once the ho-ing was over. "I can't imagine why the Duke would bring a kid like that on a trip like this."

"Well, let me help you imagine," Emily said, obviously relishing the opportunity to pass along more high-grade gossip. "The way I hear it, he only got sent along because he was *this close* to getting kicked out of Cambridge. He's a queer one, he is. Dreamylike. Couldn't keep his mind on his books. The earl—his father—he's hoping this trip will wake the lad up. Get him interested in something. Make a man out of him. Well, he's interested in something alright. You've seen the way he's taken to dressing? Ho! But as for making him a man . . . well, I daresay *that* hasn't happened yet."

Being quicker than my brother to recognize the setup for a funny, I was the one who replied.

"Oh? And why's that?"

"Because I've been traveling with the boy almost a month, and he hasn't tried to pinch me *once*!"

The maid busted out with a laugh like the nerve-jangling blast of a steamboat whistle.

"So," Gustav said through a feeble smile, "Brackwell said he heard the gunshot last night. How about you?"

The glee fled the girl's face.

"Oh. Well, I . . . I may have heard something."

Her words came out at a limp rather than the usual stampede, and I had to wonder why speaking of a noise in the night should leave her tongue-tied for once.

"Did you happen to make note of the time you 'may have heard something'?" my brother said.

"After midnight—one o'clock maybe. Really, I was asleep again so fast I could hardly say."

Old Red's eyes went kind of unfocused, like he was doing some tricky figuring over a hand of poker. While he cogitated, I jumped in with a thought I was chewing on myself.

"You weren't scared?" I asked. "Everyone else was upstairs in bed, right? So you were down there on the first floor all by your lonesome."

"Oh." Emily sounded surprised, as if the thought hadn't even occurred to her. "No, I . . . I wasn't . . . I wasn't scared."

Something about the girl's hesitation seemed to snap Gustav from his daydream.

"Well, I guess you wouldn't have felt *entirely* alone," he said. "Thanks to the Duke."

Emily glared at my brother as if he'd just complimented her on her magnificent bosoms.

"What's that supposed to mean?" she snapped.

"You said yesterday the Duke gave out derringers to everybody before you came West," Old Red explained quickly. "Sometimes the company of a gun can be a real comfort."

"Oh, that little thing," Emily said dismissively, the sting instantly gone from her voice. "I forgot I even had it."

"Really?"

Gustav's voice was full of a wonderment I shared. Emily either possessed nerves of steel or a brain of pudding.

Or she was lying.

"My goodness, but you Britishers are a calm lot," I said. "Usually when folks from civilized parts come out here to the 'Wild West,' it doesn't take more than a mouse fart to send 'em screamin' for cover, if you'll pardon my sayin' so. Yet y'all hear gunfire in the middle of the night, and the women don't bat an eyelash and the men don't bother rousin' themselves to take a peek outside."

"I didn't know it was gunfire. It was just . . . a noise, that's all," Emily said. "As for the men, Brackwell wouldn't have been any use even if he *had* pulled himself from bed, what with all the drink Lady Clara and the Duke poured down his throat last night." The maid's words picked up steam as she went along, and she looked glad to be talking about folks other than herself again. "Edwards came back from that tour of theirs barely able to walk. His back was giving him such pain he couldn't even make it to the loo—and I should know, because *I* had to empty out the chamber pot. Oooooo."

"And the Duke?" Old Red asked.

"Old Dickie?" Emily shrugged. "That one's as lazy as a fat cat once he's in his chambers for the night. Nothing less than a fire could pull him from bed, and even then he might choose to burn alive rather than fetch a pail of water."

"Just how long have you worked for the Duke, Emily?"

The girl's wide eyes narrowed, and when she spoke her tone was wary again. "I've been in the St. Simons' employ for two years. Why do you ask?"

"Well, from what I've seen, you do most of your work for Lady Clara. Yet you seem to know the old man's habits real well. I was wonderin' how you'd—"

Before Old Red could do that wondering out loud, there came the tinkle of a small bell from inside the house, and Emily stiffened up like she'd heard a bear growl behind her.

"I have to go," she said, somehow managing to look both annoyed and relieved at the same time. She turned and scurried inside to wipe marmalade from the Duke's whiskers or chew Edwards's eggs for him or whatever it is maids do for folks at breakfast time.

Old Red went all daydreamy again the second the door shut, and he spent the next few moments staring at an invisible speck of nothing that seemed to hover a few inches beyond the tip of his nose. By this point, I knew better than to ask what he was thinking—one more warning against theorizing and *theoretically* I was going to rip off his mustache and sprinkle it over his head like pepper.

So I just stood there, not saying a word. To help the time pass, I began whistling "Bury Me Not on the Lone Prairie."

Old Red blinked like a fellow coming out of a spell cast by a tent-show mesmerist.

"Can't a man stand here and *think* a moment?"

"Can't a man stand here and *whistle*?" I replied.

Old Red growled and stepped around me. "Mr. Holmes gets Dr. Watson, and what do I get?" he mumbled as he stomped away. "A goddamn canary."

"Hey," I said as I hustled along after him. "Where you goin' now?"

There was no need for Gustav to answer, for he reached his destination in less than a dozen strides.

"Stay out here and keep watch," he said as he pulled open the double doors to the storm cellar and hurried down the steps, disappearing into the dingy gloom. "If you so much as *smell* a McPherson, call out quick."

He didn't have to explain why he wanted me on lookout. We had reason enough to fear Uly and Spider when we were out in the open. If they were to get us cornered in the cellar, we'd never make it back into the sunshine.

"See anything?" I called down into the dark.

"Just spiderwebs and dirt," Old Red replied.

A small, orange light flickered to life—my brother firing up a lucifer.

"Hel-lo," he said. "Somebody got here before us."

"How can you tell?"

"Footprints, for one thing. And there's a nice, square depression here in the dirt."

The glow of the match went out, and Gustav stepped from the shadows and climbed out of the cellar.

"Somebody had a box tucked away down there—a heavy one," he said as he shut the doors behind him. "But it's gone now."

"A box of papers, maybe?" I said, thinking of the sheet of paper Old Red had seen Boo take from the cellar the day before.

As my brother didn't rebuke me for theorizing, I figured he was thinking the same thing.

"Come on," he said, moving off around the house. He stopped when he reached the southwestern corner, poking his head around and peering at the corral and bunkhouses.

"Any sign of the McPhersons?" I asked as I came up behind him.

Gustav shook his head and got on the move again. He was headed toward the corral, where the Hornet's Nesters were doctoring more cows.

We were headed out into the open, and I didn't like it.

"Uly and Spider are gonna spot us for sure."

"We'll attend to them when the time comes," Old Red said.

I didn't say so, but I couldn't help thinking that time he spoke of was coming mighty quick—and it was a lot more likely the McPhersons would be attending to *us*.

Twenty-one

FRIENDS AND FOES

Or, We Separate the Men from the Hornet's Nest Boys

s we walked toward the corral, I saw that Tall John and Crazymouth were the lucky hands that day. They were the ones on horseback, leaving Anytime and Swivel-Eye to smear oil and acid on the latest batch of maggots.

So it was only natural that Anytime and Swivel-Eye should look about as pleased as a fellow who's fallen face-first into a dung heap. And yet they looked even *more* disgusted when they glanced up and saw us.

"Well, ain't this a surprise," Anytime said. "Big Red and Old Red comin' round when there's real work to be done. I thought they'd still be off playin' Sheerluck Jones or Morecock Bones or whatever the hell that feller's called."

"Sherlock 'olmes," Crazymouth said.

Anytime nodded. "That's the one. Holmes. I'd forgotten all about that dandified fraud till Old Red here started puttin' on airs."

Tall John rode toward us as we came in through the gate. "Maybe we oughta stop callin' him Old Red and start callin' him Old Holmes."

"Or Little Sherlock," Anytime suggested.

"Or the Sherlock Kid," Tall John shot back, fighting giggles.

"Yeah, that's it—the Sherlock Kid," Anytime snorted. "Fastest Brain in the West."

"If you're lookin' for fancy new ways to goldbrick!" Tall John said, his tittering turning to outright guffaws.

Swivel-Eye and Crazymouth watched silently, neither joining in the hilarity nor taking issue with it.

Gustav didn't have much of a reaction, either. In fact, he didn't so much as blink. Before that day, such mockery could've shriveled him up like a prune. But being a genuine consulting detective—at least for the moment—seemed to make insults irrelevant. They wouldn't help him crack his mystery, so they just slid off his ears like water over an otter's ass.

I wasn't immune to all the japing and jeering, however. But the air of purposeful calm that surrounded my brother seemed to reach out and wrap itself around me, and I managed to resist the temptation to grab Tall John and Anytime by the neck and play their heads like maracas.

"Is that what *you* think?" Old Red said, turning to Crazymouth. "Sherlock Holmes is a fraud, and I'm a goldbricker?"

The English drover ambled his mount closer, looking first at Old Red, then at Anytime and Tall John, then back at Old Red.

"No," he finally said. "I gave Blighty the dodge five years ago, and you wouldn't find 'olmes in the fish-and-chips then. But you'd hear of 'im if you knew the wrong people. I 'ad friends in low places in them days, and more than one ended up in gaol thanks to that geezer. So he ain't any kind of fraud, I can vouch you that."

Crazymouth tipped back his hat and squinted at Old Red for a moment before continuing.

"As for you, you ain't lazy. Crazy maybe, but not lazy. If you want to stick your neck in the gander, mate . . . well, I'll wish you a drake, that's all."

Gustav turned his gaze on Swivel-Eye. "What do you think?"

Swivel-Eye nodded at Crazymouth. "What he said."

Of course, none of us understood half of what had come off Crazymouth's tongue. But the sentiment was clear enough. He wasn't against us, but he wasn't exactly with us, either.

Old Red took all this in with the air of rueful disappointment he had honed to perfection on me.

"Alright, fellers. I see how they lay," he said. "All the same, I need your help. Nothin' bold, mind you. I've just got questions I need answered. But I wouldn't feel right askin' without first hoppin' off something I've been sittin' on."

"And what would that be?" Anytime sneered.

"That Tall John's been spyin' on us for the McPhersons."

For a few seconds, every man there was frozen stiff as a stamp iron. Tall John broke the silence with a razzing laugh.

"Looks like you were right, Crazymouth! He's lost his damn mind!"

"How 'bout we let the boys decide on that?" Old Red replied, unruffled. "I have a feelin' they've been thinkin' along the same lines. Not that *you* were a spy, mind you, but that *someone* was. That was clear enough after what happened to Pinky. There wasn't nobody at the table that mornin' but Hornet's Nest boys. So how'd our conversation make its way back to Uly and Spider? And how'd they know Pinky'd nipped some hooch when they hadn't laid eyes on us that day?"

"The Swede was there," Swivel-Eye said, and from the way he jumped in it was clear he had indeed been cogitating on Pinky's misfortune.

"That he was," Gustav said. "But chew on this: What kind of spy would the Swede make? I've known four-year-old Comanches with a better grip on English. In fact, I think that's the only reason Uly hired the man. His ears don't pick up the lingo good enough to eavesdrop, and his mouth don't speak it well enough to gossip. And don't tell me it's an act. He's about as suited to be a spy as he is a dance-hall gal. Which brings us back to Tall John."

"Now listen, you—" Tall John growled, but that didn't slow my brother.

"After what happened to Pinky, I *knew* someone from our dog-house had been whisperin' in Uly's ear. But I didn't get the list of suspects whittled down till Uly sent Big Red to ride bog a few days back. You see, my brother and I started doin' a little eyeballin' around here even before Boudreaux turned up dead. You know why. There's somethin' about this ranch more crooked than a broken-back rattlesnake. I think Uly was startin' to catch on to us—and he wanted to find out what we'd dug up and who we'd done the diggin' with. And you all know my brother's as windy as a Texas tornado."

"Hey," I said, but Old Red was the one with the wind behind him now, and he wasn't ready to stop blowing.

"So when Big Red got sent off with Swivel-Eye and Tall John, I figured one or the other was gonna try to coax some talk out of him. And that's exactly what happened. Ain't that right, Swivel-Eye?"

"That's what happened alright," the drover said, giving Tall John one of the twisty-eyed stares he was named for.

"That don't prove a damn thing!" Tall John protested, but though he was the one on horseback it was Gustav who rode right over *him*.

"Later that day, after the Duke and them others showed up, my brother tried to make himself at home in the house," Old Red said. "But within minutes, Spider came chargin' in to herd him out. Now how'd he know Big Red was even there? Only Tall John, Swivel-Eye, and maybe the Swede had any idea where he was."

"See there!" Tall John cut in. "The Swede!"

"Alright then," Gustav said, nodding at Tall John agreeably. "Back to the Swede. I'd say he's a right fine cook, as ranch coosies go. It's a cryin' shame all them lords and ladies had to steal him away from us.

And who does Uly put in his place? A feller who doesn't know his salt from his pepper. Y'all have had Tall John's cookin'. We're gonna have to soak our tongues in turpentine for a year just to get the taste of it out of our mouths. So tell me—why would Uly leave *him* in charge of the cookshack?"

"You tell us," Anytime said, and though he didn't sound any friendlier now, he at least waited to hear my brother's reply.

"Well, you know privacy's a hard thing to come by around here. You can hardly cop a squat without at least two fellers ribbin' you about the smell. But once he started rollin' biscuits, Tall John had plenty of time alone. Why, twice a day he'd leave us to our chores so he could come back to the cookshack. And who's to say Uly or Spider couldn't meet him there? Before that, Tall John probably had to do all kinds of sneakin' to talk to the McPhersons. But with him in the kitchen and us workin' cows, there'd be no need for sneakin' at all."

Being unaccustomed to such lengthy speechifying, Old Red had to pause here for a breath, giving Tall John another chance to get a say in.

"Bullshit!" he blurted out so loud it sent his horse into a nervous shuffle beneath him. "You ain't got nothin' but probablys and maybes and who's-to-says."

"Well," Gustav said, sounding as cool and quiet as Tall John was loud and lathered, "there is one more thing."

Usually my brother lets such statements float for a moment for the purpose of drawing me into featherheaded guesses. But Anytime cut through that so quick for once I actually appreciated the man's natural-born spite.

"Spit it out then, why don't you?"

Old Red nodded. "Boudreaux was a Negro."

This observation came so completely out of nowhere the first "Huh?" that followed was from my own lips. Tall John broke into a flimsy grin, no doubt thinking my brother was about to prove himself as loco as Hungry Bob Tracy.

"Now think back, fellers," Old Red said. "All the way back to the first day the Hornet's Nest boys came together in Miles City. Think back and ask yourselves, 'Why ain't Jim Weller here?' "

I hadn't given the Negro drover a second's consideration since the day Uly passed him over in the Hornet's Nest. By the time we ran into Boudreaux at the VR, I'd already forgotten Weller's lack of luck landing a job, being more concerned with my own lack of luck with the job I'd landed. I can only assume the same was true for the other fellows, for no one ever bothered to ask why McPherson should blackball one Negro but make another a top hand. No one but my brother, that is.

"We all pushed and shoved our way into a line, you'll recall, and Uly counted off seven men from his left to his right," Old Red said. "But he skipped over Weller, a top-rail puncher and one of the best bronc busters in Montana. That don't make any sense unless the VR don't hire Negroes. But it does. So there must've been another reason to pass over Weller. And you can see it plain as day if you just move on down that line with Uly. His plan was to count off seven fellers for jobs at the VR, and that's just what he did. He didn't give a shit who got hired as long as one particular man was among 'em—the seventh and last man hired. The man who'd let himself get jostled around to the *eighth* place in line. Tall John Harrington."

As the boys listened to my brother roll out his deductions, their expressions began to change, heating up to a bubbling boil like coffee on the fire. The only exception was Tall John himself, who seemed to shrink under the heat of his bunkmates' glares. By the time Old Red wrapped up, *Tall* John didn't look any bigger than a prairie dog.

"Now look here, boys," he began.

That's as far as he got. Some fellows are born with huevos so large they could bluff their way out of hell itself. Tall John was not such a man. A fox with a mouthful of chicken feathers could hardly have looked more guilty.

"You best clear out, Harrington," Swivel-Eye said.

"But—"

"Go on!" Anytime snarled, taking a step toward Tall John. "There's the gate. Get yourself through it or I'm gonna pull you down off that horse and shove your head so far up your ass you'll be wearin' your breakfast for a hat."

Whether Anytime could make good on this threat was something Tall John chose not to test. He wheeled his mount, keeping his eyes on the former compadres who were now staring arrows at his heart, and managed to lean down and get the gate open without dismounting. Once he was out of the corral, he spurred his pinto to a gallop.

"Yeah, that's it—ride!" Anytime shouted after him. "And don't come back alone, if you know what's good for you!"

Being a man for whom hurling abuse comes as natural as growing hair, Anytime wasn't satisfied to stop there. He launched some spit, a couple cow patties, and a long string of profanities at the fleeing traitor's backside. As we watched Anytime run out his conniption, I got the feeling he hadn't had so much fun in months.

The same could have been said of my brother. His face beamed prideful pleasure, with a heap of relief piled on for good measure. He'd obviously been sitting on his suspicions about Tall John for a good reason: He didn't trust himself to be right.

But right he was, and that had *me* looking pretty relieved myself just then. Gustav had cooked up a deduction worthy of Sherlock Holmes, and for the first time I entertained the notion that the McPhersons might have as much to worry about as we did. And apparently I wasn't the only one to think so.

"Alright, Old Red," Swivel-Eye said as Anytime's cursing wound down to a raspy mumble. "You said somethin' a minute ago about havin' questions. Well, go and ask 'em. I'll provide what answers I can."

"I'll do the same," Crazymouth said.

"Me, too," Anytime added as he walked back toward us.

"Thanks, fellers," Old Red said. "I've got the same request for all of you. Tell me everything you remember about last night—*everything*—from the moment we put the lamp out to the time the sun came up."

"You mean like how many times I stepped out to take a piss?" Anytime asked.

He was joshing, but Old Red didn't treat it like a joke. "Exactly. That's just the kind of data I'm lookin' for."

"Data?" Anytime asked.

"Facts," I translated. "Information."

"Well, why the hell didn't he say so?" Anytime said.

Answering that question would've dragged us into another conversation entirely, so I did my part to herd things along by sharing my memories of the night—which didn't amount to much more than sleeping, more sleeping, and finally waking up, with the sound of a distant gunshot mixed in there somewhere. Crazymouth's account was much the same, though phrased with more color. But Swivel-Eye stirred the pot when he threw in his recollections: He heard the shot, too—and he managed to notice the time, more or less. It was just before dawn, he said. Anytime backed him up, saying the sound of gunfire woke him and he didn't grab more than another hour of sleep before it was time to roll out for the day.

I turned to Old Red. "Didn't Emily—?"

"That's right," my brother said, cutting me off.

"Didn't Emily what?" Anytime asked.

"She said she heard the shot, too," Gustav replied, still playing it cagey.

Only I knew what my brother wasn't adding. Emily had put a very different time on that gunshot: after midnight, perhaps one o'clock. It can take sound a while to travel from one place to another, of course, but I had my doubts that even the laziest echo would need all of three hours to mosey from the castle to the bunkhouse.

"None of you took a look around when you heard the shot?" Old Red said, hustling things along before anyone could ask *him* another question.

"All I saw was the insides of me eyelids," Crazymouth said.

"Same for me," Swivel-Eye added. "I just rolled over and went back to sleep."

"I looked," said Anytime.

My brother's eyebrows shot up so fast it's a wonder they didn't hit the brim of his hat. "What did you see?"

"The bunk above mine—I was on my back."

"You didn't peek to see if anyone was missin'?"

"Why would anyone be . . . ?"

Anytime's gaze turned granite-hard as his words slowed to a stop. Beside him, Swivel-Eye and Crazymouth took on the same look of surprised suspicion. They were realizing that they'd all assumed wrong—as had I.

We'd figured Old Red wasn't trying to pin down *who* killed Boudreaux. He was just trying to work out when, where, and why the McPhersons did it.

But my brother had more suspects than Uly and Spider. He wasn't counting *anybody* out—including the Hornet's Nesters.

"How about before the shot?" my brother said, his voice a touch softer now. He knew he was putting his bootheel down on his bunk-mates' toes. "Y'all notice any comings and goings?"

Crazymouth just shrugged and shook his head, his mouth sealed tight. Swivel-Eye stayed silent, too—though his googly eyes had something to say, shooting a glance over at Anytime.

"I went outside to piss," Anytime spat. "What of it?"

"Did you go to the privy?" Old Red asked.

"Why would I do that? I let 'er fly right outside the bunkhouse."

"Did you see anyone else while you were out there?"

"Come to think of it, I did. Caught a glimpse of the Swede. *He* was headed for the privy."

Gustav chewed on that a moment, looking either intrigued or skeptical—or both. Maybe Anytime really had seen the Swede. Or maybe he was just trying to dodge my brother's rope by pushing someone else in its path.

"And this was before the gunshot?" Old Red asked.

"That's right," Anytime said. "Just before daybreak."

"Just before *daybreak*," Gustav repeated, giving his head a slight shake. He shot me a glance, and I nodded, letting him know I felt just as flummoxed as he did.

We were walking the mystery through pretty much as Holmes would, far as I could tell, yet we weren't getting closer to the solution— we were getting further away. Not only did we not know who killed Boudreaux, we couldn't even be sure where and when they did the deed, not to mention why. The only thing we really did know was the how of it, thanks to the bullet hole in Boo's head.

"Alright then—that's all I needed to hear," Old Red announced, pumping up his voice with as much confidence as he could. "Y'all have been a big help, and I thank you."

"So who do you think did it?" Swivel-Eye asked.

"Yeah, tell us, Sherlock," Anytime threw in, some of the nasty snap back in his voice. "Who killed Boudreaux?"

"Well . . . I reckon there's certain fellers I'd like to point my finger at," Old Red replied, obviously choosing his words with considerable care. "But you gotta consider all the answers—even the ones you *don't* like—if you're gonna dig out the truth."

"Just let us know if there's more we can do," Swivel-Eye said.

Old Red smiled grimly. At least one Hornet's Nester was still solidly behind us. Then my brother noticed something over Swivel-Eye's shoulder, and his smile faded. I followed his gaze and saw six men moving toward the corral on foot—Uly, Spider, Tall John, and three other McPherson hands.

"There's more you can do," Gustav said. "But this ain't the time. What Big Red and I gotta do now, we gotta do alone."

"And what exactly is it we gotta do?" I asked, my eyes on the McPhersons and their boys as they drew closer.

My brother has a habit of answering questions with more questions and making comments that get a man scratching his head. But what he said now left no room for deep thought or confusion.

"Run!"

And that's exactly what we did.

Twenty-two

EDWARDS

Or, The McPhersons Stay on Our Heels While We Get on a Gentleman's Nerves

We didn't bother with the gate—we just scrambled over the fence and took off in a sprint the second our feet hit the ground. Of course, I knew what we were running *from,* but I quickly realized I had no idea where we were running *to.* Old Red supplied an answer by making a beeline for the castle.

We didn't make it. When we were still a good twenty feet from the porch, the front door opened, and out stepped Edwards, his bulky frame wrapped in one of his heavy tweed outfits.

"I would have a word with you!" he said when he saw us.

I was of a mind to keep on running. But Gustav skidded to a stop, so I did, too. As Edwards came down the steps toward us, I peeked over my shoulder at the McPhersons' little lynch mob. They were outside the corral, talking to the Hornet's Nest boys and throwing glares our way.

"You're still pursuing this 'investigation' of yours?" Edwards asked. He was moving slowly, obviously still hurting from his ride the day before. In fact, he appeared to be so weak that the small, covered basket he carried with him was enough to pull him off-balance, giving him the slightly tilted gait of a rummy stumbling from one saloon to the next.

"Yes, sir—still pursuin'," Old Red said. "In fact, I think you'll soon be out two hundred of them *pounds.*"

My brother gave Edwards the kind of salty, ribbing grin that comes more naturally to men like Anytime.

"You have a theory, then?" Edwards asked. "A notion as to which man is responsible?"

Old Red nodded, still doing his best to look smug. "I do."

Edwards waited a moment, obviously expecting more.

"Well?" he said.

"Well what?"

"What's your explanation? Whom do you suspect?"

"Oh, I shouldn't say just yet. But be patient. You'll hear my conclusions soon enough."

It was plain Edwards didn't like hearing "just be patient" from a social inferior. His face, already pink as watermelon pulp from hours in the sun to which a man of his station isn't accustomed, burned even redder.

"You refuse to tell me?"

"'I follow my own methods and tell as much or as little as I choose,'" Old Red said, quoting you-know-who. "'That is the advantage of being unofficial.'"

For a second, I wondered if Edwards was going to heft up that basket of his and bring it down on my brother's head. He settled for a dismissive sneer.

"Be obstinate if you wish. It doesn't matter to me anymore. For your information, I've withdrawn my wager."

Old Red's put-on cockiness almost gave way to genuine surprise, but he managed to keep a smile on his face.

"Backed out, did you? I suppose I oughta look upon that as quite a compliment."

"You shouldn't. My decision had nothing to do with your chances for success—though my opinion on that subject hasn't changed."

"Well, your opinion on *somethin'* must've changed."

"Yes, well," Edwards huffed. "It's simply that upon further reflection I realized that this whole charade is in the most abominable taste. A man is dead. He may have been some sort of a Negro grotesquerie, but that doesn't turn his death into a proper subject for sport."

"So it's a matter of principle, huh?" Gustav replied. "Well, I commend you on that, Mr. Edwards. You're absolutely correct. Any death should be treated with all due seriousness. Which is why I know you won't mind answerin' a few questions."

"You wish to question *me?*"

"Yes, sir."

I was almost as surprised as Edwards to hear that Gustav wanted to drag this conversation out further. We had places to go and people to get the hell away from. I took another look over my shoulder and saw the McPhersons and their crew looking right back at me from the corral.

"Don't be ridiculous," Edwards said. "What could I possibly know about this tawdry affair?"

"Just give me a minute, and we'll find out."

Edwards looked at my brother like he was a mosquito who'd just told him to drop his drawers and bend over.

"You took back your bet, but the Duke didn't," Old Red said before Edwards could spit out a firm no. "He still expects to collect two hundred pounds when this business is done. I'm sure he'd be mighty disappointed if Mr. Brackwell had cause to not pay up . . . like, say, because certain people didn't give me all the information I needed to—"

"What do you want to know?" Edwards cut in sharply.

Old Red stared back at him as if the man had told him a great deal already.

"Well," my brother said, "first off, I'm wonderin' if you heard or saw anything out of the ordinary last night."

Edwards nodded so impatiently his pince-nez went crooked. "Yes, yes. I was awakened by a noise—a sort of thud."

"A thud? Not a pop?"

"A *thud*. I didn't know it was a gunshot, of course. It could've been someone slamming a door or dropping a book for all I knew."

"Did it sound close by or far off?"

"I couldn't say. You Westerners may be accustomed to the constant sound of gunfire, but I'm not, so I have little basis for comparison."

"What time was it you heard this 'thud'?"

I pricked up my ears, hoping Edwards might help us pin down exactly when the shot that killed Boo was fired: around one o'clock, as Emily said, or closer to dawn, as Anytime and Swivel-Eye claimed. Unfortunately, Edwards couldn't—or wouldn't—help us out.

"I have no idea," he said. "I was asleep again within moments."

"You didn't get up to have a look-see?" Old Red asked.

"I saw no reason to"—Edwards took on the appearance of a man trying to swallow paint—"'have a *look-see*.'"

"And I suppose you weren't feelin' your most spry just then."

"No, I wasn't."

"That ride yesterday really took it out of you."

"Yes, it did."

"But today you're feelin' better."

"Yes, I am."

"You ain't sufferin' from the same malady as young Brackwell?"

"I should say not. I know how to handle my drink."

"And the boy don't, huh?"

"Lady Clara is overindulgent with the young man. His Grace wished to toast . . . our satisfaction with the Cantlemere. The lady encouraged Brackwell to join in with excessive enthusiasm."

"Got him drunk, did she?"

"Yes," Edwards hissed through gritted teeth.

"Just how far back do you go with the Duke and his family?"

"I've known the St. Simons for three years and have been an investor in the Cantlemere for two," Edwards said. "Are you finished? It seems to me you've strayed from any pertinent line of inquiry."

"Oh, have I?" Old Red said, blinking with wide-eyed innocence. "I beg your pardon. How about this: Your room's on the second floor, ain't it? Next to the Duke's room?"

"Our rooms are separated by a linen closet."

"Right, right. Well, have you heard any prowlin' about at night while you been here?"

"What do you mean 'prowling about'?"

"Footsteps, whispers, doors openin' and closin' at odd hours—that kind of thing."

"No," Edwards said, a strange, wary quality creeping into the disdain he'd been beaming at my brother the past few minutes. "And I don't see how that's any more relevant than your other questions."

"Well, like I said when we were all lookin' at the body earlier—the man was wearin' spurs. My guess is he aimed to clear out. Now if he was gonna do that, wouldn't it make sense for him to snag a few valuables to hock in town? And where were the real valuables around here? In the house."

"Oh. Yes," Edwards said, his irritation fading into some deeper, murkier emotion. "I see what you mean."

And then he did something that put a shiver down my spine faster than a blue norther: He smiled.

"Perhaps we got off on the wrong foot. I'm sure I seem quite the frightful prig to bluff fellows like yourselves." Edwards was attempting a jocular tone he couldn't quite pull off when using phrases like "quite the frightful prig." "Keeping up appearances, that's all. It's what one has to do around . . ." He nodded back toward the castle, rolling his eyes and making a face halfway between a grimace and a grin. "You know."

"Sure."

"Oh, yeah, sure," I said, following my brother's lead. "We understand."

"Of course you do. Just like I understand what it must be like for you. The hard work, the monotony. And then along comes a chance for a break from the routine, a little excitement, and you grab it. Who wouldn't?"

Gustav shrugged. Neutral as the gesture was, Edwards seemed encouraged to continue.

"But you know, you're not going to accomplish anything mucking about in people's affairs, except perhaps annoying your employers—never a wise thing to do. The Duke's not a man to trifle with, I assure you. So just to show that I'm not a stuffed shirt, I'm going to help you. I can go inside and lay hands on a bottle of wine or Scotch—even real English gin. Whatever you want. I'll bring that out, and you can go 'investigate' it someplace private. I daresay that would be a better use of your time than asking a lot of silly questions. What do you think, hmmm?"

Edwards's words had taken on a strangely twangy quality, and he was almost finished before I realized what he was trying to do—speak like us. His accent wasn't very convincing. His offer wasn't, either.

"I don't drink when I'm on a case," Gustav said. His right eye twitched ever so slightly, throwing out a wink so quick only a brother could catch it.

"You're a fool," Edwards snapped back, his voice reverting to its normal haughty tone. And with that he stepped around us and limped off toward the corral with as much speed as his aching muscles could manage.

"Mr. Edwards!" Gustav called after him. "Just one more thing!"

Edwards turned stiffly.

Old Red pointed at the basket dangling from the man's right hand. "Are you goin' on a *picnic*?"

Edwards's only response was to point himself back toward the corral and hobble off again. Once he reached the McPhersons, a quick conference followed, and a couple of Uly's men sprinted off to the barn where the wagons and buggies were kept. Edwards shuffled after them.

"I think he *is* goin' on a picnic," Gustav muttered.

I nodded. "Peculiar."

My brother raised an eyebrow. *"Suspicious."*

We'd been standing there staring at the McPhersons, and now they suddenly turned to stare at us. And they did more than stare, too—they headed for us again.

All the turning tail we'd been doing that morning was beginning to wear on my nerves. Yet I figured standing our ground might be even harder on my hide.

"Inside?" I asked my brother.

"Inside."

We hustled up the steps and into the foyer, the noise of our hurried entrance drawing Emily out of the dining room to gape at us. Then the door behind us opened again, and she had even more to gape at.

Uly and Spider were coming in after us.

Twenty-three

DE OOTHOOSE END DE DOOBLE-OO KAY

Or, Gustav and the Swede Talk . . . and Neither One Makes Much Sense

Id Red didn't wait for the McPhersons to rope us like a couple of steers. He started toward Emily, and I followed.

"Fetch His Grace—quick," my brother barked at the startled maid as we swept past. "Mr. McPherson has important news!"

"Don't you—" Uly began, but Emily was already scurrying away. From behind us came the sound of quick footsteps and the opening of a door—undoubtedly the one to Perkins's office—and then the Duke's booming voice.

"What now, McPherson?"

"Well, sir . . . uhhhh . . . you see . . . ," Uly stammered as we hurried up the hallway.

We found the Swede rolling dough in the kitchen.

"Oh, boyce!" the old fellow moaned, looking miserable. "Peer-kens dead, Boo-de-row dead. Aront here iss getting planty bed, hey?"

The Swede's accent was molasses-thick even under the best of circumstances, but now it was as if someone had left the jug outside on a cold day. I was still trying to strain some meaning from the syrup when Gustav replied.

"Plenty bad indeed. Got a minute to talk about it?"

"I ken be speaking mit yew boyce unteel dat leetle kronjon Eem-ily iss returning."

Fortunately, the Swede nodded as he spoke, which cut out the need for a word-for-word translation.

"So tell me—did you notice anything out of the ordinary last night or this mornin'?" Old Red asked.

The Swede nodded again. "Dere iss in de hoose downstairce a dooble-oo kay, but Eem-ily says it iss too much in de murning mit de noice. Not for herself, you know, but for the . . ." The Swede crooked a thumb at the ceiling—and the bedrooms above it. "So I em going always to de oothoose when I am to be making with the plop, yes? End I—

"Wait, wait, wait," Gustav said. "A 'doo bell oo kay'?"

"Yes, a dooble-oo kay."

Just to show how profoundly befuddled my brother was, he actually turned to me for help.

"Oh, come now, Gustav. Don't tell me you don't know what a 'dooble-oo kay' is," I said. "Why, every modern home's got one."

"So what is it?"

I shrugged. "Damned if I know."

Old Red turned back to the Swede with a snort of disgust.

"Dooble-oo kay," the Swede repeated, making symbols in the air with his fluttery, flour-covered hands.

The symbols couldn't mean anything to my brother: They were letters, which left the deciphering to me.

"*WC*—water closet."

"Oh," Gustav said, looking chagrined.

"Well, that sure was a good use of time," I said. "At this rate, it shouldn't take more than a month to find out what the Swede had for breakfast. If you'd like, I could go ask Uly and Spider to wait to kill us until we've—"

"*So,*" my brother said to the Swede, "you went to the outhouse early this mornin'."

The Swede nodded, and I noticed Old Red's eyes narrow just the slightest bit. *Anytime wasn't lying,* he was no doubt thinking.

"Boot someone iss to it before me," the Swede said. "It iss still dark mostly, so I em not seeing who. But ass I come closer to de hoose I voot-stops end maybe voices em hearing. End den *slak*! De door is shut slammed."

"You heard movement by the outhouse?"

"Vootstops, yes."

"And voices?"

"I tink maybe."

"And *then* the door slammed?"

"Yes. Slak!"

"Slak?"

"Slak!"

"And after the *slak*?"

"I em knowing Eem-ily eef I em too early de dooble-oo kay using iss complaining, yes? So I em knocking on de oothoose door end I em saying, 'Hallo! Will you soon be done?'"

"And . . . ?"

"End nothing. I em getting no answer."

"Had you tried the door?"

"Yes. It wass locked."

"And this was about what time?"

"Four thirty maybe, I tink."

"*Four thirty,*" Gustav repeated.

He pointed a cocked eyebrow at me for the briefest flash of a moment. It looked like the Swede was backing up Anytime and Swivel-Eye's version of events: The gunshot was fired just before dawn, not just after midnight. Before I could sink my teeth into that for a thoughtful chew, Old Red was pressing on.

"And then what?" he asked the Swede.

"I em no choice having. I go inside de hoose end I em de dooble-oo kay ussing. Den I get to work. Eem-ily, she tells me yesterday de Duke sausages iss wanting. Sausages! Where em I sausages getting unless my own hands I em making dem with? So dat's what I do. I em making de fat kukhuvud hiss sausages—chopping, grinding, chopping, stuffing. End den . . . *skrall!*"

"Skrall?"

"*Skrall!*"

"The gunshot."

"Yes. Only maybe I shouldn't *skrall!* be saying. It wass more maybe of a . . ." The Swede lowered his voice and put his hand over his mouth. "*Poop.*"

"A pop?"

"Yes. A *poop,* not so very loud."

"Did you step outside to take a look?"

"No."

"*No?*"

"No. I em in sausage up to my elbowce, end I em tinking, 'Ahhh, dat Brackwell. One day he is shooting soomebooty when with those fancy gunce he is playing.'"

"Had you seen Brackwell?"

"Well, no."

"Had you seen *anybody* when you were outside?"

"No."

"How about in the house? Any sign folks were up?"

"Not yet. Dat Eem-ily—always overlate she iss sleeping. Never em I seeing her out of her room before de sun. End den de—" The Swede hooked a thumb at the ceiling again. "Dey are not getting up fur anoother hour."

"Now this is very important, Swede," Old Red said, speaking extra-slow to drive home his seriousness. "How much time passed between your knockin' on the outhouse door and your hearin' that gunshot?"

"Five minutes, I em tinking."

"Five minutes?" my brother mumbled. "*Five minutes.* Just enough time for someone to—"

Just who might be doing what I didn't learn, for some other *who* came barging through the door behind us. My hand shot down to the hogleg at my side, bringing it up and cocking it as I whipped around.

What I found at the end of the barrel wasn't the steely-eyed McPherson I'd expected. It was a wide-eyed, terror-stricken maid.

"Jesus, I'm sorry, Emily," I said, holstering my .45 before she could scream.

The girl had been so shocked to find a peacemaker jammed in her face, for once she couldn't put words together. "B-bloody . . . h-hell . . . ," she panted.

"Hold that thought," Old Red said. "I've got one more thing to ask our friend here."

He was talking at a streak, as if he had to hustle out the most important question of all before Emily grabbed us by the seat of the pants and tossed us from the castle.

"Swede," he said, "did you pack a picnic for Mr. Edwards just now?"

I had to clinch my jaw to keep it from dropping to my chest. Here we were tracking a killer, the McPhersons on our tails, and my brother was curious about Edwards's *lunch*?

The Swede nodded and shrugged at the same time, looking as perplexed by the question as I felt. "He iss coming into the kitchen soon ago, fur bret end cheece asking. So I em giving him dese things."

"But not packin' 'em yourself? Just puttin' 'em out for Edwards to take?"

The old cook nodded again. "He is de food in hiss basket putting, yes."

"Thank you, Swede."

Emily cleared her throat. "Your presence . . . ," she began, taking on the stiff, brittle tone she used when she was talking like a nobleman's maidservant and not a giggly girl.

Old Red spun around to face her almost as quick as I had a moment before. "You told us you heard the shot around midnight or one o'clock. You sure about that?"

The snap in Gustav's voice—or perhaps the chance to trade in more gossip—seemed to drag the real Emily out of her servantish shell. "I'm sure," she said. "I should think I know what the dead of night looks like, and this was the dead of night."

"No, no," the Swede butted in. "It was mooch later."

"Oh, don't listen to *him*." Emily rolled her eyes, then leaned in closer to Old Red. "And I'll tell you something else, Mr. Detective— that dead darky wasn't just creeping about outside last night. He came right into the *house*."

My brother perked up like a hound catching the scent of something rotting and ripe. "How do you know?"

"Because I went into the linen closet upstairs not ten minutes ago, and an iron and some pillows were *missing*."

Gustav squinted at Emily as if she were a mirage shimmering in and out of view. "Pillows and an iron?"

The girl nodded. "And that's not all. He also took Lady Clara's—"

As those last words left her lips, Emily sighed and sagged. She quickly straightened up again, and I knew what was coming next. She'd remembered what she'd been sent after us to do—throw us out.

"Your presence . . . ," she said, launching back into the sentence she'd begun a minute before.

. . . will no longer be tolerated in this house is what I expected to hear. What actually came out was very different indeed.

". . . is requested in the parlor. Lady Clara wishes to speak with you."

Twenty-four

MY LADY

Or, An Angel Pleads for Mercy, and Old Red Plays Devil's Advocate

Lords and ladies are not accustomed to waiting for anything, let alone a pair of no-accounts with dirt under their fingernails and dung on their boots. Yet by sidetracking Emily with his questions, Old Red had put Lady Clara in just such a position, and when we entered the parlor I feared we'd find my dream girl's shimmering hazel eyes aboil with indignation. I needn't have worried, for she graced us with a heavenly smile as we entered.

But that smile couldn't conceal the lady's obvious anxiety. There were lines around her eyes and mouth I hadn't noticed before, and her proud, perfect posture had drooped, causing her to sag like a dying flower bent by the weight of its own beautiful petals.

"Gentlemen," she said. "Please sit down."

These four words showered upon us an honor I would never have dreamed possible. We had been invited to seat ourselves in the presence of a bona fide aristocrat. As Old Red and I brought our denim-clad backsides down upon the divan, I was overcome by such an intoxicating mix of humility and pride that my head felt light as a leaf on my shoulders. I stole a glance at Gustav, but he appeared to be little moved by the uncommon courtesy being afforded us. He seemed to have overcome his shyness around females, as well, for he looked more curious than bashful.

"Amongst those of my country and class, there are subjects that are regarded as unsuitable topics of discussion for a respectable woman," Lady Clara said. "But as Americans of the frontier have a reputation for . . . relaxed attitudes in matters of propriety, I hope you won't be shocked if I speak plainly."

I nodded vigorously, while beside me Old Red stayed perfectly still.

"As my father can attest, I have always spoken my mind on finance, politics, and other matters that supposedly fall outside the feminine sphere," the lady continued. "Murder would be one such topic— especially murder of the sort discovered here today. A Negro found dead in an outhouse? Some would say it's beneath my notice. But I feel that a man's death is *never* beneath one's notice. Nor should it be the subject of jokes or idle amusements. Wouldn't you agree?"

This question was directed at me, perhaps because Lady Clara saw that I wouldn't dispute any statement she should make, whether it be to criticize her father's bet or to insist that the sky is red, blood is blue, and my own hair green as grass. Old Red wasn't under such sway, however.

"My investigation ain't no joke," he shot back.

"And we couldn't agree with you more, my lady," I added quickly, trying to smooth things over. "Why, my brother said much the same thing to Mr. Edwards not twenty minutes ago. 'Ain't nothin' funny about death,' he said. 'Serious it is, and serious it oughta be treated.'"

"Then you'll both understand why I find this wager between my father and Mr. Brackwell so distasteful," the lady said.

I nodded again, but Old Red just sat there like he was carved from wood.

"I'm told the proper authorities should arrive no later than noon tomorrow," Lady Clara said, her warmth toward us starting to cool. "Surely any investigating can wait until professionals are here to pursue it."

She paused, giving my brother another opportunity to do the gentlemanly thing and put a bullet in the bet—by giving up his detecting. Instead, he made use of that pause to take himself off the spot and put the lady there in his place.

"If you're as partial to plain-speakin' as you say, you won't mind if I ask you a question of a personal nature."

The worry lines on Lady Clara's face appeared to grow deeper before my eyes. But true to her breeding, the lady remained unflustered.

"You may ask."

"Thank you," Gustav said, his voice softening up a touch. "As you're a woman who don't let notions of propriety stand in her way, I find it strange that you'd object so strongly to the Duke's wager on moral grounds—callous though that wager may be, I grant you. It makes me think there's another reason you wanted to talk to us . . . and maybe it has somethin' to do with that hunk of money your father put up for grabs."

The lady stared at my brother for a moment as if she were still waiting for him to ask his question. Then she nodded slowly and sadly.

"It shames me to admit it, but it *is* the money that concerns me."

"Two hundred pounds is a lot of cash, I gather. And cash is somethin' your family ain't exactly flush with anymore, is it?"

I blushed with embarrassment, horrified that Gustav should rub Lady Clara's dainty nose in the gossip we'd heard from Emily and Brackwell.

The lady sighed and sank into an even more pronounced slump. "Do even the Red Indians know of our troubles by now? Yes, our fortune is not what it once was. The two Cantlemeres—this one and our estate in Sussex—are all that remain. As you know so much already, there's no reason not to tell you what brought us down so."

A ripple of emotion spread across Lady Clara's usually placid features, revealing an anger that lurked just beneath the surface.

"It was gambling," she said. "On cards, on horses, on whether a fly would alight on a lump of sugar. Between my father and my brothers, it's a wonder my family has anything left."

"The ranch here don't bring in enough to keep you afloat?" Old Red asked.

The lady tucked away her bitterness behind a wry smile. "The Cantlemere Ranche is what men of finance would call a break-even proposition—with the possibility of failure hanging over it at all times. Sometimes I think that's why my father remains committed to it: It's his last grand gamble. He has great hopes that things here will take a sudden turn for the better."

My brother cocked an auburn eyebrow at that. "Based on what exactly?"

"As I've said," Lady Clara replied with a shrug, "he is a gambler."

"Which is why he wouldn't give up on the bet he made this mornin'—even though you've asked him to."

"That's correct. William—Mr. Brackwell—is a gentleman and a friend, and of course he was willing to renounce the wager."

Old Red's gaze turned iron-hard, but the lady didn't seem to notice.

"Unfortunately, the Duke refused to release him from his bet," she went on, her smoldering resentment again burning its way through any attempts to smother it. "If my father wins, he means to collect. And if he loses, he means to pay. The Duke of Balmoral won't have it said that he isn't good for his debts—if those debts are incurred through gaming. After all, a man who reneges on one foolish wager might be denied the privilege of making more. And the Duke can't have that."

My instinctive dislike for the old man had now been fanned into outright hatred, and I was ready to hop up, seek him out, and box his ears. Old Red, on the other hand, simply leaned back and shrugged.

"I'm sorry to say it, ma'am, but your father's bet ain't my concern. I'm anglin' to catch a killer. Whether money changes hands is beside the point, from where I sit."

"I understand entirely," Lady Clara said, instantly regaining her natural poise. "I must seem like a selfish old harridan to think of my own petty problems at such a time."

"Oh, no! Not at all! It's only natural you should be concerned for your family," I assured her. "Why, it would just break our hearts to pieces if we should bring any misfortune upon you and your kin. Ain't that right, Gustav?"

Old Red took a deep breath that might have been a stifled sigh.

"Yup," he said. "Break our hearts."

Lady Clara gave us a small, almost wistful smile. "You're very kind. I can see that."

She looked back and forth between Gustav and myself as she said it, but I fancied her words were intended for me alone. This was about to draw from me some hayseed ejaculation on the order of "Awww, shucks," but fortunately the lady spoke again before I could embarrass myself.

"Since you're moving ahead with your investigation, I may as well offer my assistance. As you say, the wager should be a secondary concern. There's a murderer loose, and it would be heartless indeed for me to stand in the way of his capture, no matter what the price. If I can aid you in any way, you have but to ask."

At that moment, I came to understand how women in romantic melodramas can be made to "swoon" by the mere sight of their beau's heroic deeds. I felt like swooning myself. This was proof positive for me: Lady Clara had not only the face of an angel, but the soul of one, too.

"As it so happens, you *can* help me," Old Red said, and I knew exactly what words would leave his mouth next. "Tell me—did you notice anything out of the ordinary last night or this mornin'?"

"Actually, yes. Two things. First, I heard a noise last night—from my conversations with the others, I gather it was the gunshot that killed that poor man."

"Did you make note of the time?"

I leaned forward, anxious to have the dispute over the timing of Boo's killing resolved at last. Anytime, Swivel-Eye, and the Swede disagreeing with Emily—well, that was something to think about. But if Lady Clara disagreed with Emily, why, then the matter was settled, far as I was concerned. In fact, if the lady disagreed with *everyone* and said the shot had been fired thirty seconds ago, I would've been inclined to believe her over all the others.

"It was pitch-black, that's all I know," she said.

"So it was the middle of the night?" Old Red persisted. "Midnight maybe? One o'clock?"

The lady shook her head. "I really couldn't say."

My brother and I both sank back into the cushions. The *when* of Boudreaux's death was still a mystery.

"And you didn't get up to investigate?" Old Red asked, forging on.

"No. I went back to sleep. I assumed someone had merely bumped into something in the dark."

"Oh? There's been a lot of sneakin' around at night, has there?"

"No," Lady Clara said, her tone turning a tad snippish. "I simply meant that I had no reason to assume it was anything sinister."

Old Red conceded the point with a nod. "And the other thing you noticed?"

"I wasn't the one who noticed it, actually. It was Emily. Just a few minutes ago, she discovered that my valise had been stolen."

Gustav sat up like a man who just felt a strike on his fishing line. "Your *valise*? That's a handbag, am I right?"

"Yes, though a little bigger."

"More like a carpetbag?"

"I suppose they would be similar in size, yes." The lady's expression soured ever so slightly—carpetbags being for people who couldn't afford luggage made from more tasteful material. "I had no use for the valise while we were here in the country, so it was stored with our luggage in the upstairs linen closet. Emily noticed an iron and some pillows missing, so she conducted an inventory. The only other missing item was my valise."

"What was in it?"

"Only what one would expect—a small amount of money, a few personal items of the sort women carry with them."

"I see," Gustav said, though I doubt he really knew much about what "personal items" ladies tote about. "And you think Boudreaux— that's the dead feller—you think he took this *valise* of yours?"

"That was Emily's assumption." Lady Clara shrugged, imbuing even such a mundane movement as that with grace and refinement. "I'm not so sure, myself. Perhaps this Boudreaux encountered the thief and tried to stop him. I hope that's *not* the case, however. I hate to think of anyone losing his life over some meager possessions of mine."

"Um-hmm, um-hmm," Old Red mumbled absently. His eyes went fuzzy, losing their focus as they will when his vision turns inward.

"Is there anything more you wish to ask?"

"Well, yes and no, Miss St. Simon," Old Red said slowly, pulling himself back to the here and now with visible effort. "I ain't got more questions for you, but I do have a request."

"And that would be?"

"Could you fetch your father for me? I'd like to ask *him* a few questions, too."

You might have thought my brother had just requested a peek at the lady's petticoats, her eyes shot open so wide. I couldn't blame her, for my eyes did a little popping themselves.

Men like us aren't meant to speak to men like the Duke lest it's to say "Dinner is served" or "Yes, sir—right away!" I couldn't see the use of pestering the old man with questions. He was a hive of bees I preferred not to poke.

Lady Clara recovered more quickly than I, effortlessly smoothing her lovely features back into a mask of composed gentility.

"Wait here."

She rose and left the parlor, heading across the foyer to Perkins's office. When the door shut behind her, I turned to my brother.

"What're you playin' at? You know that tub-gutted son of a bitch is just gonna stomp out here and holler at us—if he comes out at all."

"I've got my reasons," Gustav replied calmly.

"Well, I'll be damned if I can see 'em. Why you'd persist in houndin' every soul in the castle instead of sniffin' after the McPhersons or maybe Anytime is beyond—"

The office door opened wide, and Lady Clara stepped out again. She was followed by the Duke and Young Brackwell, who'd traded in his buckskin finery for a dark frock coat more suitable for a junior nobleman. While I was impressed by the lady's power of persuasion in convincing her father to grant us an audience, that wasn't what set my heart to pounding and my brain to racing.

The office window was opened wide, and a breeze blew through it, sweeping past Lady Clara and the others to bring the smell of smoke into the parlor. And not just any smoke. It had a scorchy, sulfurous aftertaste about it that I knew well.

It was the smell of *gunsmoke*.

Twenty-five

OLD DICKIE

Or, Gustav Needles the Duke, but It's My Brother Who's Cut to the Quick

I peeled off a peek at Old Red to see if he'd caught wind of that oh-so-familiar yet oh-so-surprising smell. He clearly had, for his face wore an expression of such unbridled self-satisfaction it would have made a strutting gamecock appear humble by comparison.

I knew what he was thinking: We'd found "the scene of the crime." But it seemed to me it was nothing to get cocky about, as the discovery raised more questions than it answered.

Why didn't anyone in the castle recognize the gunshot for what it was? Why move the body to the *privy* of all places? And, knottiest of all, was it possible one of our visitors had killed Boudreaux—and if so, why?

The first place to start hunting for answers was in the office. But there was a considerable obstacle between it and us—an obstacle who wasn't pleased to see us.

"Well?" the Duke demanded as he entered the parlor. He moved with the plodding confidence of a saloon strong-arm about to roust a drunken deadbeat, but his appearance wasn't quite as intimidating as he seemed to think. His hair was thick but gray, his body heavy with muscle turned to blubber, his face flushed not just with indignation but with heat and strain. He was, in a word, *old*—and he apparently didn't know it.

He didn't bother taking a seat, and I could tell from the way his eyes burned into us he wasn't pleased to see us on our rumps while he remained on his feet. But my brother kept himself buried butt-deep in cushion, so I did the same.

"Thanks for makin' time for us, Your Grace," Gustav said, his words coming out so offhanded and relaxed he might have been gabbing with another hand over a plate of beans. "I got a couple questions to ask you. Just tryin' to be thorough, y'see."

"Yes, yes. Get on with it, then," the Duke grumbled.

"Okeydokey," Old Red replied cheerfully. He turned to me, throwing a casual nod toward the old man. "Maybe you'd like to get this rollin', Brother."

This unexpected honor put a grin on my face—as did my suspicion that it was being granted merely to annoy old Dickie. I cleared my throat and looked thoughtful for a moment.

"Tell me, Your Grace—did you notice anything out of the ordinary last night or this mornin'?"

Gustav nodded his approval, while Lady Clara and Brackwell kept their eyes on the Duke like a couple of railroad stokers watching a boiler they half-expected to explode.

"I did not," the old man said.

I opened my mouth, then quickly closed it again. I'd had my next questions all set—"What time did you hear it?" and "You didn't step outside to take a look?" But now it looked like this interview wasn't going to follow the same trail as the last few, and I found myself at a loss for words.

"Uhhh . . . you didn't hear a sort of . . . well . . . *bang*-type sound?"

The Duke glowered at me, his bushy eyebrows pushing down so hard I had to wonder if he could see anything through the foliage.

"I heard nothing."

I recalled what Emily had said about the unrousable depths into which the old man fell once in bed. But for all their lack of size, derringers don't entirely lack for *sound*. They might be easier to muffle than your larger artillery, but they'll still put out a pop. The gun that had been fired last night—inside the house, if the smell from the office was any indication—had kicked up enough noise to awaken Emily on the first floor and Lady Clara, Brackwell, and Edwards on the second. Could the Duke have really slept through it?

"Ummm . . . you sure?" I asked, unable to think up a more subtle way of getting at my doubts.

"Of course I am!" the Duke barked. He didn't top that off with *you imbecile,* but his tone said it plain enough.

I shot my brother a panicky look that pleaded with him to grab back the reins of the conversation. He took them, alright—and jerked them in a whole new direction.

"Did Mr. Perkins know you were comin'?"

"What?" the Duke said, so taken aback he momentarily forgot to bellow and fume. Behind him, Lady Clara and Brackwell looked equally bewildered.

"Did Perkins—or anyone else here at the ranch—know you were comin' thisaway?"

"No. What has that got to do with—?"

"No, you say?" Old Red frowned and shook his head, making a big show of his apparent confusion. "Well, why was the house stocked up with fine linens and wines and whiskeys and whatnot? I don't think the hired help was meant to live so soft."

"The board had instructed Perkins to be ready for a visit at any time."

"A 'visit'? Don't you mean a 'surprise inspection'?"

The Duke gave Old Red a look that suggested he was reappraising just what kind of insect my brother was—and in what manner he should be squashed.

"I say what I mean. We were traveling to Chicago for the Exposition and I decided to *visit* the Cantlemere. It was a mere whim, a sudden fancy."

I found it hard to imagine the Duke acting on a "sudden fancy." Gustav apparently had the same difficulty.

"Your Grace, Chicago is more than five hundred miles east of here. That's a mighty long way to travel on a whim."

"What in blazes does this have to do with that dead Negro out there?" the Duke demanded.

"I ain't sure yet. I'm just collectin' data."

"'Collecting data'?" the Duke repeated with a grimace of disgust, apparently finding this phrase more objectionable than any comment one might make about Jesus Christ, excretion, or the physical act of love.

"Exactly," Gustav said. "Like this, for instance—how long's it been since the Bar VR turned a profit?"

"This is impertinent, irrelevant, and an utter waste of time!" the Duke roared.

"Alright, let's say it is," Gustav threw back at him. "That oughta make you mighty pleased."

"Why in heaven's name should I be *pleased*?"

"Because if I'm wastin' time, every minute I'm at it brings *you* another minute closer to two hundred pounds."

The Duke blinked at my brother as if he'd just switched from speaking English to Chinese. Then he shook his head and spat out a laugh. It wasn't a jolly, "Well spoken, my good fellow" kind of laugh. It was a laugh that aimed to pull down your britches, knock off your hat, and spit in your eye—a *mean* laugh.

"You are an insolent jackanapes, but I must admire your cheek.

You're using your own incompetence to justify a few more minutes of idle gossip in comfortable surroundings. Just look at you! Stretched out in the shade while your friends toil outside. Would you like a glass of lemonade?" The Duke laughed again and looked back at Brackwell. "What do you think of your champion now? He's half-simpleton, half-lunatic, and all rascal, I'd say!"

Brackwell remained silent, though the sour expression on his face made it plenty clear what he thought of the Duke.

Beside him, Lady Clara didn't look too pleased, either. She took a step toward her father and put a hand on his arm. But before she could admonish the crotchety old toad—or bring the interview to an end—Old Red spoke again.

"Ain't no harm in humoring a 'lunatic,' is there? So why not answer my question? Is this ranch profitable?"

The Duke snorted at my brother the way one might chuckle over the fumblings of a particularly clumsy kitten.

"Fine. Why not, indeed? The Cantlemere *was* profitable—until six years ago. The winter of 1887 hit our stock hard. We've struggled to return to profitability since then. I expect us to succeed quite soon."

Gustav cocked an eyebrow at the old man. "What makes you think that?"

Brackwell and Lady Clara suddenly became so attentive they all but leaned forward on their tiptoes and cupped their hands to their ears.

"I have an instinct for these things," the Duke said, his jowly cheeks stretched tight by a smug smile. "Our luck is about to change."

"Well," Old Red said, plainly finding the old man's answer less than satisfying, "six years is a long time to hang in there waitin' for your luck to change. How'd you manage it?"

"Cash reserves, new investors."

"From what I hear, you ain't got much in the way of cash reserves."

The Duke's grin dimmed, and a new, hotter light took to shining in his eyes, but my brother pressed on.

"As for new investors, I assume you mean Mr. Edwards. He bought in . . . what was it? Two years ago? That wasn't too long after you had your little run-in with Mr. Sherlock Holmes, was it? I bet you would've been able to herd a fair amount of cash into your 'reserves' if that had turned out different. But with the wedding called off and—"

"*Enough!*"

The Duke had gone wild-eyed at the mention of Holmes, and it was a wonder his shout didn't shatter every window in the castle. Yet his earsplitting wrath settled into a quiet seethe with surprising speed.

"Enough," he said again. He took a deep breath, and by the time he was through exhaling, a hint of his spiteful smile had returned. "Your name is . . . Apple-something, isn't it?"

"Amlingmeyer," Old Red corrected.

The Duke nodded. "It just so happens, *Amlingmeyer,* that the Montana Stockgrowers Association is meeting in Miles City in three days' time. I assume you're aware that the Association maintains a list of men who are not to be employed by its members—a blacklist. The name Amlingmeyer is going to be placed at the very top of that list. And it won't end there. Most of the ranches in this state are owned by English peers like myself, and that same group of men controls the cattle trade in Wyoming, Texas, Colorado, New Mexico—the entire West. It won't be difficult to have you blacklisted *everywhere.* Once my wager with young Brackwell is concluded, I plan to see you and your oafish brother escorted from the Cantlemere without a penny in your pockets, and you won't find a ranch within a thousand miles willing to spare you so much as a crumb of bread."

Old Red had been giving the Duke a little push to get the man's dander up and his mouth open, but obviously Old Dickie could push back a hell of a lot harder. Gustav's a proud, even conceited fellow in his own quiet way, yet I saw real fear in his eyes now, or at least the realization that he wasn't as slick as he'd thought.

The Duke saw that look, too, and his smile grew larger.

"I suppose you'll be needing a new livelihood. Well, I wouldn't suggest continuing your misadventures as a consulting detective. You attempt to ape Sherlock Holmes, that's obvious. But I've encountered the man's work firsthand, and I assure you, you possess neither his subtlety nor his cunning. And even if you did . . . well, just look what happened to *him*."

Gustav's eyes had slowly been drawing closed, perhaps to mask the panic they might reflect. But they popped wide now, and Old Red found his voice again.

"What're you talkin' about?"

"You mean you don't know?" The Duke peered at my brother for a moment before cutting loose with another of his acid laughs. "Oh, you poor, ignorant buffoon!"

"What?" Gustav demanded. "What don't I know?"

"Your hero is no more," Old Dickie choked out between guffaws. "Sherlock Holmes is *dead*!"

Twenty-six

MR. HOLMES

Or, Old Red Goes into Mourning, and I Go into Shock

When I was twelve, my father and my brother Conrad were carried off by smallpox, and it fell to Gustav and me to bury them. The only words we spoke as we did so were on the order of "Over there?" and "That's deep enough" and "*Vater* first." Gustav left the farm not long afterward, sending back cash from ranches and cow towns up and down the Old Western Trail. The next time I saw him was four years later, at a train station in Dodge City. Our mother and our sisters were barely one month gone, as were our last remaining aunt and cousins and even the farm itself, all washed away by a flood so merciless it hadn't even the decency to leave behind the gravestones in the family plot.

And after all that, Gustav just looked me up and down, nodded once, and said, "I got jobs lined up for us at the Cross J in Texas. Can you keep yourself atop a horse?"

I said yes, and that was that—no eulogizing, no weeping, not so much as a sigh.

I don't relate this to suggest that my brother is a heartless man, but simply to illustrate that he's not a fellow who's given to displays of sentiment. I'm certain that a loving soul lurks within him, for there's no other way to explain why he's stuck by me all these years. He could've cut me loose after that flood, as I was all of sixteen at the time and had some of the skills—if none of the wisdom—a man needs to make his own way in the world.

Yet my brother chose to saddle himself with a big, clumsy kid who couldn't ride, rope, or shoot any better than a cross-eyed catfish. And when that kid got fired from his first two jobs, Gustav quit and stayed alongside him, teaching him what he could, rolling his eyes at the occasional foolishness, and never once complaining of any burden. True, dark moods and long silences there were aplenty, but tears I never did see.

So you can imagine my dismay when I saw them there in the castle. Not that Old Red busted out bawling upon hearing of Mr. Holmes's death. But his eyes did get to glistening, with droplets of moisture pooling and threatening to spill out over the lower lashes.

The notion of Gustav Amlingmeyer shedding tears over a stranger's demise was at first so unbelievable I dismissed the evidence presented by my own eyes. Yet when my brother spoke, I heard in his voice such a tremor of raw emotion I had to accept that what *looked* like tears must indeed *be* tears.

"What . . . ? Did he . . . ? Who . . . ?"

"You want to know how, hmmm?" the Duke said, taking obvious delight in Old Red's distress. "Well, I'm pleased to report that the man's meddling finally did him in. Oh, the exact circumstances aren't known—that damnable quack Watson may feel entirely at liberty to besmirch whomever he chooses with his lurid scribblings, yet on this subject he has remained silent. But details have emerged. It was in Switzerland, apparently. Holmes was persecuting some poor continental, I suppose, and he ended up going over the side of a mountain, never to be seen again! Pushed or pulled or something else, no one knows. Well, Watson perhaps. If so, he'll write about it eventually, I assure you, for the opportunity to squeeze a few guineas from his friend's death will surely overwhelm whatever stunted sense of propriety he might possess."

"When?" my brother asked, the word coming out barely more than a whisper.

"Oh, ages ago," the Duke chortled.

"Holmes has been dead two years," Brackwell said. He gave Old Red a look I'd never seen directed at my brother before—pity. "I assumed you knew."

Gustav shook his head slowly, his watery eyes aimed at the space between his boots.

"So, Amlingmeyer," the Duke said, "now you see the risks you take when you interfere in the affairs of others. A pity you and Holmes couldn't 'deduce' what snooping will get you!"

Old Dickie was toying with my brother like a cat with its claws in a half-dead mouse, and Lady Clara and Brackwell looked sickened by the old man's cruelty.

"Of course, it's too late for you to renege on your current obligations," the Duke said. "Though I suppose it's never too late to *concede*."

His tone turned mild and fatherly with these last words, and the change brought Gustav's gaze up from the floorboards. A little jolt seemed to run through Brackwell, as well.

"Watson's swill about 'the great Holmes' filled your head with foolish notions, and you overstepped your bounds," the Duke continued soothingly. "It's forgivable . . . if we put this unpleasant business behind us as quickly as possible."

Brackwell's face turned bright red, the expression upon it curdling into barely concealed contempt. I was a few seconds behind him in untangling the real message in what the Duke had just said.

"This unpleasant business" was not the murder—it was Old Red's investigation. My brother had poked a thorn in the lion's paw, and now the only way to pull it out before he got a swat was to call the whole thing off. But if Gustav were to "concede," the Duke could declare victory.

Old Dickie was trying to bully his way to that two hundred pounds, and he wasn't even bothering to do it behind Brackwell's back.

"Your Grace, if you please, sir," my brother said. He sprinkled no spice on the words, loathsome and toadying though they were, and it tore at my heart to hear him grovel so. "I wonder if I might have a moment alone in the office with Mr. Brackwell. I . . ." He looked at our youthful patron, his eyes heavy with the promise of disappointment soon to be delivered. "I feel I owe him an . . . well . . . we need to talk."

The Duke nodded and smiled, finally showing a hint of the supposed "grace" for which people addressed him.

"Of course."

Gustav rose slowly, reaching out to nudge me softly before trudging toward Brackwell and the office door. I got up and followed, feeling as though I was marching my brother to an execution. His dreams and his pride were about to be strung up side by side like a pair of horse thieves. I was tempted to take a poke at the man who'd supplied the rope as I walked past him, but bloodying the Duke's bulbous nose wouldn't do anything more than scotch the deal for which Old Red was sacrificing all his hopes. No more detecting, and we'd be allowed to go on drovering—until, that is, the McPhersons saw to it that our *breathing* days were over.

Lady Clara beamed compassion upon us as we passed, but I was so utterly downhearted I could take no comfort from her show of sympathy. My brother had just lost his hero, and it had crushed his spirit.

Somehow, I knew exactly how he felt.

Twenty-seven

THE OFFICE

Or, A Sleuth Is Reborn from the Ashes

"Alright, Amlingmeyer," Brackwell snapped the moment I'd closed the office door behind us. "What is it you have to say?" His tone was both resigned and angry, and he looked ready to stalk right back out of the room the moment Gustav finished his first "I'm sorry."

"Well, I suppose I oughta . . . ," Old Red began, each word coming out quieter than the one before it. His gaze dropped, and I could hardly believe I was witnessing the day when my brother couldn't look another man in the eye. He sniffed loudly, and I figured he was about to start weeping on top of everything else.

As mortifying as such a sight might be, I couldn't really blame Old Red for squeezing out a few tears. He'd tried turning maverick, but now he had to accept that he'd been branded for life.

Cowboy, the brand said.

Laborer.

Nobody.

"Yes? Go on," Brackwell demanded.

Rather than explain, Old Red dropped to his hands and knees.

For a second there, I thought he was going to wrap his arms around Brackwell's ankles and beg for forgiveness. But my brother had something very different in mind. He let out a low whistle and started crawling toward the fireplace at one end of the room.

Brackwell and I gaped at him, goggle-eyed.

"Hel-lo! Someone's sure been busy here," Gustav said, combing through heaps of gray ash under and around the grate. "Ol' General Sherman himself couldn't have done more with a match." He pushed his nose in so close to the cinders it's a wonder he didn't dust his mustache gray. "Fresh," he said, sucking in a whiff. "The fire died out not more than seven, eight hours ago."

"Amlingmeyer . . . what *are* you doing?" Brackwell asked, sounding more perplexed than peeved.

"Detectin'!" Old Red replied. He began picking small bits of singed paper from the fireplace and depositing them gently in his left hand.

"You ain't quittin'?" I said.

"Quittin'? Brother, you know me better than that. I ain't gonna 'concede' squat to that blustery old son of a bitch."

"And you ain't all broken up that Mr. Holmes is dead?" I asked, strangely pleased that my brother wasn't pulling our necks from the Duke's noose after all.

"Oh, I ain't happy to hear someone say it," Gustav said, still sifting ash. "But sounds to me like they didn't find a body, and you know what Mr. Holmes himself says about jumpin' to conclusions. It wouldn't surprise me if he's just takin' a nice, long holiday somewhere, lettin' the folks back home assume what they will."

I was so tickled Old Red wasn't turning tail I didn't bother pointing out how childish this wishful thinking was. If believing the great detective was alive kept Gustav's spirits out of the dirt, I wasn't going to argue against it, no matter how silly the notion might be.

"You might just be right," I said.

"I try to make a habit of it," Old Red replied. "I apologize if I threw a scare into you, Mr. Brackwell. I needed to figure a way in here, and givin' the Duke what he wanted seemed like the quickest way to go."

Brackwell had already brought out a grin that made him look almost as relieved as I felt. "*Appearing* to acquiesce to the Duke while doing as you please is a sound strategy. His children have been doing it for years."

"Is that a fact?" Gustav muttered, taking the remark with a gravity it didn't seem to warrant. "So tell me, Mr. Brackwell—you have any idea who lit up a bonfire in here last night?"

"I haven't the foggiest."

"I didn't suppose you would. It couldn't be *that* easy." Old Red swiveled around and moved to Perkins's desk, walking on his knees with a small pile of burnt paper in his hands. "You fellers havin' more of an eye for words and such, I'll let you look this over."

He spread the char-edged scraps on the desk.

"And what exactly are we looking *for*?" Brackwell asked.

Gustav cocked an eyebrow at me.

"The paper Boudreaux took out of the cellar yesterday?" I said.

My brother flashed me a here-and-gone smile. Then he dropped onto his belly and took to crawling around the room like a baby, his nose no more than three inches from the floor. Brackwell and I couldn't help but stare at him a moment.

"I'm sorry—I still don't understand what we're looking for," the Englishman said when we finally turned to the task at hand.

"All I know is it's a piece of paper," I had to admit. "And it's important . . . for some reason."

Brackwell gave the scraps before us a dismissive shrug. On most of them, blocky, typeset lettering was still visible.

"Well, I don't see anything *important* here. Just a shredded newspaper—used as kindling, I expect."

"Yeah," I said, sifting through the singed paper. "There ain't nothin' here that . . . hold on!"

One of the scraps was different from the rest. It was charred up good, but there was enough left—a circle a little smaller than a man's palm—to see that it wasn't from a newspaper. It was blank.

When I flipped the paper over, I found scratchy, blurred writing on the other side. Most of the words had disappeared into the fire, but a few letters and numbers remained:

ill of Sal

nnuery 20, 1893

tallo

oo — payed

cfersin

klin Dammers

" 'Bill of Sale,' " I said after I'd read everything out for Old Red. "It's a receipt. And it ain't hard to figure out it's made out to McPherson, even if this Dammers feller couldn't spell worth a damn."

"That'd be Franklin Dammers, manager of the Diamond 8 Ranch in Wyoming," Old Red said from the floor. "Now why do you think Uly'd go all the way down there just to buy tallow? That ain't nothin' but animal fat, and he could boil down all he needed from cows here."

I shrugged. "Lord knows he didn't use it to make soap. Until the Duke's bunch came along, I don't think he'd even heard of the stuff."

"I'm sorry," Brackwell said. "I'm quite confused. Could one of you please—"

"Well, hel-lo there, stranger!" Old Red called out. He plucked something off the Turkish rug that covered about a quarter of the office floor. He turned to show it to us, displaying the little ditty proudly, like a boy holding up a foot-long trout he's just pulled from the river.

It was a tiny bit of scorched fluff—another feather, just like the one Gustav had found pasted to the hole in Boudreaux's head.

"I knew it," I said. "We got us a killer *chicken* on the loose."

"I'm afraid I'm not following this at all," Brackwell said, looking so bewildered by now he was almost woozy.

"Don't worry," I told him. "I ain't really followin' it myself."

Old Red was too busy—and in too good a mood—to chastise me for my foolishness. He was running his fingers over a round depression in the rug near where he'd come across that feather. The fabric had been worn away or crushed by some friction or heavy weight.

"This is it," Gustav announced.

Not far from the dimple in the carpet was a twin. Each spot was about two inches across, and they were separated from each other by another foot and a half.

You didn't have to look far to see what had made the marks. An ottoman was pressed up against the wall nearby, and the distance between the legs perfectly matched the distance between those indentations.

Old Red looked up at me.

"Would you be so kind?" he said, seeing that I'd added things up as he had.

I gave the ottoman a push, sliding it just enough so the legs covered those grooves in the carpet—grooves they had themselves created by resting in the same place for months if not years. Gustav squirmed around my feet to see what the ottoman had been moved to conceal. There was no need for him to get up so close, however, for the stains in the rug were plain enough from where Brackwell and I stood.

"Surely that's not—" the Englishman began.

"Oh, but it is," Old Red said. "That's blood. Last night y'all hosted a murder in this house, and you didn't even know it."

"Here? In the . . . ?" Brackwell shook his head as if he could decline this disturbing news with a polite "No thanks." "I don't understand. The noise I heard didn't sound like a *gunshot.*"

"Gunshots can be muffled—especially from a little gun like a derringer." Gustav hopped to his feet and hustled toward the other side of the room. "Anyway, don't you worry about understandin' it all." He pulled back the drapes and peeked out the window toward the bunkhouses and the corral. "That's my job."

My brother had been delivering one surprise after another that day, so you might think my capacity for astonishment would have dropped dead from exhaustion by now. But it proved to be in good working order still, for I found my eyes again popping and my jaw again dropping when Old Red slid that window open and climbed on through.

"Well, I found what I aimed to—and then some," he said once he had his feet planted outside. "I reckon the Duke's gonna come bustin' through the door any second now, so we can't dawdle. I'm gonna be gone for a few minutes. Otto, until I get back, I need you to do what you do best."

"What's that?"

"Talk—and don't forget to listen while you're at it, cuz it's what Mr. Brackwell has to say in reply that I'm interested in."

"Talk about what?"

"Edwards, mostly. And how he ties in with the Duke. And the Sussex Land and Cattle Company. And Lady Clara."

"What's there to say? Edwards is another la-di-da fool with too much money, that's how he ties in with the Duke's crowd." I turned and gave Brackwell an apologetic nod. "Not meanin' any disrespect to yourself or the lady, of course."

Brackwell nodded back, a slight, rather distracted-looking smile creasing his thin lips. "Of course."

"I suspect there's a good bit more to say about the man than you think, Brother," Old Red said, taking a quick peek over his shoulder. When he was sure no one was behind him getting a bead on his back, he continued, "Edwards seems a tad out of place amongst highborn English folks like the Duke and Clara and Mr. Brackwell here, don't he? Yet the old man treats him like a bosom pal—almost like family, you might say. I'd like to hear the why of it."

"Maybe he won the Duke over with his sparklin' personality and natural warmth," I suggested.

Gustav rolled his eyes.

"No, Otto," Brackwell said, some weary despair weighing down his words. When I looked over at him, I found him shaking his head sorrowfully. "It's Edwards's substantial bank account that has endeared him to the Duke. And his ambition. I know what your brother's asking about. I can tell you all about it."

"Alright, if you say so." I swiveled around to face the window again. "So, Gustav—what'll you be . . . ?"

There was no point finishing the question. There was no one there to hear it.

Old Red was gone.

Twenty-eight

CONNECTIONS

Or, I Learn More About a Certain "Noble Bachelor"—and Two Not-So-Noble Ones

Your brother is an extraordinary man," Brackwell said.

"So's Hungry Bob Tracy, but you won't hear his family braggin' on it," I replied, though the crack came more from habit than my heart. "Now what's this about Edwards and the Duke and Clara and what all?"

Brackwell took a seat on the ottoman and stared down at his clasped hands.

"It's something I'd normally prefer not to discuss. You must understand—Lady Clara is a dear friend. I've known her practically all my life. Her brothers and mine, they're cut from the same cloth. Their father's sons, I suppose. But Lady Clara and I have always been *different*. I almost think of her as . . . an older sister. I don't wish to betray any confidences or traffic in spiteful gossip."

I sympathized with his tender feelings toward the lady, of course. But either Old Red or the old man were going to come barging back into the room any second, and I didn't wish to face either one without getting the answers my brother wanted first.

"I'm sorry, Mr. Brackwell—we don't have much time. Whatever you got to say, you need to go on and say it," I prodded as gently as I could. "Tell you what. Why don't you start with Edwards? I bet you wouldn't mind bandyin' about some spiteful gossip *he's* attached to."

"Oh, there's an ample supply of that," Brackwell spat with a vehemence that caught me by surprise. "As much as he puts on airs, he'll never be accepted as a true gentleman. Not when all of respectable society knows how his family made its fortune."

"Which was how?"

Brackwell grinned bitterly. "Are you familiar with something called Dr. Edwards's Feminine Regulator?"

As you might imagine, I don't have any use for patent medicines of such a sort myself. But anyone who's been in a drugstore or glanced at the ads in the *Ladies' Home Journal* knows of Dr. Edwards's cure-all elixir.

"Our Edwards is kin to Dr. Edwards?"

"Well, yes and no. 'Dr. Edwards' was his father. But the man wasn't really a doctor at all—just a druggist with a flair for commerce. Mix together a pinch of this, a pinch of that, and a liberal dash of alcohol *et voilà*—you've got a 'feminine regulator.' Whatever that might be."

"And apparently you've got yourself a bundle of loot to boot." I shook my head, marveling at the cockeyed things men will do to make money—and sometimes succeed doing it. "But I suppose cash can't buy you respectability, can it?"

"No. But not everyone knows that. For instance, *Mrs.* Edwards, widow of the good 'doctor,' craves social standing above all else. She was frozen out in Boston, so she took her son—and her fortune—to Europe."

"Where nobody'd ever heard of Dr. Edwards's Feminine Regulator."

"Or so she hoped. She dragged her son this way and that across the Continent trying to make connections with the right sort of people. Utterly without success, I might add."

Brackwell snorted, obviously disgusted by such hubris and pleased that it had come to naught. Before then, he'd struck me as a gentle-souled sort of fellow, but I could see now that his gentility didn't apply where Edwards was concerned. The young nobleman didn't just resent or dislike Edwards—he hated him.

"Boston's old families have long-standing connections of their own throughout Europe," Brackwell went on. "All it took was a whisper here and there to dash the Edwardses' chances for social climbing. That is, until they met Old Dickie. In Monte Carlo, of course."

"Yeah, I suppose the Duke would feel right at home there—except I'm bettin' nobody's written any songs about his luck in the casinos," I said, referring to a tune that had been all the rage in the music halls a year or so before—"The Man Who Broke the Bank at Monte Carlo." Apparently, it had been popular over in England, too.

"I can assure you, the Duke was far from breaking the bank," Brackwell said. "Quite the opposite, in fact. And he was already quite close to broke to begin with. He'd gambled away much of his wealth, and his holdings in the West had seen devastating reversals."

"Sure. The Big Die-up hit all the 'cattle barons' hard."

Brackwell blinked at me as if I'd taken to speaking backward.

"The winter of '87," I explained. "The year all the stock froze to death on the range."

Brackwell shook his head and shrugged. For a fellow who'd been sent to inspect a cattle ranch, he sure didn't know much about ranching.

My thoughts must have showed themselves in my expression, because Brackwell set about explaining himself.

"You must understand—in 1887, I was at a preparatory school in Hallamshire studying Latin, maths, and sonnets. I had little contact with my family and I certainly wasn't privy to updates on the status of our various speculations. Which was perfectly acceptable to me . . . on both counts."

Brackwell looked embarrassed by his own words, and he waved one of his long hands in the air, dismissing what he'd said.

"In any event, Edwards and the Duke became fast friends—all the faster after Edwards began backing Old Dickie's wagers. With such men, the talk inevitably turns to finance sooner or later, and it didn't take long for the Duke to secure an eager new investor for the Sussex Land and Cattle Company. So the old man and the board gained an infusion of new capital, while Edwards gained access to—though not necessarily the acceptance of—England's highest social circles. It was what I learned in school to call a *quid pro quo.*"

"Sort of a one-hand-washin'-the-other type of deal."

Brackwell smiled. "Yes, that sums it up just as neatly." The smile faded quickly. "Except Edwards and the Duke aren't satisfied to leave it at that. They both wish their connection to become even more . . . formalized."

"What do you mean? They wanna get married?"

I'll admit that my jokes are frequently something less than hilarious, but it's not often they cause actual physical pain. Yet Brackwell grimaced as if I'd just punched him in the gut. And in a way, I suppose I had.

"You can't mean . . . *no,*" I said, probably grimacing a bit myself. "A fine woman like Lady Clara yoked to a crap pile like Edwards? It wouldn't be right."

Brackwell nodded sadly. "I couldn't agree more with your assessment. Unfortunately, the lady has few options when it comes to matrimony."

He paused, clearly reluctant to spell out just why that should be so. But he sighed and continued before I had to do any further persuading.

"There's little chance she could make a match with a respectable man. Clara is thirty-three years old—well past her prime, as the bounders and shrews in London see it. And what's more, she's been touched by scandal."

"You mean Mr. Holmes's 'Noble Bachelor' case? When the Duke tried to hitch up one of her brothers to some rich American gal? Why, it ain't fair to splash any of that mud on her. She had nothin' to do with it."

"I'm afraid Clara has a scandal all her own, Otto—though one, I'm glad to say, that Dr. Watson never had reason to write about."

Brackwell's shoulders drooped, and he sort of melted across the Ottoman, suddenly looking exhausted.

"It was a man, of course," he said, stretching out his beanpole legs and staring up at the ceiling with dreamy distraction. "Nathaniel Horne. I even met him once. I can't say I blame Clara for succumbing to his charms, no matter what the cost. He was tall, blond-haired, blue-eyed, smooth-skinned. More than handsome. Beautiful. He could have had the pick of any woman in his class—or below it. But certainly not above it. Not so high as *her*."

"Didn't have himself a fortune or a fancy title, huh?" I huffed, sympathizing with this Horne fellow.

Brackwell coughed out a short burst of weary laughter. "Oh, it was much worse than that." He brought his gaze down to meet mine again. "He was the Duke's *secretary*."

I tried to imagine how the old man would react to the proposition of an employee becoming an in-law.

"Ohhhhhhh my," I said. "So what happened to this Horne? Was he hung or burned at the stake?"

"Sacked. And blacklisted to boot. Dickie saw to it that he couldn't gain employment as so much as a stable boy in all England. Horne probably had to go to Canada or Australia or even here to America to find a respectable position again."

Of course, that very day the Duke had promised to have me and Old Red blackballed in much the same manner. It put a mighty tight knot in my stomach to realize the old man wasn't just blowing smoke when he made such threats. I tried to untangle that knot by focusing my thoughts on misfortunes other than my own.

"I suppose word got around about Lady Clara's little fling."

Brackwell nodded. "The family name had already been tarnished by her brother Robert's escapades—as if his disastrous attempt at marriage hadn't been bad enough, he'd become entangled with a dancing girl at the same time. There have been other . . . indiscretions, as well, and the St. Simons found themselves with a reputation for dabbling with those born beneath them. Clara managed to remain above it all until her flirtation with Horne came to light. After that—"

"No 'respectable' gent would have her."

"Just so. Not that she'd be interested in such a match were it to present itself." Brackwell's eyes took on a wistful look. "She loved Horne—and she says she has no intention of marrying any other man."

"Well, good for her," I said, though my foolish heart was stinging. I knew I had no chance with a woman of Clara's caliber, yet a part of me wished her to be at least tempted by the notion of "dabbling" with someone as miles beneath her as myself. "I wonder if she's said as much to Edwards."

"Apparently not," Brackwell grumbled. "Or if she has, he thinks he can change her mind. And . . . well, perhaps he can. She does seem to be warming a bit to—"

And then the inevitable happened. I'd become so wrapped up in Brackwell's gossip I'd forgotten just how inevitable it was, and I grabbed for my .45 before I realized what was going on.

"Of all the damnable insolence!" the Duke howled as he barged into the room. "I'm not some servant to be kept waiting about at your pleasure, you know!"

The old man had worked himself up into such a state he didn't notice that I'd almost put a slug in his considerable belly. In fact, he was so ablaze with indignation he kept on hollering for a good half minute before he even realized Gustav wasn't in the room. Lady Clara had entered on her father's heels, and she was showered with such a torrent of foul language it was a wonder her delicate ears didn't singe to a crisp and drop right off.

"What's going on here?" the Duke asked once he'd run through his full deck of vulgarities.

The answer didn't come in words—it came as a whistle that turned us all toward the window. Outside, Old Red was ambling up astride Sugar, the calico cutting horse Crazymouth had been riding in the corral earlier that day. Another pony, a top-rail night-horse called Brick, Gustav was leading by the reins.

"Time to go, Brother," Old Red said. "And don't forget to bring our 'ill of Sal' with you."

Any opportunity to distance myself from the Duke and his spluttering was welcome indeed, so I snatched the paper, got through the window, and climbed atop that horse without asking any questions.

"What do you think you're doing?" the old man squawked as I made my escape.

"I'm doin' what I set out to do—catch me a killer," Old Red shot back. "It just so happens I have to go to Miles City to do it."

"Miles City?" Brackwell exclaimed.

"Don't you worry, Mr. Brackwell," Gustav said. He gave Sugar's neck an affectionate rub. "We got a couple of fast mounts here. Plus, we won't be tempted to stop off at any saloons while we're in town, as McPherson's man might. If we ride hard, we can find what we need and still get back here in time to win the bet for you."

Old Red got his pony moving, so I did likewise. But before we could kick the horses up to a trot, a cry of "Wait!" stopped us. I turned back toward the castle to see Brackwell climbing out the window.

"Please," he said as he dropped from the windowsill and hurried toward us. "Take me with you."

Gustav let the young man get all the way to his horse before he leaned down and spoke to him, his voice so low I could barely hear the words.

"I'm sorry, pardner," he said, putting a hand on the younger man's shoulder. "You ain't dressed for it."

Then Old Red straightened up and got Sugar going again without waiting for any arguments. After just a few trot steps, he fanned her to a gallop. It wasn't hard to figure why, for I'd turned to give Brackwell a wave, and beyond him I saw Uly and Spider back at the barn, watching us. It was a sure bet they'd be on our trail before our dust had even settled.

I kicked Brick into as fast a gallop as he could manage—though I knew it wouldn't be speed that would keep the bullets out of my back. It would be sheer *luck*.

Twenty-nine

THE SPREAD

Or, I Set Off on a Race but End Up on a Tour

Old Red kept pushing Sugar hard, and poor Brick had a devil of a time keeping up. Although he'd been weighed down with a heftier load to tote—me—Brick had heart, and he didn't let Sugar's backside slip out of sight.

We finally got our chance to catch up after an hour on the trail that winds northwest out of the Cantlemere. Sunday Creek, the little trickle of water that cuts through the spread, was swollen with recent rain. Though still not large enough to require a swim to cross, neither was it a puddle you could take with a standing jump. Gustav was waiting for us as Brick and I reached the edge.

"Here's what we're gonna do," he said by way of hello. "Ease on out to the center of the creek, then turn and ride with the water. After a quarter mile, the creek'll bend south. We'll hop out there on the far side."

Old Red's plan made a certain sense, as it would get us off the well-worn trail and force the McPhersons to do some hunting before they could jump us. Yet there was one respect in which it made no sense at all—it would take us east and south when Miles City lay north and west.

"We ain't goin' to Miles?"

"Nope," Gustav said, and he pushed Sugar out into the Sunday without another word.

As we were aiming to untangle ourselves from anyone tracking us, we rode Indian fashion—single file and closemouthed. When we were through splashing along the creek, my brother quickly got Sugar up to a gallop again. He headed over a row of hills at the first opportunity, putting some cover between us and the creekbed. Yet we continued to follow its path south, and before long we were a ten-minute ride east of ranch HQ.

We'd come full circle.

Old Red took us down to a trot then, for though the ground wasn't bone-dry, a hard-charging horse might still kick up a trail of dust you could spot a half mile off.

"So what'd Brackwell say after I slipped out to fetch our mounts?"

Anyone watching us would have assumed Gustav's question was directed at a field mouse or a clump of grass, as my brother's eyes were pointed at the sod sliding by beneath us as we rode.

"He said plenty. And I'll tell you all about it . . . if you tell *me* something first."

Old Red brought his gaze up slowly.

"What do you want to know?"

"Oh, just *what the hell is goin' on*?"

My brother fixed his eyes to the ground again. "You'll have to cut that deck a little deeper."

That's a drover's way of asking a fellow to be more specific.

"Well," I began, realizing then just how narrow my question had been. Where was Gustav supposed to start?

There was Perkins's death. There was Boudreaux's death. There was the Duke's "sudden fancy" to visit the VR and Edwards's solitary "picnic" and a thief who took pillows, handbags, and irons. There was Hungry Bob and the McPhersons and feathers and a half-burnt receipt for beef fat and a stray nose and . . .

There was a *lot*.

"Start with Boo then," I said. "I thought I had some ideas as to who might've put that hole in his head, but what we found back there in the office . . . it's got me all jumbled up. If you were able to make something of it, it would be a comfort to hear it."

"Theorizin'," Old Red warned me, saying the word the way you might say "sharp" when a two-year-old reaches for a knife.

"Gustav, let me be plain: I don't give a shit about 'biasin' your judgment' just now. I am sick of runnin' around like a chicken with its head cut off. Tell me what's goin' on."

"Otto, you know Sherlock Holmes don't go blabbin' his every thought to Doc Watson. He keeps his notions to himself until—"

"You ain't Sherlock Holmes, and I ain't Doc Watson, alright? So just *talk*, God damn it!"

Half a minute passed in silence before my brother realized I was serious: no theorizing from him, no new data from me. He finally heaved a sigh and gave in.

"Boudreaux had a horse waitin' last night, so it's safe to figure he was goin' someplace—probably leavin' the VR," he said, still aiming his words straight down. "But first he stopped at the castle. He was wearin' his spurs, which ain't somethin' a man's likely to do if he's on the prowl. You know how them things kick up a jingle. So I ain't inclined to believe he snuck up to the second floor and went rootin' around in the closet for an iron. No, he stayed on the first floor, in the office—cuz he was meetin' somebody there. And that somebody up and shot him."

"But if Boo was killed in the office, the folks in the house would've heard the shot plain as day," I pointed out. "I mean, what about Emily? Her room was right down the hall."

Old Red nodded. "True enough. But it looks like the shot was muffled, either by a couple pillows or a passin' duck. I'm thinkin' it was most likely the pillows."

"Hold on, Gustav. You lost me right around the part about the *duck*."

"Well, why do you think there was a feather on Boudreaux's forehead? I never saw the man in a Cheyenne warbonnet, did you? Nope, that was pillow down. Pillows would've swallowed up the powder flare, too, which would explain why Boudreaux didn't have any scorch on him."

"So before the killer shoots Boo, he says, 'Thanks for comin'—now would you mind sittin' here with these pillows over your face?'"

I half-expected my brother to respond to my snipping by snapping, but instead he just shrugged. "Yeah, that's a hole in the bucket, alright. Still, Boudreaux was killed in Perkins's office, of that I'm sure."

"Well . . . let's say you're right. That means I've lost my favorite suspects."

Old Red peeked up from the turf beneath our mounts just long enough for me to see the amusement in his eyes.

"I started off sure it was Uly or Spider," I explained. "And if not them, one of their boys. And if not one of their boys, then maybe Anytime—he hated Boo from the second we hit the VR. But there ain't no way any of them would've done the deed in the castle. They could've killed him a lot more easily someplace else."

"Good deducin'," my brother said. "So the question is, who was Boudreaux meetin' in the house and why? The *who* we'll have to leave for later. But the *why* falls into place with just a little jigglin'. It stands to reason the killer lit up a blaze in the fireplace to try and cover the smell of gunsmoke—and destroy that 'Bill of Sale' in the process. So the receipt's the key."

"But, come on . . . a receipt for *tallow*? Why would anybody kill a man over that? It's fat, not gold."

I leaned back and shook my head, suddenly understanding the problem with theorizing. It doesn't just bias the judgment—it drives a man crazy.

"And how does that nose in Boo's pocket tie in?" I said. "And the missing iron and handbag from the closet upstairs? And why can't anybody agree on the time of the gunshot? And why move Boo out of the office just to dump him in the *outhouse,* for Christ's sake?"

"The answers to them questions are 'Damned if I know,' 'I ain't sure,' 'I am utterly confounded' and 'All I've got is a guess.'"

"A guess, huh? Well, that's better than a 'Damned if I know.' Let's hear it."

Old Red snuck another quick peek at me, almost looking embarrassed by what he was about to say.

"It was an accident."

"Come again?"

"Just stroll through it with me," Gustav said. "The Swede told us he heard someone sneakin' around the privy not long before he heard the gunshot. Now he was comin' *toward* the house at the time, and if someone was movin' the body *from* the house, the two might cross paths. So the body got stuffed into the jakes until the Swede passed by. But you know the door on that privy's always had a mind of its own—let it slam, and it drops the latch."

My brother shot me another peek, apparently gauging how crazy I thought his guess to be. I sure as hell didn't have a better guess of my own, so I told him to keep going.

"The latch drops, and the body's stuck in the outhouse," he said. "And though somebody fought with the door a bit—there were fresh scratches in the wood, remember—whoever it was needed tools and more time to pry it off. It was almost mornin' by then, and before long the Swede wouldn't be the only man up and about, and breakin' through the door was bound to kick up a ruckus. So throwin' the gun in there to make it look like suicide—that was just someone doin' some clever thinkin' on the fly."

For a man who'd resisted theorizing for so long, my brother sure looked like he was enjoying himself. I couldn't join in the fun, though. There were still too many unanswered questions churning my brain to butter.

"Well, that would explain a lot," I said. "Not everything, though—not by a long shot."

"Yeah, we still got quite a ways to go before it all makes sense." Gustav reached up to tap the side of his Stetson. "But wheels are turnin'. Just give me a little more data and a little more time to cogitate, and I'll cook up some answers that'll sit better in both our stomachs. Speakin' of which, I think it's time you told me what Brackwell had to say back in the office."

I nodded. Old Red had held to his side of the bargain. Now it was my turn.

So I told him the tale—about Edwards's hunt for respectability and how Lady Clara's fall from grace could land her right in the man's clutches. Though my brother had been uncommonly chatty just moments before, he held his tongue for the next several minutes, offering no commentary beyond the occasional nod or grunt as I dredged up everything I could recall from my conversation with Brackwell. When there was no detail left to dredge, I shifted into spirited speculation on Edwards's chances of wooing the lady—chances I stacked up unfavorably against a snowball's chances in hell.

"Alright," Old Red finally cut in. "That's enough gossipin' over the fence, Mabel. It's time we got serious about ridin' again."

Though kicking a man in the seat of the pants while both you and he are mounted would be a difficult and perhaps even dangerous task to undertake, I considered it seriously for a moment there. But instead of lashing out with a boot toe, I lashed out with my tongue.

"How can I be 'serious about ridin'' when the Sherlock Kid over there won't even tell me where we're headed?"

Gustav glared at me like I'd just called him the Son of a Bitch Kid.

"I'd have thought it was clear enough," he growled. "We're gonna keep followin' these tracks."

"Tracks?" I said—and I instantly regretted it, for upon bringing my gaze to the ground I beheld a trail Helen Keller herself would have no trouble following. I'd been so caught up in conversation I hadn't even noticed it.

I stared at the tracks now, trying to make sense of them. They were made by wheels, that much was clear, and they cut across the prairie to the southeast—toward a section of the Bar VR the McPhersons had warned us Hornet's Nesters frequently and forcefully to avoid. Other than that, I wasn't sure what to think. There were so many crisscrossing ruts of varying depth and freshness they all mashed together into a jumble in my head.

I knew Old Red was seeing something else entirely, however. There'd be no jumble for a master tracker like him.

"Well?" I prompted him.

"Four fresh trails, new and light," he said.

I stared back down at the flattened grass and exposed dirt slipping by beneath Brick's belly. It was still a jumble to me.

"*Four* new trails, you say?"

"Two trips in a buggy," Old Red replied. "Out and back, then out and back again, all within the last day."

"Well, the Duke's little expedition would account for one set of tracks," I said. "But what about the . . . oh. Edwards?"

Gustav nodded. "He must've headed this way for his 'picnic.'"

"Why would he come all the way out here?"

"Only one way to find out," Old Red said, and he got Sugar going before I could slow him down with more talk.

We were able to make good speed, for there was no science to staying on the trail. It took us far deeper into the VR's grazing land than we'd ever been before, and we rode across open range and up and down gently sloping hills that would have made for pleasant riding if I hadn't been worried about someone putting lead in our livers. Following the buggy tracks kept us exposed to view, making us easy targets for any unfriendly fellow with a Winchester in his scabbard.

Though the wind was at our backs, I eventually began to sense by way of my nose that we would soon be in the company of cattle. We found them not long afterward, perhaps a thousand strong. They were meandering unattended across a long, narrow strip of grassland at the bottom of a rocky punch bowl formed by the surrounding bluffs. From the way the grass had been flattened throughout the valley, it was clear they'd been packed in pretty tight. The Duke's party seemed to have taken pains to drive straight through the center of the herd, and many a cow pie had been squashed beneath buggy wheel and horse's hoof.

At the far end of the valley, a stand of trees ringed a largish pond around and in which perhaps fifty cows were cooling themselves. It appeared that this modest prairie oasis held some appeal for one of the VR's two-legged residents, as well, for the trail split here—one set of buggy ruts cut straight over to the pond, while the other kept on to the south, out of the valley. Gustav eased his horse to a halt where the trails separated.

"The tracks down to the water must be from Edwards today," I said. "The trail's fresher. The patties it runs through ain't even baked hard yet."

I had no doubt my brother had already noticed that. I just didn't want him thinking I *hadn't*. He acknowledged my trail-reading with a nod, then unhorsed himself.

"Hold on to Sugar. I wanna look at somethin'."

I dismounted and stood there holding the horses. They wished to get at that water, but Old Red didn't want them mussing up the ground before he'd had a chance to look it over. He followed the buggy tracks to the pond, walking so bent-over his face would've been dead even with the buckle of his gunbelt had he been wearing one. It was pure luck that kept him from charging hat-first into a heifer's hindquarters, as he didn't look up to make sure the cows were clearing out of his way. When he got about ten feet from the water's edge, he dropped down to one knee.

"What ya got, Brother?"

"Footprints," Gustav said. "Cows've already made a mess of 'em, but . . ." He crawled closer to the marshy muck that ringed the pool. "Edwards took himself a little stroll down to the water here." Old Red hopped up and planted his feet firmly in place. "This is as close as he got. Didn't want to muddy his pretty shoes, I reckon."

My brother stayed there staring out over the water. Several cows stared back at him.

"Then what?" I asked.

"Then he left. Got in the buggy, wheeled around, and headed back to the castle."

"Well, it's plain to see why he'd go to such trouble to visit a spot like this." I nodded at the murky brown water and the poop-pocked ring of hoof-trampled mud that encircled it. "This here's a regular Garden of Eden."

"Yeah," Old Red said, slapping away some little winged pest that was making a run at his neck. "Only things that'd wanna *picnic* around here are horseflies and mosquitoes."

"So why do you think Edwards really came back here? To meet somebody maybe?"

"Nope. No other tracks."

"You can't tell me he came all the way out here to eat cheese and bread with a bunch of cows."

"I ain't tellin' you nothin', Brother. I don't have anything to tell—not till I've had a chance to do some serious thinkin'."

Gustav picked up a clod of dirt and threw it out into the pond. He spent a moment just watching the ripples spread before he turned and spoke again.

"Alright—you can let the ponies get 'em a taste now."

I dropped the reins, and Sugar and Brick hurried over and dipped their muzzles in the pond.

"Don't drink too deep," Gustav said, giving Sugar's haunch a friendly pat. "We got a lot of ridin' yet to do today." He peered off to the northwest—back the way we'd come.

"Anybody followin' us?" I asked, not bothering to pretend I had eyes as sharp as his.

"A *few* somebodys," Old Red said. "Not that I see 'em yet. I don't. That won't last forever, though."

"You think they'll figure out we ain't gone to Miles?"

"Not if we're lucky. But I ask you—when was the last time an Amlingmeyer got lucky?"

I pondered on that a moment before speaking again.

"We best get movin'."

We let the horses ease back into their work, heading up out of the valley at a canter. As we crested the far ridge of the punch bowl, the valley beyond popped into view—as did a dark line that cut across it.

"Hel-lo!" Gustav said.

He was greeting another clue—or a little nest of them, more like.

That dark line was barbed wire, and the buggy tracks headed straight for it. A thin plume of gray smoke wound its way skyward from the other side of the fence.

Deep in the VR's most forbidden corner, someone was cooking dinner.

Thirty

THE BEAST

Or, We Discover the Bar VR's Secret—and the Secret Discovers Us

The territory we were moving into lacked the smooth flatness of the valley we'd just left, and rolling hills and rocky bluffs soon blocked our view of what lay ahead. In addition, late-afternoon was turning to dusk as we rode, and each minute stole from us a bit more light by which to follow the trail. It was easy enough to find the gate through which the buggy had passed, however, and Old Red opened it up and waved me through.

Once on the other side, heaping turds and hoofprints soon dotted our path, and as we approached a particularly steep hill each became more abundant. The tracks, in fact, grew so heavy it got to looking like a herd two thousand strong had recently rolled through on the run.

The buggy ruts we'd been following led up to a rocky bluff nearby. There they stopped, though the hill didn't round off for another thirty feet or so. Down below, the cattle tracks wound snug around the base of the hill.

"It almost looks like the Duke and his pals had a front-row seat for a stampede," I said.

"Why *almost*? I think they did." And with that Old Red gave Sugar his heels and steered the horse over to where the stampede—if that's what it had been—had kicked up a band of turf about a hundred feet across. When we reached the cattle trail, my brother got to riding along it.

Now when a herd gets spooked, there's no figuring which way that avalanche of beef will tumble, which is why so many punchers pass through the pearly gates looking like strawberry jam. All the same, there's one thing you can count on cattle *not* doing without being pushed to it, and that's circle up.

Yet that was precisely what had happened here. That trail hooked right and hooked right and just kept on hooking right until it brought us all the way around the hill to the spot we'd started from. As we finished our little ride on the merry-go-round, Gustav bent over practically double in his saddle. I thought he was looking for more clues amongst the dirt until his giggles worked themselves up into guffaws. I couldn't join in, as I had no idea what the funny was in the first place.

"Uly brought the Duke and the rest of 'em all the way out here just so they could watch a bunch of cows run around a hill?" I asked.

Old Red's cackling wound down into mere snickering, and he drew in a deep breath and sighed with the satisfaction of a man who's just enjoyed a choice steak after a week of jerky. "You might say that."

"I *did* say it. Now why don't you explain it?"

My brother nodded, happy to oblige for once.

"There's an old trick the Sioux used to pull. Or maybe it was the Cheyenne. Or the Apache. Depends on who you hear tell it. Anyway, they might have twenty warriors in a raidin' party, but they could make it look like a *hundred* and twenty if they got some troopers pinned down in the right spot—a box or blind of some kind. The braves would get to ridin' circles around them bluecoats until there was no way a man could keep track of the numbers. Used to scare the crap out of them poor army fellers. It looks to me like the McPhersons pulled the same trick. They got the Duke and the others up on the bluff and then they ran a few hundred critters around in so many circles they looked like a river of cattle instead of a mere trickle."

"Now wait a second," I said. "It's plain enough Uly's boys salted the trail down here with herds to give the Duke and them others the impression the spread's overflowin' with beef. Alright. Makes sense. But why the show here? What would this do that the ride down didn't?"

Gustav peered up at the bluff above us, which was by this time little more than a dim outline against the darkening sky.

"That's a good question, Brother. I reckon we'll find the answer a mile or so to the southeast."

I thought of the curlicue of smoke we'd seen drifting up over the hills. "You think Uly's got more men down here?"

Old Red nodded. "Only one way to find out. Let's go."

"So let me ask you . . . ," I threw out before my brother could give Sugar his heels.

"Yeah?"

"Do you want me to salute when you give an order, or will a simple 'Yes, sir' suffice?"

"Try the salute," Gustav sighed. "The less talkin' you do, the better."

He quickly got his horse up to a pace that seemed a touch speedy for night riding, but the added risk must have been worth it to him, for it kept us from conversing for a good fifteen minutes. By the end of that time, a rank, musky odor was assaulting my nostrils. It was the smell of a thousand wet dogs rolling in manure.

"You catch a whiff of that?" Gustav asked as he brought Sugar to a stop.

"Hell, yes. That ain't *my* nose in your pocket—though I almost wish it was if it'd spare me a snootful of this."

"The herd must be nearby."

"Yeah, but a herd of what—polecats?"

"Whatever they are, we don't wanna rile 'em up and get ourselves spotted. We'd best take the last stretch afoot."

I saluted. Old Red ignored me.

We left the horses behind a thick tangle of huckleberry bushes in a shallow gully. We hadn't taken a dozen steps before a strange, raspy squeal froze us in our tracks.

"Boar?"

"No," Old Red answered, the word coming out slow and uneasy.

We took a few more steps before another bleating cry stopped us.

"Sheep?" I asked.

"No."

We started off again—and again the sound of something braying or bawling close by glued our boots to the ground.

"Uhhh . . . goat?" I asked, though I knew better.

"No."

"Well, you can't tell me that's no *cow*."

Yet when we finally got out of the gully and saw a long stretch of grassland laid out before us, it did indeed appear that the caterwauling had come from cattle. Dotted here and there across the moonlit plain were the hulking silhouettes of maybe four hundred beeves bedded down for the night. They seemed to be brahmas, having dark hides and an uncommonly lumpy look about them. As we drew nearer, however, I could make out what appeared to be clumps of fuzz on the closer specimens, and they lacked the wrinkly, low-hanging wattle for which brahmas are known. Though we were still a good fifty feet from the nearest of them, the musky scent of the herd was clogging up my nose like rancid oatmeal.

"What the hell *are* these shaggy—?"

Gustav shot me a shush and pointed off to our right. Perhaps a quarter mile away a rectangle of flickering orange pierced the nighttime blackness—firelight in an open doorway. I gave it a long squint and managed to make out the boxy outline of a smallish cabin.

"Come on," Old Red whispered.

We moved slowly along the outer ring of the herd, the animals' choking squalls sending fingers of ice up my back. As we approached the shack, a different noise drifted out to greet us—the sound of conversation. Two rough male voices ran into and over each other, with a third, quieter voice joining in from time to time so soft I could barely make it out.

Before long we were close enough to pick out words and phrases, though what we heard was hardly helpful.

"When we *mumble mumble mumble* Miles City *mumble mumble* eggs and taters!"

"First *mumble* the Gaities *mumble* whiskey *mumble mumble* Squirrel-Tooth Annie! How 'bout you, *mumble?*"

"Whisper mumble whisper mumble mumble whisper mumble."

It sounded like typical bunkhouse bullshit—cowboys blowing wind about the restaurants, saloons, and whores they'd patronize upon their return to town. Yet Gustav kept creeping closer, no doubt hoping the talk would turn to something useful. Before it could, however, our eavesdropping was interrupted by a hulking black shape that loomed up before us.

Now most cattle, even your he-stuff, lean more toward meek than mean. Jittery they can be, but they're rarely truly ornery unless they have a reason.

But this was plainly no ordinary critter. It hauled itself off its huge haunches and greeted us with a distinctly unfriendly grunt.

What a man doesn't want to do in such a situation, much as he might feel the urge, is turn tail and run. An angry bull will take this as an invitation to a square dance under the fellow's hat, and big as that steer may be, he's fast enough to get there before the party's over. So Old Red and I had no choice but to stand there and stare at the big beast.

He was horned and hooved and four-legged, but there the similarities to your average beef ended. His skull was broad and round and so large a man could practically stretch out and take a bath in it were it be upturned and filled with hot water. A hump rose up behind the head like a dark, distant mountain. And the whole of the creature was matted with thick fur, a long black beard of it dropping from under his chin almost to the ground.

In short, the thing appeared to be half-bull, half-bear—a combination that didn't bode well for us.

"When he charges, we split up," my brother whispered.

"You really think he's gonna—?"

I had neither the opportunity nor the need to finish my question, for at that moment the beast lowered his horns and came at us. Gustav sprang right, I sprang left, and that freight train of flesh passed right between us, coming so close I could feel the creature's hot breath on my back.

As bulls have a turn radius akin to that of a covered wagon— meaning they require a stretch of space the size of Arkansas just to turn around—I should've had a decent chance of escape once I'd dodged that first run. Unfortunately, in hurling myself away from one danger, I put myself in the proximity of a hundred more. My mad dash had progressed but four steps when I realized I was running *into* the herd.

A black mound of hair blocked my route, and I was moving so fast that getting around it wasn't an option. So I took it with a jump, stretching my legs out and sailing above it like a jackrabbit hopping over a log. As beautiful a hurdle as it might have been, I had no time to revel in the glory of it, for I heard the pounding of hooves behind me, and another dark shape was huddled up ahead.

I leaped again, clearing this newest obstacle by a mole's whisker. When my feet hit dirt, I saw that I had enough space before me to turn back out of the herd. Only one more critter stood between me and safety, and I approached it with the speed and confidence of a steeple-chase champion. I'm sure I would've cleared it, too, had the thing not stood up with a startled gurgle just as I made my jump. I smacked into its mangy hide like a snowball dashed against the side of a barn, coming down hard on my saddle warmer with my legs splayed out in a wishbone U. Naturally the frightened animal took to running, and one of its hind hooves stamped the ground so tight on the inseam of my trousers that I could hear my unborn children crying out in mortal terror.

I sat there in a daze until my brother's frantic "Otto! Behind you!" snapped me out of it. I looked around just in time to see that bullish, bearish beast coming at me again, his stubby horns at the perfect height to catch me through the eyeballs. Being flat-ass on the ground, all I could do was roll—which I got to with gusto, not minding the patties I flattened so long as the creatures who'd made them didn't flatten *me*.

Heavy hooves pounded the ground, missing me by a distance so slim you could bottle it in a thimble.

"Over here, Otto! *Over here!*"

I crawled toward Old Red as fast as my belly could take me. He'd managed to get himself into the gully from which we'd emerged minutes before, and he urged me to join him in his usual warm, fatherly fashion.

"Get up and run, you damned idjit!"

I hopped up and took to my heels, managing to cover the last few feet of ground before my innards decorated the grassland. Once I was safely hunkered down next to Old Red, I looked back at the chaos I'd left in my wake. Big black shapes were awhirl in the dim light, squealing and bellowing as they barreled this way and that. As eerie a sight as this was, it didn't chill my blood half as cold as looking over toward the cabin, for framed in the doorway glow was the outline of a man. A straight line of shadow cut across his midriff, and even without catching any glint of steel I knew it was a rifle.

I turned to tell my brother, but before I could pop out a word he opened his mouth and produced a truly remarkable sound—a long, loud howl so convincing I had to wonder if the Amlingmeyer family had at some point diluted its pure German blood with a few drops of lobo. Gustav cut off his cry with a *yip-yip-yeowow* so sudden and piercing-high it sounded as if it came from a different animal entirely.

Though this little ruse might convince the fellows in the cabin it was a pack of wolves riling things up, not a couple of nosy brothers, I didn't see how that would save us. Surely these were line-camp hands we were dealing with, and they'd grab their guns and lanterns and hustle out quick to protect the herd.

Yet the man in the doorway did no such thing. We were too far away now to hear any talk, but from the way his shadow went thin then wide, thin then wide, it was plain he was conversing with his companions inside, swiveling back and forth between them and the darkness in which we cowered. My brother cut loose with another *yip-yip-yip,* and the shadow disappeared entirely. The man had stepped back inside.

"I don't understand," I whispered. "Why don't they—?"

"First things first. Let's get the hell out of here."

I didn't bother with a salute this time, as I was too busy running. The tetchy bull-creature that had fanned up all the fuss was moving toward us yet again.

As Old Red and I retreated back to where we'd left the horses, I was still wondering just what kind of beast this was—and hoping I would never see its like again.

Thirty-one

THE CAMP

Or, Old Red Lights a Fire for Me, and I Light a Fire Under Old Red

or safety's sake, we withdrew a good mile from the cabin before settling down to make camp. A feather bed and silk sheets being unavailable, we had to make do with a small clearing amongst the thicket and bramble nestled against an outcropping of ice-cold rock. The night had turned nippy, and after weathering my grousing about the cold for five minutes straight, Gustav built a miserly little flame out of brush and twigs and a single dried cow pie.

"Careful with that bonfire," I said once he had it leveled off to a dull smolder. "If it gets any bigger, it might actually *warm* somethin'."

The fire gave off such a puny glow I couldn't quite make out the expression on Old Red's face, but the snap in his voice filled in the picture well enough.

"We got two choices—cold or dead. You want a bigger fire, you head off a mile or two before you build it. I'll follow the smoke to your body in the mornin' and give you a decent burial."

"Well, fine! We'll deprive the McPhersons of the pleasure of

shootin' us by *freezin'* ourselves to death. Or maybe we'll die of starva-
tion first. Damn it, Gustav! If you knew we weren't goin' to Miles, why
didn't you grab—?"

Old Red reached into his war bag and produced a small, white
brick, which he threw across the fire into my chest. By the time I'd figured out it was a biscuit, a leather pouch filled with pemmican came flying behind it. I set to gnawing at the strips of dried meat while my
brother pulled out a couple of airtights, drove his knife into one, and
started sawing. A minute later he handed over the tin can, and I took a
satisfying slurp of briny water. Big chunks of stewed tomato were
afloat in the thick liquid, and I fished one out and popped it into my
mouth.

"Alright then," I said as Gustav began cutting open the other can.
"We've got a campfire—or a few camp-*embers,* anyway. We've got food,
for which I do thank you. There ain't nobody around to eavesdrop.
And for the next few hours, we ain't goin' nowhere. So how about if
you did a little more talkin'?"

Old Red speared a hunk of tomato and took a bite out of it. In the
dim orange light of the fire, he was little more than a shadow chomping
into some dark, pulpy mass, and if I hadn't been half-starved, thoughts
of Hungry Bob Tracy would surely have put me off my feed.

"What would you have me talk about?" Gustav asked.

Now we had plenty of mysteries to talk over still, that's for sure.
And yet the more I'd thought about them that day, the more one stood
out from the others like an elephant running with a pack of coyotes. It
was something I'd made my own deductions on, but I had yet to hear
Gustav offer a single explanation of his own.

"Brother," I said, "why'd you stick us in the middle of this mess?"

Old Red answered the question with a shrug. "You're free to leave,
you know. You could just *ride*. You don't have to see this through."

"But you aim to."

He shrugged again.

"Even though it might get you killed."

He shrugged *again*.

Of the two of us, my brother usually serves up the long-suffering sighs. Now it was my turn to heave a big one.

"Gustav, would you please just answer the damn question?"

Old Red threw more brush on the fire. When it flickered up into flame, I could see that his lips had a little curl to them—almost as if he was *smiling*.

"You remember the time I asked Uncle Franz why we weren't Calvinists?" he said.

This was a mighty strange time to be reminiscing over family history. But I knew what Gustav was speaking of, and it almost had me unpacking a sad smile myself.

The Germans populating the little corner of Kansas from which we hailed came in two varieties: Calvinist and Lutheran. The Amlingmeyers and our *Mutter*'s family, the Ortmanns, were Lutherans without exception, and my brother had once wondered aloud why this should be so.

"Becauze vhen you are burnink in hell, Gustav, it vill be becauze *you* zent yourzelf dere, not *Gott*," our uncle had told him.

Even with no more light to go by than a lightning bug produces from his butt, Old Red knew exactly what I was thinking just from the wistful way I shook my head at the memory.

"Yeah, ol' Franz could sure talk crazy," he said. "But he had a solid enough point that day. The Calvinists, they talk about 'predestination.' You don't work your way to heaven—you're either born wearin' golden slippers or you're not. That idea wouldn't sit too well with the likes of Franz. It sure don't sit too well with me, and you know I don't even *believe* in heaven."

I did know that, actually, though I'd gathered it more from inference than deep conversation, as Gustav brings up religion about as often as a Zulu chief brings up baseball.

"But I don't know," Old Red went on. "Maybe there is such a thing as destiny. If there is, I'll tell you what a feller like me's supposed to be—dirt-poor and dumb. A farmer, a cowboy, it don't matter which. We're born to use our hands, not our brains. And God damn it, Brother, I just don't accept it."

My brother got to poking at the fire absentmindedly, and as the silence that followed stretched on, I got the feeling he didn't know what to say next—or he knew and he didn't like it.

"You're afraid, ain't you?" I said, talking at the tiny, flickering flames between us. "Not of the McPhersons or the Duke or whoever killed Boo. You're afraid you won't crack the mystery—afraid of what that says about *you*."

"You're right, Otto."

My gaze shot up from the fire, seeking out my brother's face in the gloom. I could see little more than an outline, but his eyes pierced the darkness, sparkling at me like twin stars. He was staring at me, unblinking, and I knew that my ears had not deceived me. For the first time, my brother was giving me an honest look into his heart.

Don't get me wrong: I knew my brother—knew him damn well. But not because he'd ever done much talking about what he felt or what he believed. I'd just sort of soaked up a knowledge of the man by spending all my time in his company, almost like the way a drover gets to know his best cow pony. You don't expect to have a heart-to-heart with your horse, and I'd never really expected to have one with Gustav. Until now.

"I'm tryin' to be something I'm not, and I'm more scared of failin' than dyin'," Old Red said, his words heavy with as much raw feeling, as much raw *fear*, as I'd ever heard in his voice before. "Does that make me crazy? Does that make me Uncle Franz?"

"Uncle Franz thought he could walk on water," I said.

"You know what I'm sayin'."

Now I've often fallen into a lazy sort of call-and-response with Old

Red. He'll snip at me, I'll snap at him, and so on, achieving little beyond mutual irritation. But I was setting that aside now. After our years on the trail, Gustav was finally seeking my counsel as a *man,* and I had to live up to the honor by offering whatever degree of wisdom I could muster.

"You ain't crazy, Gustav. You're just . . ."

I took a deep breath before moving on. Filling the air with words is usually no challenge for me, but picking out the right ones now was proving tricky indeed.

"It's like this. Most cowboys stick to droverin' cuz they ain't got a better idea what to do with themselves. For you it ain't like that. You been lookin' for somethin' different—somethin' more. And I think those Holmes tales showed you what it was. You ain't just a *hand.* You're a *mind.* And whether that mind's filled with book-learnin' or not, it's damn sharp. That ain't no accident. Maybe it's your *destiny* to be a detective. The only way to know for sure is to wrap up all the riddles around here in as neat a knot as Mr. Holmes could've thrown. So that's what you gotta do."

"And what about you?" Gustav asked. "What is it *you* gotta do?"

I'd been sailing along alright there, but now my words lost their wind, and I drifted to a standstill.

As for me . . . what? Even if Old Red was fated to be a detective, that didn't tell me what *I* was supposed to do.

My brother and I locked eyes on each other. It might have been a trick of the fluttering firelight, but Old Red's seemed to be glistening especially bright and moist.

That gave me my wind back. For a long while, I'd been tagging along behind Gustav out of pure habit. It was different now. My brother wasn't just tolerating me. He *needed* me—and he respected me enough to show me.

For the first time, I didn't feel like Old Red Amlingmeyer's kid brother. I was just his *brother.*

"I guess I'm like most punchers," I said. "I don't hear any particular call for myself—except to stick close to the only family I got left. So you just do what you got to, and I'll be there to back you up . . . no matter what."

Old Red nodded, and for a moment the only sound was the quiet crinkling of the burning brush in our campfire. Then my brother stuck his hand out. I grasped it, and we shook.

"You're a good man, Otto."

"I've had a good teacher."

Gustav nodded again, then let go of my hand. We shared a few silent minutes, basking more in the lingering warmth of our conversation than the scanty heat that little fire put out. Then Old Red slapped his knee, drew himself to his feet, and announced, "I feel me a piss comin' on." And with those decidedly unsentimental words he tramped off, wrapping himself in the thick shroud of darkness that enveloped our campsite.

I tried to pass the time by reviewing the "clues" and "suspects" we'd collected, but my mind stuck firm to one and wouldn't budge free. It was Lady Clara, of course. Hearing from Brackwell that she and Edwards might be making a love match had been unsettling. On the other hand, learning that she shared her family's taste for romantic entanglements with the lower classes was fodder for fantasies of an admittedly ludicrous (but altogether satisfying) sort.

After several minutes, this distracting line of thought was interrupted by the rustling of bushes nearby.

"Well, it's about time!" I called out. "You said you had to water the grass, not fertilize an acre or two with a big load of—*shit!*"

The rustling I'd heard had materialized into a large, whirling, panting shape that suddenly burst from the shadows. I had just enough time to recognize my brother in a life-or-death grapple with another man when the two of them crashed to the earth, kicking and cursing. Their spinning bodies rolled over the fire, smothering its meager flame and casting us all into utter blackness.

Thirty-two

HUNGRY BOB

Or, A Fight in the Dark Sheds New Light on Our Case

Under normal circumstances, a man of my considerable size doesn't need much time to end a fight. These weren't normal circumstances, however, since it's pretty hard to end a fight you can't *see*. For nearly a minute, Gustav and our surprise caller rolled this way and that while I followed by the sound of their grunts and muffled blows, unsure which head to hit or back to kick when I managed to catch a glimpse of them.

The men's tangled forms finally came to a stop pressed against the rocky outcropping beside which we'd bedded ourselves. One of them ended up beneath the other, and from the familiar sound of the yelps coming from the ground, I knew it was Old Red who'd been pinned.

But being on top proved to be no advantage to Gustav's attacker, for it gave me the opportunity to determine the exact location of his face and send a punch flying smack-dab into it. A loud groan was followed quickly by the dropped-potato-sack sound of a man collapsing to the earth.

"Thanks, Brother," Gustav said, sounding winded and shaken as he pulled himself up.

"My pleasure. So who'd I just whack the bejesus out of, anyway?"

Old Red began dusting himself off and picking bramble from his hair. "I have no idea. I heard someone creepin' around, so I made like I had to let off a sprinkle and circled round behind him. He's got some good ears on him, though, cuz he heard me comin' and jumped me first."

"Maybe it's one of the McPhersons," I said, hoping I'd just belted Uly or Spider.

"Let's find out."

Old Red pulled out a lucifer, fired it up, and moved the small flame down toward our prisoner. The light of it shimmered off a black, broad, and strangely familiar face.

"Well, I wouldn't have guessed that one," Gustav said. "What the hell is *he* doin' here?"

"What the hell is *who* doin' here?"

I leaned in to give the Negro sprawled beneath us a closer look just as his eyes snapped open and his hands shot up to clamp around my neck. Gustav dropped his match and began struggling to break the powerful grip that was suddenly cutting off my breath.

"Jim!" Old Red said. "Stop! It's Old Red and Big Red! The Amlingmeyers! Stop it, Jim! *Stop!*"

The pressure around my windpipe eased.

"Old Red?"

The voice had a touch of Kentucky drawl, and I recognized it straight off: It was Jim Weller, the Negro puncher Uly had refused to hire in the Hornet's Nest more than two months before.

"Yup, it's me," Gustav said. "And that's my brother you're stranglin'."

"Hey . . . there . . . Jim," I wheezed.

The hands at my throat disappeared, and shortly thereafter the three of us were gathered around the rekindled campfire like a bunch of old chums. Weller had brought with him fresh, strong Arbuckle grounds and flavorful Durham tobacco, and by way of apology for trying to throttle Old Red and me, he treated us to the best java and smokes we'd had in months. From the enthusiastic reception this received, Weller guessed that life on the Bar VR had not been silk and velvet, and I was about to launch into our tale when Gustav got his lips working first.

"Oh, it ain't as bad as you might think," he said. "The work's hard, the food stinks, and the foreman's a son of a bitch, but you could say the same of most outfits. So what brings you out our way?"

Weller stared into the fire. "I'm ridin' the grub line. Miles has been bone-dry job-wise, so I thought I'd try my luck over in Wibaux."

If you're headin' to Wibaux, what're you doin' this far south? I could've said. Or *I would've thought the grub line went* around *the VR these days, not through it.* But I held my tongue and let Old Red do the talking, for he seemed to be digging around for answers in his own way.

"Travelin' alone, are you?"

"Just me and my horse."

"Oh?" Old Red replied. "Ain't that a bit risky—a man on the drift alone in these parts? It's not enough you got the McPhersons to worry about, but there's Hungry Bob on the prowl, as well."

Weller chuckled. "Awww, Old Red—I thought you were a level-headed man. Yet here you are spreadin' around the heebie-jeebies like them gossipy hens back in Miles. All this talk about Bob Tracy's just a big bucket of nothin'. He's either up in Saskatchewan or down in hell by now."

"I ain't so sure. I got a feelin' he's a lot closer than that."

"Oh?" Weller's dismissive smile went weak at the knee. "And how'd you come by this feelin'?"

"For one thing, I picked up some tracks a week or so back. Looked like one feller on his own, afoot, livin' rough and lyin' low."

Weller laughed with a little too much gusto. "Is that all? Hell, if I got spooked every time I came across bear sign, I'd sell my saddle and take up knittin'."

"Gustav knows bear sign when he sees it—and this wasn't it," I said, leaping in to defend my brother's honor. He thanked me for the support by ignoring me, as did Weller, who just kept right on laughing.

"For another thing," Old Red continued, "there's you."

Weller's laugh choked to a halt. "What do you mean?"

It was Gustav's turn to smile now, and he favored Weller with one of his sly little smirks. "I've been sittin' here tryin' to figure why you'd be skulkin' around the Bar VR given its less-than-hospitable reputation, and it occurred to me that all the bad talk about the VR might actually *attract* a certain kind of person. Or two kinds of persons, actually—a man on the run and a man on his heels. Tell me, Jim—what's the bounty on ol' Bob up to these days? I sure bet you could use the money."

The expression on Weller's face seesawed between dismay and disgust before finally settling on the latter. He sighed and threw his cigarette in the fire, looking like a fellow who'd just had his bluff called on a fifty-dollar bet.

"One thousand dollars," he said with sulky irritation. "And yeah—I *could* use the money."

"Well, don't worry—we don't aim to horn in on you," Old Red assured him. "We got our own business to attend to, and I just had to be sure you weren't mixed up in it."

Weller was plainly relieved to hear this, though it didn't cheer me up any. I'd already done the arithmetic necessary to divide a thousand dollars into three shares, and the resulting figures had been tempting indeed.

"So what makes you think Bob's around here, anyway?" Gustav asked.

"It's pretty much like you said," Weller replied, his tone still a tad wary. "I turned bounty hunter when I couldn't hunt up a job. Headed down to Biddle cuz word was Hungry Bob had passed through there a few weeks back. I managed to find an old mule skinner who'd spoken to him—or someone like him—in a roadhouse. Said this feller was *very* interested when he heard about the Bar VR—its size and its reputation for unfriendliness in particular. And that got me thinkin' the VR'd be the perfect place to hole up, cuz most fellers like me would be too scared to set foot there."

"So you came up here and got to trackin'."

"That's right."

"And?"

"No sign of Hungry Bob—though I was sure I'd finally caught up to him when I saw your fire here." Weller grinned. "And I stumbled across something other than you two fellers, as well."

"The cattalo," Old Red said.

"You seen 'em, too?"

"Not just seen 'em—Otto here almost got himself pulped by 'em."

Weller laughed, and it was such an infectious sound I had to join in even if the merriment was at my expense.

"So them hairy things back there was cattalo?" I said, pleased that I'd finally laid eyes on the rare critters.

Cattalo is hybrid stock, a cross between cattle and buffalo. Breeding them had been quite the craze out West—until folks figured out what a stupid thing it is to do. The buffalo blood gives you big, meaty offspring that can withstand winter cold better than any steer. But it also gives you unsightly, unpredictable brutes that are as foul-tempered as your average cow is dull-witted. On top of that, cattalo calves take a harsh toll upon their mothers, their buffalo humps presenting challenges of delivery cow anatomy is not designed to overcome.

If raising cattalo was just plain dangerous—which it is—no one would bat an eye. But so many of the calves and mothers die in labor it makes the whole business unprofitable, which is why cattalo ranching

came and went in the blink of an eye. Exactly why a herd of the misbe-
gotten creatures should be lingering around the Cantlemere was but
one more mystery to throw atop the heap we'd already built up.

"Well, them big bastards sure lived up to their reputation for bein'
ugly and mean. I can see why Uly'd have a soft spot for 'em, him bein'
ugly and . . ."

A thought slammed into my gut like a fist, knocking the air out of
me. I stood, walked around the fire, and bent over, my butt cheeks
pointed at my brother.

"Kick me in the ass," I told him.

"What?"

"You heard me. Kick me in the ass. Believe me, I deserve it."

"Oh, stop actin' like a fool, Otto. Just tell me what you're talkin'
about."

"Alright, you had your chance," I said, reaching into my Levi's and
pulling out the scrap of paper I had tucked away there. I gave Weller as
quick a rundown on the receipt as I could—how it went from the cellar
to Boudreaux's pocket to the fireplace to our hands—then read it out
loud.

> *ill of Sal*
> *nnuery 20, 1893*
> *tallo*
> *oo — payed*
> *cfersin*
> *klin Dammers*

"Why would McPherson be buyin' tallow from Frankie
Dammers?" Weller asked when I was done. "You got all the beef fat you
could want right here on the VR."

"That's just what we've been thinkin'," I said. "Except I was readin'
this wrong. It's *t-a-l-l-o* on here, not *t-a-l-l-o-w*, like it oughta be. I figured Dammers couldn't spell—he sure as hell didn't know how to write
January or *paid* or even *McPherson*. But *tallo* ain't just misspelled. It's a

different word entirely—only the first few letters got burned off in the fire. What we've got here is a receipt for—"

Gustav might not know his way around the alphabet, but he figured out where I was headed quick enough.

"Cattalo."

Weller chuckled and shook his head. "You sure you don't wanna kick his ass?" he said to Old Red.

"Later," my brother mumbled, his thoughts focusing elsewhere. "Lady Clara said the VR was her father's 'last grand gamble.' I reckon that's what he's rollin' the dice on—hybrid stock."

"Who'd be dumb enough to put any money in cattalo anymore?" Weller asked.

"It ain't a matter of bein' dumb," Old Red said. "It's a matter of bein' a thousand miles away. Them folks in England only had one way of knowin' what was goin' on out here."

"Perkins," I said.

Gustav nodded. "He was probably sendin' the board one letter after another sayin' the ranch is fit to bust with big, beefy cattalo—only they had to keep it quiet so as not to tip off the competition, or some such nonsense."

"Meanwhile, Perkins and the McPhersons was milkin' the VR for every penny it was worth," I threw out.

"Could be. But don't forget—the Duke and them others have been goin' over the books ever since they got here."

For once, I was a step ahead of my brother.

"Oh, pshaw. That's easy enough to fake. You just do two sets of account books—a real one for yourself and one that's doctored-up for everybody else. Hey! That'd explain all those empty ink bottles we found in Perkins's office the night we snuck in there! And I bet that's why the bill of sale for them cattalo was in the cellar. Perkins hid the VR's *real* records down there. After Boo popped up with the receipt, the

McPhersons put a bullet in his brain and moved the ledger books to a better hidin' place."

Old Red gaped at me a moment before a small smile curled his mustache at the edges.

"That's some fine deducifyin', Brother."

I grinned back. "Well . . . I *was* a clerk for a spell."

"And that's sure come in handy lately." Old Red's smile slid off his face. "I think you're wrong, though. At least about who killed Boudreaux. Perkins knew the Duke and the rest of 'em were comin' months ahead of time. The receipt says those cattalo were bought in *January,* and the Hornet's Nesters were hired to fix the VR up a few weeks after that. So who sent word ahead? It had to be somebody who knew the board was sendin' folks out to look the place over in the spring. And I guarantee you this: That somebody's in the castle at this very moment."

"But the Duke and Brackwell and Edwards—their families have all got money tied up in the ranch. Why go to all this trouble to steal from themselves?"

"Somebody ain't ready to stop playin' cowboy."

I gave my brother the same cocked-headed look of confusion dogs give calliopes, velocipedes, or anything else they can't quite understand.

"Somebody doesn't want the Sussex Land and Cattle Company gettin' out of the cattle business," Old Red explained.

I was about to point out that Gustav seemed to know an awful lot about this *somebody* when Weller spoke, breaking his long silence.

"I ain't followin' this at all—and I thank God I don't have to. I'm sorry for whatever predicament you two have got yourselves in, but it's no concern of mine."

"I wouldn't be so sure about that."

Weller and I turned to stare at Old Red.

"Jim, you didn't happen to bring along a reward notice for Hungry Bob, did you?" he went on.

Weller nodded slowly and pulled a sheet of folded paper from his canvas coat.

"Take a look," he said as he handed the notice over. "Not that it'll make any difference. There ain't no way ol' Bob's mixed up in this mess."

I leaned in to get a look—and to offer my services as reader—as Gustav spread the paper out. But my brother didn't care what was written on that poster. His only interest was the photographs printed across the bottom. Both were of Bob Tracy, one looking straight ahead, the other in profile.

He had an unsettling look about him, with a shaved head and dazed grin and eyes alight with the inner fire of insanity. Yet it was his enormous, mole-encrusted beak of a nose that really put a shiver down my spine.

Weller was wrong. Hungry Bob was as mixed up in our mess as a man could get.

"Sweet Jesus," I whispered. "I don't believe it."

"Don't believe what?" Weller asked, blinking at the flyer in confusion.

Old Red answered him by slipping his fingers into his vest pocket and pulling out the folded neckerchief stuffed within. He unwrapped it carefully, gradually revealing the very nose depicted on that poster.

Thirty-three

SEPARATE TRAILS

Or, I Head Back to HQ Without Old Red . . . but I'm Not Alone

It being a little unlikely that even a man as peculiar as Hungry Bob Tracy would take to roaming around without his own nose, we quickly concluded that the Colorado Cannibal would be feasting no more. Naturally, Weller wanted to know how we'd come by Bob's smeller, and Old Red had me unspool the story. When I was through, Weller threw out the question that was weighing heaviest upon him.

"So . . . y'all think that nose is enough to collect the reward on?"

Even as I'd been tale-spinning, this very thought had been bouncing around the back of my mind. Having an essentially sunny, hopeful disposition, I'd leaned toward the affirmative. Naturally, Old Red was less optimistic.

"If the law paid out good money each time somebody walked in with a nose, every greedy hard case in the West would take to carryin' around sheep shears and snippin' off nostrils," my brother said. "Nope, if you want that reward, you're gonna have to go in with more than this."

Gustav patted his vest pocket, where he'd returned Hungry Bob's neckerchief-enshrouded remains.

"What more is there?" Weller asked, staring at the lump in my brother's vest as if it already contained a heap of cash. "We don't even know how that Boo got hold of Bob's nose in the first place."

"Actually, I've got a thought on that—though it takes a little *theorizin'* to lay out."

I couldn't be sure, as dark as it was around our little fire, but it looked like Old Red gave me a sly smile. I think he'd decided once for all to make a break with Mr. Holmes on the advisability of talking out your theories.

"A while back, I was dumb enough to show Spider that trail I found back up towards HQ," he said. "One man, on foot. Well, let's just say the McPhersons went out and got hold of that man . . . and it was Hungry Bob. They might feel a touch nervous about turnin' him in. They've got a lot to hide out here. So they killed him. But Boudreaux had ideas of his own, and he set off to collect the reward for himself. Only he didn't want to drag in a whole body—not with Uly and Spider likely to get on his tail. So he had the same idea as you, Jim. Try collectin' on the nose."

A part of me wanted to nod, a part of me wanted to shake my head. It was like taking a taste of underflavored soup. I knew something was missing, but I couldn't quite figure out what.

Weller had an entirely different concern. "Alright, let's say all that's true. How does it get us closer to the rest of the body?"

"Well, here's the thing," Old Red said. "I saw that trail a few days before Perkins got ground into chuck. If the McPhersons laid their hands on Hungry Bob, I'd think Perkins would want a say in what to do with him. And Uly might be a lot of things, but he ain't rash. I figure he'd want to simmer a bit before throwing away anything as valuable as ol' Bob. So if they roped Bob in, they'd probably corral him someplace for a spell before puttin' a bullet in him. And they couldn't hold him at headquarters—not with us Hornet's Nesters there."

"The line camp," Weller jumped in with a snap of his fingers. "You think they kept Hungry Bob there."

Gustav shrugged. "It's the first place we oughta look for his body, anyway."

"*We?*" Weller and I blurted out together.

"Jim' n' me," Old Red explained. "Jim's gotta go to the line camp to look for Hungry Bob. I gotta go to find out if I'm right about what Boudreaux was up to. I'm sorry, Otto—that means you'll be headin' back to HQ alone."

"Oh, does it now?" I said, peeved to find my brother sliding us this way and that like so many dominoes.

"Most likely the Peacock's gonna be back tomorrow mornin' with a marshal from Miles. You'll have to slow things up till I can get there."

"And how am I supposed to do that? Hold everybody at gunpoint half the day?"

Old Red turned away from the fire and began balling himself up in his sugan.

"You could always try *talking* everybody to death," he said through a big yawn. "I'm sure talked out, that's for sure. I'll be turnin' in now, boys. I suggest you do likewise. We're gonna need an early jump on the day tomorrow."

He was snoring within seconds—which didn't necessarily mean he was asleep. I harbored the strong suspicion that he was simply avoiding more questions.

If he was faking, he got away with it. Weller quickly wished me a good night and turned Old Red's solo snores into a duet. Though agitated, I was too tired to stay awake and stew, and within minutes that duet became a trio.

When I awoke the next morning, Gustav and Weller were already about ready to ride. I gathered my gear fast but without enthusiasm, for the prospect of splitting with my brother troubled me deeply. The McPhersons were no doubt sniffing after our trail, and it made me nervous to have Weller watching Old Red's back instead of me. It didn't settle my nerves when I noticed that Gustav—who could usually stare into a tornado without blinking—seemed a touch spooked himself.

"You be careful, Otto," he said gravely, walking up and offering me his hand as I got set to horse myself.

"*You* be careful, Gustav."

As we shook, I saw that he'd already taken steps to follow that advice—sticking over the top of his trousers was the grip of a gun, no doubt borrowed from Weller.

My brother nodded, we unclasped hands, and I hefted myself atop Brick. Moments later, Gustav and I rode our separate ways facing the unspoken possibility that we would never see each other again.

I headed east a while before swinging north, avoiding the trail we'd ridden down the previous day. I kept to gullies and creekbeds mostly, doing my best not to stay in the open for long or present a clear outline against the horizon. I thought I was doing a pretty good job, too—until Brick jerked in his bridle and began to fall.

The sound of the gunshot didn't reach me until Brick was almost to the ground, by which time another bullet was whipping off my hat and putting a crease across my scalp. I didn't even hear that second shot. I was too distracted by other sounds and sensations—Brick's scream, his body curling into the dirt, my own being catapulted from the saddle, and a sudden jarring pain across my backside as I slammed into the sod.

I rolled to a stop far beyond the VR or Montana or America or even the earth, journeying to some distant plane that knew neither light nor sound. I can't say how long I stayed there, but it couldn't have been more than a few minutes. A hum rose out of the stillness, and from that grew a throbbing, and from that formed a noise so terrible it jerked me all the way back to the Bar VR.

It was the anguished cry of a horse, close by and hurt bad. I blinked open my eyes to see white puffs of cloud lazing overhead in a perfect blue sky.

"You sure I got him?" someone said.

"You saw it," came the gruff reply. "That second shot brained him."

A familiar clop-clop grew louder, and the voices did the same. The two men were mounted, and they were headed my way.

"There's Brick," the first fellow said. Thanks to my still-scrambled brains, the words echoed in my head like a shout from a well. Yet I caught enough of the man's speaking to know I'd heard his voice before.

My body was atingle with pain and shock, but somehow I managed to get my hand moving down to my holster. When it got there, however, it found nothing to grasp. I'd lost my iron in the fall.

"His body must've—" the second man said, his words cut off by another whinny of pain from poor Brick.

". . . over there," the first man was saying when the horse quieted down again.

I rolled over on my stomach and took a look back toward Brick. He was lying about twenty feet away, kicking his legs in a feeble attempt to right himself. Smack-dab between us was my gun.

I snaked toward it slowly, still so woozy from my tumble I feared I'd pass out before I could be shot to death.

The sound of approaching horses grew louder.

I stretched out my hand.

I don't know if the first fellow saw me or heard me, but he called out "Hey!" just as my fingers wrapped around the gun's grip. I looked up and saw a gray Stetson appear over Brick's heaving belly.

I pulled the trigger, sending a slug as low into that hat as I could.

The Stetson sank out of sight, and I heard a squeaking of leather and a dull thump that told me a man had just slipped from his saddle.

I kept the gun pointed over Brick, waiting for another hat to sling lead at. But the only target I got was empty sky. The sound of pounding hooves filled the air, growing fainter with each second. I pushed myself to my knees just in time to see a man on horseback disappear over a nearby ridge. I caught only the briefest glimpse of him, but that was all I needed.

I'd just missed a chance to kill Spider McPherson, and he'd just missed a chance to kill me. I encouraged Spider to keep going with another shot from my .45. Given the distance between us, it was a pointless gesture—though one I took satisfaction in making.

After that, I began creeping slowly around Brick. The horse lived only a few more moments, dying in agony before I could bring his suffering to a merciful end myself. When I rounded his heap of a body, I found that fate had been kinder to the man I'd shot.

It was Tall John Harrington, and from the mess that had been made of his head, it was plain he couldn't have experienced a single second of pain. Lying next to his body was a Winchester carbine.

I'd killed men twice before and felt neither pride nor remorse—both instances had simply been matters of strict necessity. I didn't feel any more moved now, even though I'd once considered Tall John a compadre. I couldn't help but be disappointed in the man, but that's as deep as my sorrow ran. I was a lot more broken up about what had happened to Brick.

Despite all the noise, Tall John's horse hadn't run far off, being trained like all good saddle ponies to stay put anywhere the reins are dropped. Pausing only to collect my hat, the carbine, and as much of my wits as I could, I got myself into Tall John's saddle and resumed my ride. I was determined to reach headquarters—but just as anxious to avoid Spider on the way. I moved north cautiously, circling around west of the castle before daring to get in close. As a result, I didn't make it back fast, though I did at least get there without losing another horse.

Once I was within sight of HQ, I reconnoitered from high ground. A glint of sun drew my eyes to the castle, and I saw Brackwell out by the western side of the house, alone. He appeared to be practicing his quick draw again, for he was wearing all his cowboy finery, including both his shiny six-guns. The remaining Hornet's Nesters were around the corner from him, loading up a buckboard parked near the front steps. In the wagon's bed was a slowly growing mountain of luggage.

Our guests were preparing to depart.

I spied the McPhersons' men in the corral doctoring cows but caught no sight of Uly or Spider themselves. I had a good idea where they were, though—somewhere nearby, waiting. If I was going to make it to the castle without getting bushwhacked, I'd need one hell of a diversion.

I was crouching in the brush trying to dream one up when it just came riding down the trail for me. Two men on horseback passed no more than a hundred feet from where I was hiding. As soon as I recognized them, I horsed myself and galloped after them.

Just as I got up behind them, two more riders appeared—Uly and Spider. They took up positions on either side of me, escorting me in toward the castle just as I was escorting the other two men: the Peacock and Jack Martin, deputy U.S. marshal.

I'd made it back too late. Brackwell had lost his bet.

And what's more, Old Red was about to lose his only chance to clear up all the mysteries around the Bar VR—and get us out of there alive.

Thirty-four

NOTHING (ALMOST)

Or, Justice Appears to Be Not Only Blind, but Deaf and Dumb, as Well

Martin and the Peacock didn't even notice they had a caravan until they brought their horses down to a trot and heard us riding on their tails. The Peacock turned back toward us first. As usual, he was dressed up fancy, wearing a red silk shirt and striped trousers and boots adorned with ornate stitching—though the gleam of all this finery was dulled under a layer of trail dust.

"Boss," he said to Uly. Then his gaze slid over to me, his blue eyes going frigid cold despite the gloating grin on his face.

I could feel another stare on me, this one scorching hot, and I turned to face Spider. The look he was giving me said he'd soon finish what he'd started. The look I gave *him* invited him to try.

"McPherson!" Martin spat as he swiveled around and saw us. "You better tell me you got Hungry Bob Tracy hog-tied in that bunkhouse up ahead or I'm gonna be mighty pissed."

"Ain't nothin' in there but smelly blankets and hungry lice," Uly replied cheerfully.

Martin began swearing about his long ride to nowhere for nothing. As he ranted, I put the spurs to my brain, desperate for a way to slow things down until Old Red could arrive.

I got a little help from Brackwell, though he didn't mean to offer it. We were right up on the castle by then, and he and all the hands came out front to meet us. The sight of the young Englishman in his masquerade-ball getup was enough to bring Martin's cursing gurgling to a halt.

"This here's Mr. Brackwell. His old man's the baron of some such," Uly offered by way of explanation.

"The Earl of Blackwater," Brackwell said, straining for a dignity his clothing wouldn't quite allow him.

"You don't say," Martin replied, looking skeptical, as if he suspected that anyone attired in such a fashion probably belonged in Hungry Bob's old cell.

Uly sent one of his men off to fetch Edwards and the Duke, then turned back to Brackwell.

"Looks like you're out two hundred pounds," he said, not bothering to drip honey over his voice. Obviously, he'd decided Brackwell wasn't worth sucking up to anymore.

Brackwell took it quietly, like a fellow who's not unaccustomed to people making sport at his expense.

"I'm sorry," I told him. "We tried."

"What happened to you?" Brackwell asked, reminding me how rough I must look—I was caked in dirt, and a smear of crusted blood stretched across my forehead. "And where's your brother?"

I glanced at Spider and found him still staring at me. He gave me a wink, and I knew it was a dare.

Tell 'em, he was saying. *Tell 'em . . . and then just try and prove it.*

"Trouble with my horse," I said. "Gustav'll be along shortly."

"Aha! So you're here at last!" the Duke called out from the castle's front steps. He looked equal parts pleased and worried, no doubt because Martin's arrival signaled both a victorious conclusion to his bet with Brackwell and the possible appearance of yet another meddler—this one wearing a badge. Edwards tagged along behind the old man like a bespectacled bulldog on its master's heels.

Old Dickie was apparently more in keeping with Martin's idea of a nobleman than Young Brackwell, and the deputy marshal quickly hunched his back and removed his hat. Though he remained astride his horse, Martin somehow seemed to be looking *up* at the old man.

"Would you be the Duke, sir?"

His Grace nodded and favored Martin with a smirky smile, obviously relieved to have finally found someone in the West who could kowtow properly. Some range-country lawmen make an art of kissing royal ass, as the cattle barons can be picky indeed about when, where, how, and for whom law and order are maintained. Martin seemed to be of this lickspittle breed, and it soon became clear that the only thing he planned on investigating was how to affix his lips to the Duke's posterior.

"It's a real pleasure making your acquaintance," Martin said. "I wouldn't have bothered comin' out here if not for you and your party. As you know, there's been some concern about an escaped lunatic. Based on what I've been told, I doubt the . . . uhhh . . . *problem* y'all have is tied up with our madman. But I thought it best to ride out and see for myself. It's not every day Montana is blessed with such distinguished guests, and I could hardly take any chances with your well-being, now could I? In fact, just to be on the safe side, I'd be happy to escort your group back to Miles City for the Stockgrowers' sit-down once we've cleared this all up. Folks are already arrivin' from far and wide, and you'll want to—"

"We won't be staying for the Stockgrowers Association meeting," the Duke cut in, obviously irritated by Martin's windiness. Since the deputy marshal had so quickly revealed himself to be an utter toady, the old man clearly wouldn't have to bother offering him such sops as courtesy or respect. "We will be returning to Chicago on the earliest available train."

"Oh," Martin said, looking confused. I couldn't blame him—I was thrown myself.

Each year, the biggest cattlemen in Montana send representatives to the Stockgrowers Association meeting in Miles. I'd assumed the Duke's arrival at the VR just days before the convention couldn't be a coincidence. But now he was going to hop a train back East without bothering to attend?

"So if you would examine the body . . . ," the Duke prompted, plainly anxious to hustle Martin in and out so he could move on to more important concerns—such as securing a promissory note from Brackwell.

"Of course. If someone would be so kind as to lead me to it."

"I'll show you, Deputy," Uly said, flashing Martin a smile the lawman didn't return.

Those of us on horseback dismounted, and soon the McPhersons were leading Martin toward the outhouse. The rest of us formed a small herd and followed quietly.

"Ain't you gonna say anything to Martin about what's been goin' on out here?" Swivel-Eye leaned in close to whisper.

"Let's see how things play out first," I replied.

That satisfied Swivel-Eye—he gave me a grim nod and walked on in silence. But *I* wasn't satisfied. I had no idea what I would say should it befall me to speak up. The McPhersons were but one worm in a whole squirming can, and I'd been counting on Old Red to sort them all out. I stole a glance off to the south but saw no sign of anyone approaching.

These worries were chased from my mind by a pungent odor that singed my nose hairs as we approached the outhouse. The unsettling hum of tiny wings vibrated through the door.

"We didn't want to muss anything up before an experienced lawman could arrive," Uly explained genially as he pulled off his bandanna and pressed it up over his nose and mouth. "So we left him just as we found him."

I followed Uly's lead with my neckerchief, as did the others. Naturally, Edwards and the Duke substituted silk hankies for bandannas.

"Alright then," Martin said glumly as he stepped forward and wrapped his hand around the door handle.

Even with the inside latch broken off, the door still stuck a bit, and Martin had to do some tugging to get it free. When it flew open, two things emerged: a swarm of flies and a stench so fierce it ate straight through my bandanna and clamped its jaws around my lungs.

Most of us cursed and turned away, but Martin actually found the fortitude to step in to get a good look—though he wasn't happy about it.

"Good God almighty," he spluttered, the words almost buried under the flies' deafening buzzing.

"So—what do you think, Deputy?" Uly asked from a safe distance away.

"Well, he's got himself a gunshot wound to the head, alright."

I was beginning to get the feeling that Jack Martin wouldn't be taking Sherlock Holmes's place as the world's greatest living detective.

"So it would be suicide," the Duke coughed from behind his hankie.

"It sure ain't how Hungry Bob's known to do things," Martin replied. "He's more the stabbin' and hackin' kind."

"Yes, yes. It's settled then," the Duke persisted. "The man killed himself."

Martin saw which way the wind—or at least the Duke—was blowing, and he bent himself in the appropriate direction.

"Ain't no other way to look at it, I reckon." Martin stepped back and slammed the door shut. "Well, this surely was a damned waste of time." He offered the Duke an apologetic smile. "Beggin' your pardon for sayin' so."

"No, quite right, quite right," the old man replied, already drifting away from the outhouse. The rest of the crowd drifted with him, with one exception—me. "It was obvious from the very beginning. Still, certain parties had to be satisfied."

"Now, look," I said, knowing I had to hold my ground even if I had no idea what to hold it with. "There's good reason to think Boo was done in by foul play."

The Duke snorted.

"'Foul play'!" Edwards said, rolling his eyes. "The man sounds like a penny dreadful!"

Uly and Spider backed him up with a round of guffaws.

"I ain't in the mood for monkeyshines, Big Red," Martin said.

"I'm serious, Jack." I turned to Brackwell and the Hornet's Nesters, hoping they'd back me up. "You saw how my brother talked it through yesterday. Help me out here."

But Brackwell appeared to have resigned himself to defeat—he wouldn't even meet my eyes. Swivel-Eye looked game but tongue-tied, Anytime merely looked pissed (as always), and Crazymouth wouldn't have been much help even if he had started talking, which he didn't.

"Why'd he kill himself with a hideout gun if he had a .45 ?" I asked, turning my appeal directly to Martin. "And how come he ain't got powder scorch on his hand? And . . . ummmm . . . he's wearin' spurs . . . and . . . well . . ."

Edwards said something to Martin I couldn't catch, and the deputy marshal responded with a hearty chuckle. Then the Duke turned and began walking away—and the rest of my audience followed him. The sight of it was so agitating that every other clue Old Red had unearthed suddenly flittered right out of my head. I let loose a loud "Hey!" but no one was listening any longer.

I abandoned the outhouse then, following everyone around to the front of the castle. It was either that or make a run for my horse and simply skedaddle—which is precisely what I would have done if it weren't for my brother. I owed it to him to stick around as long as I

STEVE HOCKENSMITH

could, even if every minute I remained was another minute the McPhersons could plot my demise.

Not being men to dillydally, they got right to it. As I rounded the corner of the big house, Spider turned to me with a grin and asked if I'd join him in the corral.

"I've got some branding that needs to be done," he said, "and I can't do it without you."

I juggled different responses in my mind, ignoring him being the wisest—and thus the least satisfying. For all I knew, Gustav was already dead, and this was my last chance to see justice done. So what the hell? I'd kept a rein on my anger the last few days. Maybe the time had come to let it run free.

"You and your bastard brother can go straight to hell," I said.

Spider's grin grew wider.

"Do I have your permission to fire this man, Your Grace?" Uly asked. He was moving as he said it, taking slow steps that brought him closer to me while putting distance between himself and Spider. When I drew, I'd have to choose either him or his brother to go after.

"Fire?" the Duke asked.

"Sack," Edwards explained with smug satisfaction.

"Oh, by all means! And his fool of a brother, as well, if he bothers to return."

"Really, must you—?" Brackwell began, but his voice didn't have much wind behind it, and Uly easily outspoke him.

"You heard the man, Amlingmeyer. You're done. Just hand over that gun and I'll have my brother escort you—"

"*Ha!*" I barked. "There's only one way you're gettin' this gun off me."

That made things so plain Martin couldn't stay out of it any longer.

"Calm down, everybody," he said. He was trying to play the part of the gruff, domineering lawman, but his pose wasn't helped by his choice of position. He was fifteen feet from the McPhersons and a good

262

thirty feet from me, yet he didn't make a move to get any closer, and he certainly didn't step into the line of fire. "There ain't gonna be any of that while I'm around."

"Oh, is that a fact?" Spider said. His gaze was still on me, but it had moved downward, from my face to my hand.

My only chance was to draw before they did. I knew it, and Spider knew it. He also knew it was him I'd be coming for first. Yet his smile never wavered. The sight of it brought to mind a real spider, its fangs gleaming with poison as it closes in on a fat fly dumb enough to think it can bust loose of the web.

Yet I had fangs of my own, and the time had come to use them. I pictured it in my mind—Spider first, then jerk the barrel to the right, fan the hammer . . . and hope for a miracle.

"Come on, boys," Martin said, his voice now more pleading than commanding. With his dark, sweat-soaked hair and big buck teeth, he was taking on the look of a frightened beaver. "Don't do anything foolish."

Uly's eyes flickered to the left as Martin took a hesitant step toward us.

This was my chance. I had to use the distraction while I had it.

I had to draw now.

"What's going on here?"

Now *I* was distracted. Fortunately, Uly and Spider were just as surprised to hear Lady Clara's voice.

Each of us stole a peek toward the castle's front door, and distraction turned to outright astonishment, for by the lady's side was the small figure of a dust-coated cowboy.

"Ease down, fellers. There'll be time enough for that later," Old Red said. "Right now we've got us some talkin' to do."

Thirty-five

EVERYTHING (ALMOST)

Or, Old Red Talks Up a Storm and Stirs Up a Cyclone

The dirt on Gustav's clothes and the scrapes on his face and hands said he'd covered a lot of miles fast—and someone had tried to stop him. He looked like a man with quite a story to tell. Yet at least one person there was in no mood to listen.

"You're too late, Amlingmeyer," the Duke said. "Brackwell has lost the wager. And now I intend to have you—"

"As I recall," Old Red cut in calmly, "the issue at hand was whether I could come up with an explanation for Boudreaux's death before a lawman got here."

"And you failed!" the Duke boomed.

"Oh, but I didn't. You never said I had to give that explanation to *you.*"

"That's ludicrous! If not me, then . . . ?" The Duke turned his gaze to the woman at my brother's side, and the fire in his eyes flickered. "You? But—?"

"Amlingmeyer and I have had quite an illuminating conversation,"

Lady Clara said, her own gaze cool and distant. "I think it would be best if that illumination were shared with everyone."

"Well," Gustav said with a little cough, "maybe not *everyone*. Your Grace, Mr. Edwards, Mr. Brackwell, Jack, Uly, Spider, Otto—if you'd join us in the office, I think we could clear this up pretty quick."

The Duke grumbled, but with the lady behind Old Red he couldn't kick up too much fuss. Everyone filed inside and headed for Perkins's office. My brother pulled me aside before I could join the others, leaving us alone in the foyer.

"I spotted some buzzards circlin' on my way north," he said. He wrapped his hands around my forearms. "It's good to see you here."

"It's good to be here to be seen. That was Brick and Tall John you passed on the trail."

"Oh." Old Red gave my arms a squeeze, then took his hands away. "That's a shame about Brick."

"*So,*" I said, "have you got everything Holmesed out?"

My brother nodded, suddenly looking downright cheerful. "Everything. Well, except who was in the office with Boudreaux the other night."

I smiled back at him—until his words sank in. "You mean . . . everything except *who killed Boo*?"

"Shhhh. Not so loud."

He spun on his heel and hustled down the hallway toward the kitchen.

"Gustav! What—?"

My brother stopped, shushed me again, then opened the door to the room next to the office.

"Perkins's bedroom—just the way he left it," he said. "Looks comfortable."

He continued down the hall, and I caught up just as he pulled open the next door.

"Well, now," he said. "Comfortable this *ain't*."

265

A small chest of drawers was jammed into one corner of the tiny room, and from the comb and brush and other feminine sundries scattered about, it was obvious who'd made her quarters here.

"Poor Emily—shoved into this matchbox when there's a room twice as big one door over," Old Red said. He pointed to the bed—little more than a cot barely as long or as wide as Emily herself. "No, that'd never do, would it?"

"I don't guess a maid's got much say in the matter."

"It ain't the maid I'm thinkin' of."

Before I could take a step down that trail, my brother slapped his hands together and gave them a rub.

"Alright—can't keep 'em waitin' any longer."

"Well, maybe you should if you still don't know—"

But Gustav wasn't listening. He'd already spun around and headed back up the hall. I followed him feeling like a bull in a stampede—I didn't know where we were going, and it was too late to stop us from going there.

When we stepped into the office, we found Lady Clara and Edwards seated upon the ottoman, with Brackwell leaning one buckskin-clad shoulder against the wall nearby. The Duke had wedged himself into the chair behind Perkins's desk, and Uly had snagged the chair on the other side—much to Jack Martin's obvious annoyance. He and Spider were standing on either side of the window. Emily was over near Martin, having apparently been escorted in before Old Red and Lady Clara stepped outside to fetch us.

Gustav closed the door and gave me a *stay here* look that kept my substantial bulk planted in front of it. Then he walked to the center of the room and set loose a herd of words so massive it almost brought his lifetime head count up around mine.

There was a glow to him as he spoke that was totally unlike the crabby, quiet Gustav I'd known so well for so long. I think it was pure joy that lit him up so, as strange as that may sound given our predicament. He'd been following the trail blazed by his hero, Sherlock Holmes, and now he was but a hop, skip, and a jump from its end.

"Alright then," he said. "I guess it would be best to begin at the beginning, but this matter's so kinked up it's hard to even say where the beginning begins. So I'll just pick it up with yesterday mornin': We found Boudreaux in the privy with a bullet in his brain. The gentlemen here let me look into how it got there, and it's a good thing they did, too. Cuz after talkin' to folks, I stumbled across what you might call an *irregularity* about Boudreaux's death. The boys out yonder in the bunkhouse heard the gunshot right around dawn. But our guests here in the house heard it, too—only they say it was hours earlier, in the middle of the night. I turned that over and turned that over and turned it till it wouldn't turn again. But I couldn't make any sense of it till I realized the answer was so simple I shouldn't have wasted a heartbeat's time huntin' for it."

Gustav paused and looked around, waiting for someone to dare an explanation. No one took the bait. My brother ended his survey of the room facing me.

"Tell 'em, Otto," he said. "Assumin' nobody's lyin', how is it folks in two different places could hear the same gunshot at two different times?"

I stared back at Old Red, wondering why he'd gone out of his way to humble me by putting me on the spot.

"Well," I said, and the second I opened my mouth it came to me that I wasn't on the spot at all. My lips stretched into a grin, and Gustav grinned back at me.

He hadn't thrown that question my way because I couldn't figure out the answer. Just the opposite. He was filled with faith that I *could*.

"It's obvious, ain't it?" I said. "They weren't hearin' the same shot at different times . . . because they weren't hearin' the same shot at all."

My brother gave me a wink, then packed away his smile as he swiveled around to face everyone else again.

"Exactly. There were *two* gunshots—the earlier one closer to the big house, the later one closer to the bunkhouse. The hands didn't pay any mind to the one they heard, as Mr. Brackwell made a habit of early-mornin' target practice. But it's harder to figure why our guests wouldn't react to such a noise. Visitors from parts East are usually looking for Cheyenne braves under their beds, yet nobody so much as poked a head out after hearing a *bang* in the dead of night."

"It was more of a *thump* than a bang," Edwards said. "It didn't sound like a—"

Gustav silenced him with a raised hand. "I'll get to that. Bang or thump, no one stepped out to investigate. Well, with a little cogitation I could think of a reason for each and every person to keep to their beds. Lady Clara—she's been known to dabble in affairs usually fenced off to those of her gender, yet she still might leave any actual *danger* to servants and menfolk. As for them, Mr. Edwards had his bad back, and Mr. Brackwell . . ." Old Red shrugged apologetically at our young friend. "I do believe he was drunk as a skunk."

Brackwell returned an embarrassed shrug of his own that said, *True enough.*

"As for the Duke," Gustav went on, "I suspect he was . . . let's say 'entertaining a visitor.' "

I puzzled over which "visitor" Old Red might mean until I realized he'd skipped someone who'd been in the house that night—Emily. That brought to mind his comment about the size of her cot. And then there was her gossip about the St. Simon family's habit of dallying with the hired help, not to mention the deep sleep from which it was so hard to rouse the Duke.

My brother turned toward the maid now, and though he said nothing, his eyes blazed a question at her.

"I . . . I . . . ," she stammered before pursing her lips up tight. She said no more, but the blush that came to her round cheeks spoke loud enough.

"You disgusting insect!" the Duke spat, hoisting his girth halfway from his chair. No doubt he had more names for my brother, but he didn't get a chance to sling any of them on account of Edwards, who took the extraordinary step of interrupting the old man.

"Why should it matter who was doing what inside the house?"

"Because that's where Boudreaux was murdered," Old Red replied. "Here in this very room, in fact."

The Duke was struck dumb, and it was left to Edwards to blurt out "Preposterous!" for the both of them. The McPhersons threw out their own protests, Uly's being "Hogwash!" and Spider's a less genteel "Bullshit!"

"Nope, it ain't preposterous or hogwash either one," Gustav said, ignoring Spider's contribution to the discussion. "Jack, you get a whiff of the powder burn, don't you? Our guests might not have the nose to pick it out, but surely you can."

Martin's nose twitched like a hare's. "Well, I'll be damned," the lawman mumbled before he could stop himself.

"If you need more convincin'," Old Red said to Edwards, "there's a bloodstain about one foot beneath your behind."

Edwards bent to look underneath the ottoman. His back was obviously still paining him, for his doughy face twisted into a grimace. The Duke, Martin, and Uly all leaned forward to get a better look at the rug, as well.

"That stain could be months old!" the Duke hollered.

"Looks like ink to me," said Uly.

"He put it there himself!" Edwards declared.

Gustav sighed.

"Amlingmeyer didn't make the stain," Brackwell said, finally speaking up from his perch against the wall. "I was here when he found it."

"It makes no difference," the Duke shot back. He had his teeth sunk into that two hundred pounds like a Gila monster on a fellow's foot, and he wasn't going to let go. "This proves nothing."

"It don't?" Gustav countered with a little chuckle that turned the old man's already flushed face beet red. "I'd say it proves Boudreaux was killed by somebody here in the house."

"It *doesn't*," said Edwards, his eyes going droopy behind his spectacles, as if humoring my brother had him all tuckered out. "A stain on the rug? A scent most of us can't even smell? Please."

"Oh, there's more proof than that. You've seen it already, Mr. Edwards."

Suddenly, Edwards's eyes weren't quite so droopy.

"Of course, it's under about eight feet of water now, but all we need's a rope and a hook to drag it up," Old Red continued. "When a valise and an iron go missin' right before a feller with a boogered-up back drags himself out for a nine-mile buggy ride, all so he can 'picnic' next to a pond . . . well, it hardly requires any deducin' at all, does it? I assume there's a freshly fired derringer and a couple bloody pillows in that handbag, too."

Edwards barked out a mirthless laugh of disbelief. "Are you actually accusing *me*?"

Old Red shrugged. "I ain't the one doin' the accusin', exactly. Lady Clara just about spooned the whole thing on my plate for me."

"She *what*?" the Duke roared, whipping around to face his daughter.

She ignored him, instead fixing Edwards with a deep, unblinking gaze—a look of devotion mixed with regret.

"When Amlingmeyer came to me a little while ago, he told me he had suspicions about your buggy ride yesterday—and about my motivations in asking that the wager be abandoned. He was"—the lady's long, dark lashes fluttered, and her eyes flicked toward my brother for an instant—"extremely persistent. I finally had to admit that I knew more than I'd said."

Her eyes took on a shimmery shine as tears welled up and threatened to streak across her pale skin.

"There *were* two gunshots. I heard the second one, as well. It was faint, but I was already beginning to awaken, and the noise was enough to draw me to the window. And I saw you, George—I saw you running back to the house. When that man's body was found, I prayed that it wasn't what it appeared. But I couldn't be sure. And when Amling-meyer told me his theories . . . told me where you went yesterday . . ."

Edwards shook his head slowly. But the bellowed protests for which I steeled myself never emerged. His expression changed, righteous in-dignation giving way to something like relief.

"There's no use lying anymore," he said. "Yes . . . I killed that man."

The words were like buckets of water sloshed in our faces, and everyone came spluttering to life to gasp or mutter curses or blurt out "What?" The exceptions were Old Red, who took in Edwards's words with an unnatural calm, and Lady Clara, who was still fighting to keep her tears in her eyes and not on her face.

My brother said something I couldn't catch through the commo-tion. It must have been "Tell us what happened," for that's what Ed-wards proceeded to do.

"The pain in my back kept me from sleeping, so I came downstairs. We'd been reviewing the Cantlemere's books, and as long as I was awake I thought I'd go through a few more files. I'd been here perhaps thirty minutes when that ghoulish-looking Negro walked in—pointing a gun. He wanted jewels, cash, anything valuable. And he . . . well . . ." Ed-wards's expression turned sour, as if the next words were too bitter to hold in his mouth. "He demanded to know which rooms the women were in."

Brackwell and Martin frowned and shook their heads, and the Duke muttered, "Animal!" The men's reaction seemed to boost Ed-wards's confidence, and he continued his tale with more dramatic dash.

"I knew I had to act. I wasn't facing a mere thief. I was facing a *fiend*. Fortunately, I wasn't as helpless as the blackguard assumed. I had with me a gift from the Duke—a derringer pistol. I concocted some folderol about a safe in the desk, and when the Negro walked around to take a look, I 'got the drop on him,' as the cow-boys say. I had no choice but to shoot, for it was plainly his life or mine in the balance."

"Of course," the Duke assured him. "Bully for you, Edwards!"

"Thank you, Your Grace. But I couldn't be sure everyone would be so understanding. Law in the West is a capricious business. Every day, murderers are set free because their neighbors refuse to convict them, while honest cattlemen can't raise a finger against 'rustlers' lest they be lynched by some bloodthirsty mob. There could be no 'jury of my peers' for a gentleman like myself. If the man I'd killed was well-liked, if he had enough friends, allowing myself to stand trial would be suicide."

"You needn't have worried about that, mister," Martin said. "A man like yourself shoots a thievin' nigger? Nobody'd blink an eye."

"I wish I'd known that two days ago," Edwards said. "But I didn't, so I moved to protect myself. When no one came to the office to investigate the gunshot, I knew I had a chance to hide what I'd done. I decided to leave the body someplace outside—hopefully, it wouldn't be discovered until we'd left the Cantlemere. But before I got far, I saw the ranch cook heading toward the house. I had to hide the corpse quickly. I threw it into the outhouse, slipped around the side, and waited for the man to leave. Once he was gone, I discovered to my dismay that the outhouse door was stuck. Fortunately, I was able to keep my wits about me, and I soon had a new plan."

Whereas Edwards had begun reeling out his story mournfully, with an air of guilt about him, by now he was talking fast and with obvious pride.

"I would leave a gun with the body, and everyone would assume the man had shot himself. I couldn't leave my own, of course—it would be recognized as one of the derringers His Grace had given to his traveling companions. But I was in luck. While going through Perkins's drawers earlier, I discovered that he kept a derringer of his own. There was one problem, however: It hadn't been used. I had no choice but to fire a shot, slide the gun through the ventilation hole in the outhouse door, and run for the house as quickly as I could—which is exactly what I did. I'd already cleaned up the blood with pillows from the closet upstairs, so the next step was to cover the smell of gunpowder that lingered in the room. I attempted to do so by building the biggest blaze I could in the fireplace. After that, I had to dispose of the pillows and the gun, which I did on my 'picnic.' All the while, I played along with the Duke's wager as a show of confidence. It was pure bluff, as was my later change of heart."

"Ingenious!" the Duke exclaimed with the same chummy admiration he might use to compliment a fellow nobleman on a well-played hand of whist.

The old man's attitude rubbed off on Martin, who shook his head and grinned. "That was some pretty slick thinkin', alright."

"Oh, yes, well done, Edwards," Brackwell added, not sounding enthused even though he now had grounds to claim two hundred pounds from the Duke. "And well done to you, too," he said to Gustav with considerably more sincerity.

Old Red didn't acknowledge the salute—his attention was focused on Edwards and Lady Clara.

"Oh, George! If only I'd known!" the lady said, clutching his hands. "Can you ever forgive me?"

"There's nothing to forgive," Edwards replied. "All the shame in this affair is mine and mine alone."

Lady Clara's tears let loose now, and Edwards wrapped an arm around her to offer comfort. That had the Duke looking mighty pleased. Though he'd just lost a small fortune, it appeared he'd soon have access to a considerably larger one—through a new son-in-law.

"Well," Martin said cheerfully, "I'll have to make a report when I get back to Miles, but there won't be any need to dredge up all the ins and outs of this thing. Mr. Edwards was attacked and he defended himself. That's that."

"No, Jack. That *ain't* that," Old Red sighed, looking like a fellow who's found half a worm in his apple. "Everything we just heard is pure horseshit."

Thirty-six

THE REST OF IT

Or, The Truth Comes Out—and So Do the Guns

Almost everyone in the room blurted out "What the hell?" or words to that effect. Not surprisingly, Edwards's and the Duke's protests were the loudest, the former assailing Gustav's sanity while the latter howled and growled about my brother's "damnable insolence."

"For God's sake, let him talk!" Brackwell roared at them.

The two older men swiveled around to stare, momentarily slack-jawed with surprise. Old Red threw himself into the resulting silence while it was still there to jump into.

"I'd be happy to explain, but it might be best if we sent Emily along first," he said, turning to the Duke. "I'm sure she's got things to do, am I right?"

His Grace gave Emily a brusque nod without looking her in the eye. She curtsied and moved slowly toward the door, her ears no doubt straining to sweep up any additional dirt they could before she left. After she'd pulled the door shut behind her, Old Red's gaze jumped from me to the door and back again.

Once again he wanted a roadblock in front of the exit, and once again the roadblock was to be me. I moved to the door and leaned up against it, tucking my hands casually over my gunbelt—leaving my right hand just inches from my .45.

I figured I knew why Gustav wished Emily scooted from the room: He'd pulled from her what information he'd needed, and now he didn't want bystanders around if things got hot. And they seemed to be warming up fast.

Across the room was my mirror image—Spider, leaning against the wall next to the window, his hands resting on *his* gunbelt. Uly smiled at me from his seat, his fingers clasped loosely on his lap, ready to reach for a trigger in the blink of an eye. Martin noticed our preparations and made his own, sliding back to press himself into the wall, as if he wished to trade in his badge and take up a new career as a filing cabinet.

"Now to start with," Old Red said, "just look at Mr. Edwards here."

We obliged, but all there was to see was a sweaty son of a bitch foolish enough to wear tweed in Montana on a warm May day.

"That back of his is stiff as board, ain't it?" Gustav pointed out. "And any of you catch sight of his face when he moves? Looks like he's got wasps in his socks."

"So?" Edwards snipped.

"So how are you supposed to be draggin' dead cowboys around when you say it was your bad back that kept you from sleepin' in the first place?"

"Oh . . . well . . . a man is capable of extraordinary things in a time of crisis."

"Like sprinkling feathers around after shootin' somebody to death?" Old Red said. "We found down stuck to Boudreaux's forehead. You wanna tell me how it got there?"

Edwards sidestepped that one entirely. "I don't even know why we're listening to this little tramp any longer," he said to the Duke and Martin.

"You need a reason to listen?" Gustav asked. "Try this on: Perkins was robbin' the Sussex Land and Cattle Company blind—and Boudreaux was killed cuz he had proof."

Uly waved off the accusation with the back of his hand. "Awww, now that he's slandered every livin' person in the room, he has to go and speak ill of the dead!"

But my brother's words had hooked the Duke like a jowly trout.

"What's this about Perkins robbing us?"

"I thought that might interest you folks," Old Red said. "In fact, it's the real reason you're here, ain't it?"

"Who told you that?" the Duke demanded.

Brackwell, however, was done beating around the bush. "You're right," he said. "One of the board members, Sir Charles Appledore, owns an interest in another ranch near here. Apparently, Sir Charles had been hearing about our ranch from the general manager there. The Cantlemere was sending fewer and fewer cows to market, he said—far fewer than Perkins's reports indicated. So the board sent a party to investigate the situation personally . . . and discreetly."

"And if you didn't like what you found," Old Red said, "you could sell the VR at the Stockgrowers Association meetin' in Miles City."

"Who told you *that*?" the Duke blurted out again.

"No one told me. The timin' of your visit just seemed a touch . . . convenient."

"You're right," Brackwell said. "The plan was to find a buyer for the Cantlemere if we discovered anything troubling."

"And did you?"

"Well, aside from all the *deaths*, everything seemed to be in order."

The hint of a grin tugged at Old Red's lips. "That's right, Mr. Brackwell—death*sss*. I'm glad you haven't forgotten that we've had more than one corpse around here lately."

"Who're you talkin' about?" Martin butted in.

"Perkins, the general manager. We had us a stampede a while back, and . . . well . . ." Gustav shrugged. "You know, if any of our guests had bothered askin' questions, I could've laid out some mighty curious data about what happened. But I guess y'all ain't in the habit of chattin' with the hired help—which is exactly what certain folks was countin' on."

"You're being asked now," the Duke snapped.

"Alright then. For one thing, another man went missin' right around the time of the stampede."

"Another man?" Martin moaned. "Just how many more bodies are you gonna drag into this?"

"I guess we'll have to count 'em up when we're done," Old Red said. "Anyway, Jack, you should be pleased I'm pullin' this one in." He took a step closer to Martin, digging out his handkerchief and unfolding it just enough for the lawman to get a peek at what it held.

Martin mumbled something that might have been a curse.

"What is it?" Edwards asked.

"A . . . a man's nose," Martin told him, hardly able to believe his own words.

The Duke's bushy eyebrows jumped so high it was a wonder they stayed on his head. "A *nose?*"

"And not just any nose," my brother said to Martin. "You must've looked at the reward notice for Hungry Bob a hundred times. Don't that look familiar?"

"I'll be damned," Martin whispered. "Where'd you get it?"

Old Red wrapped the nose back up in its little shroud and returned it to his pocket. "Found it on Boudreaux. I think he was plannin' on takin' it to you."

"To *me?*" Martin looked stunned to find himself drawn into Old Red's helter-skelter theorizing.

"Well, not *you,* exactly. To the federal marshal's office in Miles. You see, that was the only proof he was able to save that Hungry Bob was dead."

"Why the only proof?" Martin asked.

"Because the rest of the body had been gummed up like a stick of chewin' wax."

For a minute there, Old Red's line of thought seemed to be zigzagging willy-nilly. But now I realized he'd been moving in a circle—right back to Perkins.

"Holy shit!" I said, so thunderstruck I forgot to watch my tongue around Lady Clara. "That body we buried the day after the storm—that was Hungry Bob?"

"It was so flat it could've been Queen *Victoria* herself and we wouldn't have known the difference." Gustav, looking intolerably pleased with himself, cocked an eyebrow at the Duke. "Except I did notice a couple irregularities. You remember, Brother. The only bit we found that wasn't trampled to a pulp was the left hand—and it was *tanned* even though Perkins never set foot outside the house. On top of that, Perkins wore a gold band on this finger." Gustav held up the finger next to the pinky on his left hand. "But it wasn't there when we found the body."

"Are you saying Perkins wore a wedding ring?" the Duke asked.

"Sure looked like one."

"Rubbish!" the old man proclaimed triumphantly. "Perkins was a bachelor! Never married! That's what made him ideal for the position—he had no family to leave behind in England."

Old Red frowned, then smiled grimly, then frowned again, all in the span of a second. "I suppose that would make him 'ideal.'"

"So," Lady Clara said, "if I follow you correctly, you're claiming that Perkins is alive?"

"No, ma'am. Not quite."

"He's *not quite* alive?" The lady's chilly tone made the words brittle as ice. She still had a hold on one of Edwards's hands, but it looked like her grip was beginning to loosen. "Whatever do you mean?"

"I'll show you," Gustav said. He turned toward Martin and pointed at the window. "Jack, do me a favor—open that up and let loose a nice, loud whistle."

The deputy paused only a moment, then did as my brother asked. It was obvious why Old Red didn't want to mess with the window himself—he was keeping his distance from the McPhersons, who'd been easing their hands ever closer to their guns.

"Perkins took out a horse called Puddin' -Foot the night he 'died,' " Gustav said, walking in a slow circle as he talked. "Gentle as a kitten. A perfect mount for any man without much horse sense."

A movement outside caught my eye. A man on horseback was approaching the house. Trailing him was another, riderless horse with a large pack slung over the back.

"Puddin' -Foot never turned up after the stampede—until this mornin'," Gustav went on. "I saw him out at a line camp a good twenty miles from here. As you might imagine, I was anxious to go in for a closer look. Fortunately, I had a friend with me, for I got into a bit of a tussle with three fellers there."

I recognized the man on horseback now. It was the friend Old Red had just mentioned—Jim Weller. The horse ambling along behind him was Puddin' -Foot.

I got a better look at the pack on Puddin' -Foot, too. It wasn't a pack at all. It was a body.

"Them three men went and got themselves dead." Gustav ended his pacing to my right, near the wall but angled out so as to have a clear view of everyone in the room. "Two of 'em I'd never laid eyes on before. The third I knew—or thought I knew."

Uly and Spider were coiled up as tight as rattlers set to strike, and given what Gustav was saying I had to wonder why they hadn't put their fangs to work. Then I caught a quick flicker Uly's eyes made away from my brother. I couldn't tell exactly where he was looking, but it gave me my answer nevertheless.

The McPhersons had been waiting for a signal from someone else in the room. Old Red was setting himself up to see who.

"Mr. Edwards, Lady Clara, Mr. Brackwell, Your Grace," he said. "Would you be so kind as to look outside?"

They all obliged, the Duke grumbling about my brother's "insolent theatrics" as he stood—until the sight of the body shut him up.

Outside, Weller had dismounted just a few yards from the house. He walked around to Puddin' -Foot, took hold of the dead man's silver-gold hair, and pulled, lifting the head up to reveal the face.

Edwards looked away. "Good Lord! What's the meaning of this?"

His three companions had very different reactions.

"It can't be," Brackwell gasped.

The Duke's knees buckled, and he sank into his seat, his ruddy face going chalk white.

And Lady Clara—she cut loose with a shriek so loud and long Edwards's spectacles should've shattered. The scream faded into a sob as she fell back onto the ottoman, her face in her hands. Rather than comfort her, Edwards turned and gaped again at the body.

"What's happening? Who is that man?"

"That's Perkins, the VR's manager," I said.

"No, it's not." Brackwell was staring at Lady Clara as he spoke, his expression mixing equal parts wonderment, pity, and betrayal. "It's Nathaniel Horne."

The lady peered up at her young friend, her face streaked with fresh tears, and held out a hand to him. "William . . ."

Brackwell moved closer and took her hand in his.

"Hold on—Nathaniel who now?" But even as the words sprang from my tongue, a memory was stirring. "You mean the Duke's secretary? The one he blackballed?"

"If I'm not mistaken, Horne was a lot more than the Duke's secretary," Old Red said. "He was his son-in-law to boot. Ain't that right, Lady . . . whoa there."

We all turned toward Lady Clara and came face-to-face with two unexpected sights. One was the composure that had chased the grief from her features. The other was the gun she'd slipped from the holster on Brackwell's left hip.

"Darling, what are you—?" Edwards began.

"Oh, do shut up, George," the lady said, her words trembling despite the mask of calm on her face. "You truly are the most colossal fool."

"Well, it's about time," Uly snickered, and he started to stand and draw his own .45.

Lady Clara turned the business end of the iron in Uly's direction. *"Sit down."*

There was no tremble in her words this time.

Uly blinked at her, his chuckles curling into a strangled cough. "What? Have you lost your damn—?"

Lady Clara pulled back the hammer with her thumb, and Uly sat down quick. I didn't blame him. It was a big gun for such dainty fingers. Should the lady's thumb have slipped, Uly would've found himself with an ugly hole where his heart used to be.

"Don't move." Lady Clara swung the barrel in Spider's direction. "Either of you."

"Now just calm down, ma'am," Uly said, managing to ooze snake oil despite an obvious—and justified—case of nerves. "Your man's dead, and that's too bad. But we're still in this together. We've got to—"

"Got to *what*?" the lady snapped. "There's no hiding our secrets now. Not without killing every man in this room—and I won't allow it." Her gaze moved to her father. "Not *everyone* here deserves that."

"Well, we can't just—"

"McPherson," Lady Clara said, sounding more tired than angry now, "speak again and I'll kill you, I swear. Our partnership died with Nathaniel . . . and I think a part of me is glad. It shames me that we had to associate with brutes of your sort for so long."

"But you needed allies here in Montana," Old Red said.

Lady Clara swung the gun his way, and for a second it looked like she was going to do more than swing it—she was going to *use* it. The look on her face made it clear she hadn't forgotten who'd killed her beloved.

But something kept her from pulling the trigger. I knew what it was when she glanced toward her father again and smiled grimly at his hollow-eyed heartbreak. There was her real enemy—and she wanted to give one more twist to the knife she'd plunged into his back.

"Yes," she said. "On his way here from England, the real Perkins was . . . *intercepted* by my husband. That was regrettable, but it made so many things possible. Nathaniel could assume his identity and take over the Cantlemere. As a general manager with a board of directors thousands of miles away, he was in a perfect position to chip away at the ranch. He allowed the herds to dwindle and struck quiet deals to sell off outlying parcels of Cantlemere land. These men"—she gave the McPhersons a curt nod—"were allowed a small portion of the profits in exchange for their help."

"But then the board sent your father out for an inspection," Old Red said. "And naturally he couldn't find Horne here to greet him instead of Perkins."

Lady Clara nodded. "I wrote to warn my husband, and he staged his death. That he had a body to use in doing so—that of an escaped lunatic who would be mourned by no one—was merely a stroke of good luck. But that hideous Negro betrayed him. He came here to tell us where 'Perkins' was hiding. The Negro found me in the office, waiting for a rendezvous with Nathaniel. I'd been separated from my husband for three years, and I was willing to take any risk to feel his touch again."

Lady Clara looked at the Duke as these last words left her lips, and she seemed to savor the wince they slapped across his face. She kept her eyes on him as she went on.

"Given that no one would be on the first floor—Emily having gone upstairs to take her usual place in my father's bed—I'd assumed the risk wouldn't be all that great."

The Duke winced again.

Gustav coughed gently. "If I may, ma'am?"

"Yes?" Lady Clara responded, equally polite despite her pointing a peacemaker at my brother's guts.

"Your husband had been sendin' the board reports of a secret breakthrough here: a new buffalo-cow hybrid that was going to be the next big thing in beef," Old Red said. "When Boudreaux came to the house, he brought proof that it was all a lie—a receipt for cattalo from another ranch. Naturally, he wanted a reward for doin' you this service. So you went upstairs and grabbed your valise. The derringer your father'd given you was inside, and you stuffed a couple pillows in there, too—to muffle the sound of a gunshot. Then you went back downstairs, brought that bag to Boudreaux like you were bringin' him cash . . . and you killed him. Some of the feathers from the pillows got sprayed about by the shot, and you tried to clean 'em up—only you missed a couple."

Lady Clara inclined her head. "It was exactly as you say."

"Damn the details and deductions! What I want to know is *why*," the Duke spat out. "Why, Clara?"

The lady's face had relaxed as she and Old Red talked, as if going over the particulars of the plot had pushed everything into the past, making it something that had happened far away and long ago. But her father's words snapped her back to the here and now. Her proud, straight back slumped, and for the first time her hand wavered under the weight of the gun it gripped.

"Revenge, of course," she said. "Revenge on the man who squandered my family's fortune on foolish wagers. Revenge on the man who humiliated my mother with disgusting debauches. Revenge on the man who did his utmost to drive away my one and only real love."

Inch by inch, the gun moved across the room until it was pointed squarely at the Duke.

"I married Nathaniel in secret a year after you tried to break us apart. I longed to tell you—throw it in your fat face. But you would've disowned me, and I would've been denied my due as a St. Simon. So Nathaniel and I set out to transfer your last remaining pounds to us. And when the Cantlemere Ranche was finally revealed to be worthless, when you were ruined completely, you would be forced to sell the *real* Cantlemere—our family estate, my home. It would be purchased by an anonymous gentleman from America. Nathaniel. And I would come to live with him openly as his wife while you rotted in the gutter."

The Duke's stiff-necked dignity melted away drip by drip under the heat of his daughter's hatred. By the time she was finished, he wasn't so much sitting in his chair as poured out over it like a lumpy mound of candle wax.

"Well," the Duke said, his eyes brimming with tears, "you've failed, haven't you?"

"There's always another way," Lady Clara replied, her own eyes beginning to overflow.

A contract was sealed between father and daughter in this last look, and the rest of us had but a split second to prepare for its execution.

I settled on Spider as my first target, hoping Old Red would go for Uly. Martin, Brackwell, and Edwards would have to take care of themselves.

My gun was halfway from its holster when Lady Clara pulled the trigger. I saw Spider's hand come up with his .45 just as the puff of powder smoke from the lady's iron threw a fog across the room. There was a blast from where Spider had been, and I pointed at it and fired twice. Glass shattered, and four more gunshots rang out in quick succession, followed by a deafening boom. I crouched down low, trying to look beneath the layer of smoke that was choking the room, but all I saw was eye-stinging soot, and I dared not fire blind lest I put a bullet in someone whose name wasn't McPherson.

For a long moment I could hear nothing beyond a high, screaming buzz, but as the smoke cleared so did my ears. The sound of groans and whimpers grew louder as the various bodies slumped around the room took shape.

Only one meant anything to me just then. It was the one closest to me—Old Red. He'd stumbled back against the door before slumping to the floor, leaving a smear of blood down the wood as he went. His hand was clutched to his side and his eyes were closed.

"Gustav!" I crawled to my brother and took hold of his arm. *"Gustav!"*

My brother's eyelids fluttered open, and he looked at me as if I'd just awakened him from a particularly strange dream. He grimaced as he placed where he was—and in what condition.

"Oh, hell," he said, staring down at his stomach. "This never happened to Mr. Holmes."

Then his eyes shut again.

Thirty-seven

THE END

Or, I Put Down My Rope and Pick Up a Pen

Someone crouched down at my side, and I turned to find Brack-well staring at me with that look of surprise men share after they've passed through some cataclysm in each other's company. It's a look that says, *We're alive . . . right?*

Together, we lifted Old Red and moved him down the hall to "Perkins's" bedroom.

The Swede showed up shouting, "Oh, my heaven! What iss happening?" just as we got Old Red settled on the bed. To his credit, the old cook got hold of himself quick and took to fussing over my brother's wound. The bullet hole was far over on Gustav's right side, just below the ribs.

"It iss not goot looking, hmmm?" the Swede said. "But the bullet iss through him going. We just should be hoping there iss no . . ." He pointed at his own stomach and waggled his fingers, frowning. For once, I knew exactly what he meant.

If the bullet had ripped or even just nipped any of Gustav's vitals on its journey, my brother would die a death as agonizing as any torture devised by man. The iron maiden and the rack offer mere tickles compared to the pain of gangrene and peritonitis.

The Swede got back to dressing the wound while I watched, feeling useless. Brackwell left, though I didn't notice until I remembered the McPhersons and their men. Then I left, too.

Spider wasn't in the house—he was in a heap outside the window, covered in glass and full of lead. Not far away stood Jim Weller, a scattergun in his hands. He'd discouraged any interference from McPherson's bunch by peppering the Peacock with buckshot, while the Hornet's Nest boys had done their part by roping two of the more persistent fellows and taking them for quick rides behind fast horses. The other McPherson men simply scattered.

As for Uly, he was still sitting in his chair, though it had been knocked over backward and he was now staring up at the ceiling, two ragged holes punched in his shirt. We never did figure out who killed him. My brother hadn't squeezed off a single shot, as Uly had aimed for him first and hit his mark. Brackwell had returned fire with his other gun—it being a blessing in the end that he'd taken to wearing two. Yet Jack Martin claimed to have fired the shot that bedded Uly down. Given the angle one would have to fire from when cowering in the corner, I had my doubts, but I didn't have the energy to disprove it with any detecting of my own.

There was no need for detective work to figure out what happened to the Duke and Lady Clara. They'd both been debrained with bullets from the same gun—the one still clutched in Lady Clara's hand. Edwards was reduced to a trembling wreck who assured us over and over that his confession had been false. The lady had come to him saying she'd been foully assaulted by a Negro and had been forced to shoot the man dead. The only hope for avoiding scandal, if the incident were to be uncovered, would be if a *man* took credit for the killing. Edwards had been all too eager to be that man, and he even agreed to dispose of the evidence. After all, it would place the lady in his debt—a debt she could pay off with a simple walk down the aisle.

The rest of the day was strange indeed. While the Hornet's Nest boys were digging graves, I just wandered around the house in a daze waiting to see if Old Red would pull through. Martin left that afternoon, saying he had to lay the whole affair out before the marshal and a judge. He didn't expect much to come of it, though. The affair was so knotted up with complications there was no hope of untangling it in court.

He didn't volunteer to fetch a doctor when he left, for we all knew the good that would do: By the time a sawbones got to the VR, my brother would either be better or buried.

The next morning, Brackwell announced that he and Edwards and Emily would be leaving for Miles, as well. He'd found the VR's real records—not the fake ones Horne had done up—in the McPhersons' bunkhouse. From the look of those ledgers, there wasn't much left to the Cantlemere, and Brackwell figured it was up to him to do what had to be done. He'd be attending the Stockgrowers Association meeting to sell off the Sussex Land and Cattle Company's last remaining land and cattle.

"You may remain here as long as you wish," Brackwell told me as he got set to go. "Whoever the new owners are, I'll make sure they agree to that. If it takes your brother days or weeks or months to recover, you stay. There should be enough food to last, and I've paid the Swede's wages through the summer. I'll pay your wages, as well."

"That's awful generous of you."

"It's the least I can do to repay you and your brother."

"Repay us? For gettin' a score of folks killed and puttin' the company out of business?"

Brackwell shook his head. Somehow he looked years older than the skinny, awkward kid I'd met not a week before.

"Change was coming anyway," he said. "You and your brother simply . . . herded it along."

He stretched out his hand, and we shook. He was wearing a proper gentleman's traveling suit when he left—and his tall, white Stetson.

The Hornet's Nesters hit the trail soon after, having been paid off the same as the Swede. They took their leave with well wishes for Old Red but also with the fervent desire to put as many miles as possible between themselves and the VR. Weller departed, too, riding out after asking me for a keepsake of our adventure together. He headed for Miles with a nose in his pocket—and a heart full of hope that he could swap it for a thousand dollars. I wished him the best of luck.

So the next day, there were just three of us left. The Swede and I drank coffee and played dominoes. Gustav did little more than sweat, groan, and sleep.

"The fever iss not good to be having," the Swede said. "It iss infection maybe."

"What can I do?" I asked for probably the one-thousandth time.

The Swede usually answered with a shrug and a suggestion for prayer, but this time he gave me something more solid to go on.

"He iss your bruder. *Talk* to him."

So that's what I did. I started by laying out my reasons for preferring him alive. As the minutes wore on, I drifted into family reminiscences meant to warm the heart. But it's hard to talk about the Amlingmeyers without the conversation turning morbid, what with nearly all of us being *dead* and all, so I decided to work another angle.

I ran out to the bunkhouse and rummaged through my brother's few worldly possessions. It took me but a moment to find what I was looking for, and soon I was back at Old Red's bedside, a copy of *Harper's* spread out on my lap. Given the manner in which Sherlock Holmes had awakened Gustav's mind, I was hoping he could now do the same for my brother's body.

I started with "The Stock-Broker's Clerk," and when that was done, I moved on to the other Holmes tales. I ran through all of them twice in the next day. I reaped no miracles from my efforts—though at one point halfway through "A Study in Scarlet" I could've sworn I heard a whispered "capital mistake" just as I reached Old Red's favorite line.

I mentioned this to the Swede when he brought more of the warm broth we'd been pouring down Gustav's gullet, and the cook nodded and smiled broadly.

"Goot, goot! He iss hearing you! Try to get him more talking maybe!"

So the next time I caught something coming from Old Red's lips—"dog in the nighttime," it sounded like—I tried to keep those lips on the go.

"Gustav," I said, "I been wonderin'. Before you corralled everybody in the office the other day, you talked to Lady Clara on the sly. How'd you know to go to her? You told me you still didn't know who the killer was."

My brother's mouth got to working slowly, though it made no sound. After a minute or so the movement stopped, and I leaned in again.

"And who dragged Boo out to the outhouse? Surely the lady couldn't have done that."

There was no response at all this time. Old Red just lay there stone-still and slick with sweat. The sight of it brought to mind my father and my brother Conrad going from fever-hot to icy-cold with smallpox. I tried to shake the vision out of my head, but it lingered there as I drifted to sleep in my chair, and I dreamed of all the long-dead Amlingmeyers welcoming Old Red into their midst.

I awoke the next morning to find my brother sitting up in bed staring at me as if *he'd* been the one keeping vigil over *me* all this time.

"Look in my Levi's," he said.

"Gustav!" I wanted to pull him out of bed and dance a jig with him, but I resisted the urge. "You just rest now," I said instead, assuming my brother was in the grip of delirium.

"Don't you want your questions answered?"

"Questions?" I hadn't had my morning coffee yet, so my brain was slow to follow his meaning. "Oh! You heard me, then?"

"I heard you. Now . . . look in my Levi's."

"Alright, alright." Old Red's denim trousers were folded up atop a chest of drawers nearby, and I pulled them down and reached for one of the pockets. I froze before my fingers could slide inside. "You didn't come across another *nose,* did you?"

"It ain't a nose," Gustav growled with remarkable vigor for a man who'd just spent three days not only on death's door but halfway inside the house. "It ain't an ear or lips or ass cheeks, neither. Just *look.*"

I looked—and found a gold locket. Inside it was a photograph of a thirtyish woman with long, dark hair and delicate features and sad eyes. A beautiful woman. A woman I knew to be dead.

"You found this on Perkins, didn't you?"

"I suppose we oughta call him Horne now," Gustav replied. "Now that we know his real name and all."

Opposite the picture, an inscription was laid into the metal in gracefully curling letters. I cleared my throat and read it out.

So you that are the sovereign of my heart
Have all my joys attending on your will;
My joys low-ebbing when you do depart,
When you return their tide my heart doth fill.
C.

Old Red nodded thoughtfully. "I was wonderin' what that said."

"She . . . she really did love that feller, didn't she?"

I closed the locket and started to put it back in Gustav's denims.

"No," my brother said. "You hold on to it."

I paused, unsure if I truly wanted such a melancholy memento. Then I nodded and tucked it away in one of my own pockets.

"So," I said, "after you found this, you knew the lady was mixed up in things."

"Yup. But I didn't know *how*. Edwards was up to somethin' with that buggy ride of his, that I knew. So Lady Clara could've been in it with him—or playin' him for a fool. I even thought maybe her father cooked up the whole thing to swindle Edwards and Brackwell, and she was just goin' along with it." Old Red shook his head ruefully, clearly chagrined that he'd underestimated the lady's cunning. "As for who moved Boudreaux to the outhouse, I reckon that was the McPhersons."

"And how exactly do you figure that?"

"Well, as the man once said, 'The grand thing is to be able to reason backward.' Now that we know who the bad actors were, it's easy as pie to piece together."

Gustav's eyelids fluttered. His words started to slur and his shoulders sag, but he forged on.

"Horne showed up after Boudreaux was killed. Remember, Lady Clara said she was up waitin' for him, and we found tracks from two horses outside—one for Boudreaux, one for the lady's caller. Clara and Horne did their best to clean up the office, but they couldn't be expected to get rid of a body, bein' respectable murderers not accustomed to heavy liftin'. And Boudreaux had his mount waitin' outside. Somebody had to unsaddle that pony and get her back to pasture. That would've been work for hands—and Horne and the lady sure as hell weren't going to fetch *us*. So they set Uly and Spider to it. I figure that's who threw that beat-up old hideout gun in the outhouse with Boudreaux, too. Clara's derringer . . . would have been . . . recognized . . ."

Old Red's strength finally gave out, and he sank back into his pillows, his eyes beginning to close. I thought maybe he was passing out, but his eyes popped open again and he hit me with a question of his own.

"So," he said, peeking down at the bloody dressings wrapped around his waist, "what the hell happened, anyway?"

I filled him in on all the deaths and departures, and he listened silently, drifting to the edge of unconsciousness once or twice before I could finish the telling of it. When I was done, he just nodded and said, "Alright then. It's over."

"That's right. It's over," I replied. "Thanks to you. You make a damn fine detective, Brother—as good as ol' Holmes himself."

"Well, I . . . don't know about . . ."

His words trailed off as he sank back into slumber—with a smile on his face.

He was awake again within the hour asking if I could bring him his pipe and read him a story. There could be no doubt after that. Old Red was back.

His strength returned slowly, but within a week he was on his feet again, and within two he was ready to ride. I didn't have much to occupy myself once my bed-sitting duties were done, so I spent the remainder of those days in the office hunched over the desk at which the Duke had died. The Sussex Land and Cattle Company no longer had any use for the pen and ink and paper I found there, so I commandeered it all for my own little enterprise.

Before we left to head back to Miles City, I read out what I'd written to my brother. It took several hours to do it, but he didn't say a word all that time. He just nodded here and there and grimaced here and there and even grinned once or twice. But when I reached the ending, all I got was a shrug.

"Well, I suppose that tells it fair enough," he said. "It's mighty heavy on words though, ain't it?"

This response didn't do much to build my confidence in myself as a writer. Yet still I'm clinging to the hope that all these *words* of mine will meet with a more enthusiastic reception elsewhere.

After all, my brother set out to make himself another Sherlock Holmes, and he succeeded—so much so that he now plans to search out the nearest Pinkerton office and offer his services. So why then can't

I be another John Watson? As I see it, I've got less of a leap to make than Old Red, for I was putting in practice as a tale-teller years before he got it in his head to be a detective.

When the time comes for us to leave the Bar VR, I'll do so with a big bundle of scribble-scrawled paper wrapped up in my war bag. Gustav keeps joking that I'll never make it back to Miles with so many trees strapped to my horse, but I've let these rare jests of his pass without reply. I'll be packing that bag tight with something new—a real dream for myself—and wherever my brother and I might ride to next, I know I can carry that with me without it weighing a thing.

ACKNOWLEDGMENTS

The author wishes to thank:

Sir Arthur Conan Doyle—for inspiration.

Elyse Cheney, super-genius (and agent)—for tenacity and good advice.

Ben Sevier, super-genius (and editor)—for enthusiasm and insight and *excellent* taste in books.

Steve Boldt, Stephanie Hanson, Mary Dell, Matt Springer, Mike Wiltrout, Cecily Hunt, Steve Bayer, Ron Hockensmith—for seeing what I couldn't.

Janet Hutchings, Linda Landrigan, Gina McIntyre, Gene Wolfe—for priceless encouragement and the timely opening of doors.

The fine folks of the alt.old-west discussion group—for putting up with stupid questions.

The Sonoma County Library—for books, books, *books*!

Alyssa and Mark Nickell—for open hearts and an open door.

John Harrington, Marcie Galick, Linda Manning, Joyce Tischler, Bob and Nancy Ortmann, Charles Best (1570–1627)—for *miscellaneous*.

Mom and Dad—for making so much possible.

Kate—for love pats and oo-mas.

Mar—for everything.